Nana's Wicker Back

Nancy-Ellen

Copyright © 2009 by Nancy-Ellen

All rights reserved. No part of this book shall be reproduced or transmitted in any form or by any means, electronic, mechanical, magnetic, photographic including photocopying, recording or by any information storage and retrieval system, without prior written permission of the publisher. No patent liability is assumed with respect to the use of the information contained herein. Although every precaution has been taken in the preparation of this book, the publisher and author assume no responsibility for errors or omissions. Neither is any liability assumed for damages resulting from the use of the information contained herein.

This is a work of fiction. Names, characters, places, and incidents either are the product of the author's imagination or are used fictitiously. Any resemblance to actual events or locales or persons, living or dead, is entirely coincidental.

ISBN 0-7414-5517-X

Cover design by Nancy-Ellen

Published by:

1094 New DeHaven Street, Suite 100
West Conshohocken, PA 19428-2713
Info@buybooksontheweb.com
www.buybooksontheweb.com
Toll-free (877) BUY BOOK
Local Phone (610) 941-9999
Fax (610) 941-9959

Printed in the United States of America
Published July 2009

This book is dedicated to:

"Muh" and Daddy – I'm blessed to have two friends who just happen to be my parents.

Linda – The best sister ever! I'll never stop missing you.

Lamont and Brandi – You can't possibly imagine how much you mean to me.

Darius – My precious "Sweetie Pie" grandson

and

John – Forever and ever…and one day more.

TABLE OF CONTENTS

Chapter 1:	*A point of reference*	*1*
Chapter 2:	*Self discovery*	*6*
Chapter 3:	*Brotha' Man*	*10*
Chapter 4:	*Where two rivers meet*	*13*
Chapter 5:	*Angie*	*17*
Chapter 6:	*What sistas do best*	*25*
Chapter 7:	*Introspective*	*31*
Chapter 8:	*"FM"*	*34*
Chapter 9:	*Nana's Wicker Back*	*39*
Chapter 10:	*Ironically, time served enslaved*	*43*
Chapter 11:	*Two separate worlds*	*50*
Chapter 12:	*Mojo*	*55*
Chapter 13:	*Finding self*	*59*
Chapter 14:	*The heart of Jordan*	*62*
Chapter 15:	*The power of pain*	*65*
Chapter 16:	*When He hears*	*68*
Chapter 17:	*Mixed signals*	*72*

Chapter 18: *Love's the crutch*	74
Chapter 19: *An answered request*	78
Chapter 20: *Gathering*	81
Chapter 21: *Traveling against her name*	86
Chapter 22: *Ten circles, plus two*	91
Chapter 23: *The mortar of men*	95
Chapter 24: *Toni's conjure*	99
Chapter 25: *Betty*	101
Chapter 26: *Pharaoh's army wears hoods*	106
Chapter 27: *The Stayers*	110
Chapter 28: *The first meeting*	116
Chapter 29: *Accidental exposure*	122
Chapter 30: *Thompson*	127
Chapter 31: *Destiny in design*	129
Chapter 32: *Composure compromised*	133
Chapter 33: *Coincidence*	140
Chapter 34: *Rebirth*	145
Chapter 35: *Round one*	147

Chapter 36: *Round two*	*150*
Chapter 37: *The Sisterhood*	*153*
Chapter 38: *Concerns from another realm*	*159*
Chapter 39: *Chess moves*	*161*
Chapter 40: *Roughing it*	*169*
Chapter 41: *Choosing sides*	*175*
Chapter 42: *North!*	*180*
Chapter 43: *Unrequited Love*	*184*
Chapter 44: *Thanksgiving Day*	*188*
Chapter 45: *Into his own hands*	*195*
Chapter 46: *"Somebody in de back chambers!"*	*201*
Chapter 47: *The 3 o'clock meeting*	*205*
Chapter 48: *Groundbreaking news*	*208*
Chapter 49: *The last Stayer*	*214*
Chapter 50: *Revelations: The Final Chapter*	*223*

CHAPTER 1

A point of reference

The large franchised bookstore was often a place of solace for Nilé. Matching overstuffed seats near enormous metal-paned windows invoked a prefabricated intimacy with which, for some odd reason, she identified. She would allow her childlike spirit to run ahead of her and escape into the endless mahogany shelves long before slinging her coat across an unclaimed chair. Then her full-figured form would timidly follow. Fingers and eyes caressing each book title that beckoned her attention. She had no favorite section, though there were some aisles she knew she would never travel.

Her love of literature came naturally. Nilé's memories would wander back to the days when her mother, father, sister, and she would pour over books on Saturday mornings. They had ooohed and ahhhed over pictures of wildlife, landscapes, or illustrations of famous people who shaped the nation. Often, Mom and Dad would relive events that they could recall, or correct the accounts of their history conveniently overlooked by Caucasian authors. Nilé's eyes would widen as Dad's animated gestures filled and warmed the room. Mom would read a line or two about the width and length of an elephant's trunk and its ability to uproot a tree from the roots—never expecting Daddy to rush up to her and her sister Eden and swoop them both up in his arms! With legs and arms dangling in the air, their giggles and screams were overshadowed by Daddy's clumsy imitation of the wild elephant, until he finally swayed them to a nearby couch and dropped them each into the sheltering arms of a pillow.

On this particular Saturday, while the smells of freshly brewed mocha lattes and blueberry scones wafted through the store and teased her appetite, the souls of her ancestral Africans had already sought out and recognized her name, despite her attempt to camouflage it with a French accent. Reluctantly, she turned down the aisle and found her very life force ahead of her, soaking in the essences exuded by her people's past. Tilting her head, she began perusing titles. *Captives and Cousins, Fire in My Bones, The Story of American Freedom.* Countless books whispered to her heart. It was *The Souls of Black Folk* by W.E.B. Du Bois that lifted her index finger toward its spine. She hesitated then boldly pulled it off the shelf. Remembering others say that this was a "good read" and anyone black and worth their salt should have it as part of their literary repertoire, she glanced at the cover and back. Thumbing through, she felt her alter ego tightening up, reminding her that this afternoon was supposed to be a relaxing endeavor, and Du Bois' provocative expression in *The Souls of Black Folk* was already making her tense. Nilé stumbled upon the author's statement regarding being black in America that read:

"One ever feels his two-ness, - an American, a Negro; two souls, two thoughts, two unreconciled strivings; two warring ideals in one dark body, whose dogged strength alone keeps it from being torn asunder."

Nilé could not remember how many times she read that sentence. She felt dense and unmovable as the words sped through shadowed corridors of her emotion on the tracks of a moan. She had no idea that a connection to such a profound statement existed in her. She read it once more, smiling as she wept, then shook her head and tried not to hate. She dare not continue to read. What she already took in was too much. Closing the book with a crisp snap, and then tucking it under her arm, Nilé decided to purchase *Souls* but read it later. Determined to find something lighter, she moved toward the novel section. Skimming through countless titles, most of which she had at one time or another heard of, she asked herself why she even chose this aisle. *Because you need this,*

Nilé...you need to know was the quiet, determined inner response. Nervously looking back toward her coat, she warned herself that she was getting too far away from home base. Then, a soft shadow of a form caught the corner of her eye.

There he stood, back erect and knees locked, forcing his calves to sway backward. He was so engrossed in reading that she could see the muscle in his jawbone straining against clenched teeth. Fat gnarly locks dropped like wisteria blossoms from southern plantation trees and framed his dark keen features. His exquisite beauty frightened her. Moving slowly away toward a cookbook aisle, she was all but clear of him when her Du Bois book decided to escape from the pit of her arm. An awkward clump interrupted the intense stillness of the aisle. "Snap!" she mumbled. He looked up and toward her. *Lord! That kind of fine should be quarantined!* she thought. Picking up Du Bois, her eyes flashed a timid apology. Then she darted through the next aisle advertising quilt making and upholstery. All she wanted at that moment was her coat and the exit sign. Ashamed of being so overwhelmed by a man's good looks, Nilé determined to make something out of her bookstore browse. So, she got in line to purchase *The Souls of Black Folk*.

Good, the line is short. I'll buy this bad boy and then head for home. I can make a cup of tea, sit by my favorite window, and cuddle up to a book that I'm sure will enlighten as well as inspire me!

The woman at the front of the line couldn't remember her husband's PIN number, and that was the only credit card that had enough money to cover her purchases. "I'll just be a second," she assured a perturbed cashier, then quickly speed dialed hubby.

"Bill, what's your PIN?" was all Nilé heard before drifting into a consumer's trance. A pleasant song came to mind. It could have been the store's background music. It didn't matter—it was pleasant. Stationery, two-inch jewel books, exotic teas, and chocolates lined nearby cases, and her eyes playfully glanced at them all.

"No, it's not the VISA one, honey; I've got the American Express card today." Impatient sighs and foot shuffling amused Nilé who had resolved earlier not to allow life's daily trivia to aggravate her. That was when the subtle fragrance of sandalwood and musk drifted lazily toward her nostrils. *Oh Lord,* Nilé thought, *this smell is too sexy to belong to that spike-haired Joe Computer-looking dude standing behind me.* Wanting desperately to confirm that it was the brother she saw in the African-American aisle, she needed to do it in a way that was not obvious. Nilé decided to feign losing something. That way she could legitimately look back toward the chair that once held her belongings. There it was dripping from his hand—her scarf! It mocked and imitated how she would limp and melt at his touch. Nilé could do nothing but stare.

"Is this yours?" "Could you move up, Miss?" Two simultaneous questions were answered with a most devastatingly obtuse "Uh...yes" that surfaced like a bubble from her slightly parted lips. Reaching toward the scarf, she stepped backward to close that infamous line gap. Everyone was now staring at Nilé, who felt her knees weaken when the brother playfully tugged and did not release the scarf. In disbelief, she sputtered, "Excuse me!"
He, in response, touted "For what?"
"For wanting my scarf!" she replied.
Joe Computer suggested he and Nilé change spaces so that (as he sarcastically bellowed), "You two can exchange scarves, roots, and digits and I can get the hell out of here!"
There was silence. Then the brother spoke.
"Yo' man, you've been in my way since the beginning of time! Why either of us should remotely care about how quickly *you* get the hell out of *here* is not a concern of mine.

Besides (initiating a gentle swinging motion between his fist, the scarf, and Nilé's hand), I kinda' like our roots, scarves, stares, smiles, and hopeful exchange of digits messin' up your day! Sista, stay right where you are. OK?" After which he tugged once more, staring hard at Joe Computer, and then allowed the scarf to slide sensuously through his fingers. Joe Computer's gradual intake of a six-foot-eight frame, foot-long locks, and plumlike complexion abruptly dampened his macho arrogance, as Nilé whispered, "Well alrighty!"

CHAPTER 2

Self discovery

Though *The Souls of Black Folk* was difficult to read from many perspectives, Nilé persevered. She found herself creating time to read it. Ordinarily her girls would take up what was left of her working day. Her kids grew up and moved out. Because of that, her place was always clean, cozy and inviting. The girls would drop by one at a time until her apartment windows dripped from the condensation of steam caused by countless kettles of tea being brewed. Her couches bowed from the abuse of voluptuous hips pressing downward upon them. She would often bark, "What am I? The KOOL-AID Mom? Why don't you hussies take yo' tired behinds home instead of comin' by my place?" Her protests were ignored. Everybody wanted to be around Nilé. Hers was an apartment like something out of an *Essence* magazine—eclectic, ethnic, eccentric. Her best friend Angie once said, "Nilé, your style is betta' than Martha Stewart! You know why? 'Cause yo' hookups got some *smell* to it!" Everyone in the room high-fived each other and hollered in agreement. Nilé's place was not only beautiful, but it could also handle a can of soda on the table or a few dishes in the sink and still look good. Rich warm colors covered her walls. Lush textures and intricate patterns adorned every nook and cranny of her apartment. She was blessed to find a place with good bones, one that came with natural hardwood floors, high ceilings and crown molding. Every room was designed to fit the character and shape of that room. While some would flinch at the acidic color of chartreuse, Nilé boldly splashed it across her dining room walls and softened the blow with mango and kiwi satin pillows and cream-colored curtains. She would replace the ceiling bowl light with an old found chandelier. Earrings that she could not find the mates to would dangle whimsically as bauble replacements, and you would wonder why the lamp wasn't made that very way in the first place. All of her rooms looked edible. Perhaps that's why Angie said they had smell.

Lately, however, Nilé found herself irritated by her girlfriends hanging around too late to watch one raggedy show after another on TV as they used to. She longed to hear only the refrigerator motor, or her cat Patwa jumping down from a ledge. She wanted to read. Admittedly, she returned weekly to the African-American section of the bookstore to look for Brotha-Man but found only books. Months later, she no longer wanted nor needed to find him, though their brief encounter had a drastic influence on her need to become more Afrocentric. Her new love was connecting to her past. The books she read had a separating effect, delicately cracking a self-made shell that distanced her from the pain and suffering of her people, and gingerly rolling her yolk (the very essence of her spirit) away from the transparent white part of her existing life. Du Bois was just the beginning. She bought coffee table books with breathtaking illustrations of men and women living and thriving in the age-old Dogon civilization. She became acquainted with Frederick Douglass' autobiography and excerpts of his arguments as an abolitionist. She read of the sacred text of Maat, an ethical and spiritual tradition developed in Kemet, and discovered that it essentially meant moral and spiritual *rightness* in relation to the Divine, nature, and other humans.

Nilé engrossed herself in Marcus Garvey's Negro Improvement Association, and his Back to Africa program introduced her to the concepts of Black Nationalism. As quickly as her library grew, so did her unrest. The books both soothed and infuriated her. Being made aware of such unimaginable injustices, as told by the slaves in *Bullwhip Days* and *Drums and Shadows*, rendered her weak with pain while it strengthened and validated her very existence at the same time. Nilé would often stare out the window, recreating scenes of sorrow, seeing herself enslaved and sparsely clad, back riddled with welts and bent over the unforgiving twigs in her imaginary "massa's" cotton fields. Thorns tearing into her calloused fingers, hating and punishing her for being born black, reminded her of the reality of her fate, while fluffy clouds larger than the crinolines of nearby white girls her age sailed overhead through the bluest of blue skies with detached tranquility.

One Sunday morning, while stepping out of the shower, Nilé caught a brief glimpse of herself. Her frame was as the kids said "thick" and for the most part she was ashamed of it. Various fad diets, free weights, and exercise balls were scattered around her place, reminders of how she tried and failed. Drying off in the bathroom (because she couldn't see her figure in the steamed mirror), she secretly argued that slavery would have at least given her the figure she longed for because she would not have been able to eat! Then, as if charmed by some ancestral matriarch, Nilé walked into her bedroom. In zombielike fashion, she slowly turned and stood directly in front of her full-length mirror. Dropping her towel in obedience to a distant command, she stared at her naked body. Eyes that used to wince at a plump form quietly inspected her image and became forgiving. The morning's sun poured playful rays through burgundy sheers making zebralike stripes of her entire torso. She felt sensuous examining heavy pendulous breasts with raisin-brown nipples ready to protrude at the slightest touch. They begged the question: "Why **wouldn't** the sight of these ripe brown melons run massa away from the red-tipped, white-skinned and blue-veined udders of a dried-out wife?" She caressed her pecan-brown satin pillow of a stomach, punctuated and pouting around an invisible belly button, and then discerned how hips that bore stretch marks resembled golden rays of an evening sunset. She began to smile sheepishly, turning sideways to inspect fat legs inherited from her momma. Her eyes finally looked toward her rear end, anxious to discover the beauty of that which she used to refer to as her laundry bag. A bold, round, hefty, and voluptuous bottom dared her to even *think* of a mean thing to say about it. Nilé literally blushed from within, feeling embarrassed that her skin tingled with excitement. What was it about today that made this happen? The energy in the room exploded with the spirits of black women laughing, singing, and celebrating their individual beauty. They roared with each of Nilé's discoveries about her body, while bragging that the features she realized as beautiful came from them. Nilé finally grasped that she was not solely responsible for the way she looked. DNA that remembered and etched the shape and size of Momma's legs into her cells was responsible as well. Her grandfather's dark rich grizzly brown skin mixed with the redbone *yallaness* of her grandmother rendered her the color that she was, and she had no more control of her big behind than she did her skin tone. Coming to terms with her appearance made her grimace at the thought that she once considered undergoing a liposuction procedure. She wondered just how many times Grandpa's head enjoyed the yielding comfort of Grandma's tummy before she settled down to sleep. As thick as Momma was, why was Daddy always wrapping his arms around her waist? She determined that he knew a round warm rump was nice to snuggle up to back-in-the-day when there was no heat. Nilé slowly applied lotion to her voluptuous frame and felt really, really good. She could feel the pride of her ancestors too. She wondered if Brotha' Man liked full-framed women. Dang! Why didn't she get his digits?

CHAPTER 3

Brotha' Man

Jordan Beslow was very tall. "You must play basketball" was often an opening line from passers-by. He wondered why his height warranted total strangers to take a shot at his occupation, since he would never ask a short person, "Do you make toys for Santa in the North Pole?" His frame was thin and wiry, although his shoulders were broad. Veins the width of computer cords wrapped around attenuated arms covered with soft fluffy hair so thick it could almost be parted. Both men and women deemed him pretty. He had deep-set eyes protected by a curtain of lashes, full and long, that seemed to weigh down his lids. He had what the old folks called "good hair," and that's exactly why he chose to lock it. Since he had no control over his height and color, he thought he could at least manage the comments about his hair. But it didn't work. Women would come up and request to touch it, commenting, "It's so pretty!" One woman exclaimed, "Lord! You look like a racehorse reared up on your hind legs! I could just ride you into the sunset!"

Jordan was the kind of person that people could always describe in two-word sets: "Pretty Nigga," "Dark fella," "Tall brotha'," "Quiet guy." For the longest time he was shy. The youngest of three siblings, the one closest to him being ten years his senior, Jordan was a loner by default. His sister Gina was sixteen years old when he was born and acted as if she were his mother. Bossy and overbearing, she kissed, hugged, and combed his hair too much. His momma worked day and night and he adored her, while his brother Darnell acted as if he wasn't there except for the times when Momma brought home goodies. Breaking a candy bar in two, or snapping a yo-yo apart, Darnell would be the first to remind Jordan that he wasn't a full brother and that half brothers should only get half. If Jordan complained or cried, Darnell would throw the toy over a roof. Later, he would whip Jordan's behind for getting him in trouble.

Darnell was the first to call Jordan black. At age four, Jordan responded with "I am not. I'm brown!" Darnell placed his 14-year-old arm next to his brother's. He seemed to win the argument instantly just because his arm was stronger and longer. Jordan's small hairless arms were as deep and rich as ox blood. He began to whimper as Darnell spoke slowly saying, "No, I'm brown; this hot dog bun is brown; Gina's face is brown, but yo' black ass is black! Look at you! You look like the toast Momma burnt up yesterday!" He'd point at Jordan, then begin to sing Stevie Wonder's *Purple raindrops, painted flowers*. Jordan would run off screaming with his hands in his ears, "Shut up! I am not a purple raindrop!"

"At least his hair ain't nappy," Gina would retort, grabbing Jordan. Then she'd commence to comb his soft dark curls and somehow this would make him feel worse. "Look at you! You're turning him into a punk, and he likes it!" Though he didn't know what punk meant, he knew instinctively that she was doing something wrong because Darnell enjoyed pointing it out. The look in his big brother's eyes would make him feel sick, and he would jerk away from Gina's arms and run into his momma's closet where it was warm, quiet, and smelled safe.

By age fourteen, things had gotten worse. Gina was married with kids of her own and Darnell was still living at home, claiming that because Momma's health was failing he had to look out for her. Truth be told, he knew that she had settled a big fat disability case from a slip-and-fall, and her checks would come in steady for the rest of her life. The house was paid for; she already got checks because of Gina and Darnell's father's death in Vietnam, and so there was no need in his eyes to go out there on his own. Momma was too tired to fight when he nagged Jordan to get a job because **his** daddy's check didn't cover Jordan's black behind.

Fortunately, it was never hard for Jordan to find work. He was bright, loved math and science, and the neighborhood clothing stores would almost beg him to work for them, because his looks would increase sales by almost 30 percent. By age eighteen, he had won a full scholarship to Pennsylvania State University where he would receive his undergraduate degree in chemistry and graduate summa cum laude. All these accomplishments were fueled by his hate for, and need to get away from, his light-skinned brother.

CHAPTER 4

Where two rivers meet

Spring in Philadelphia is best displayed on the East and West River drives. These drives flank the Schuylkill River, a tributary to the Delaware. East River Drive was later renamed Kelley Drive in respect for a Philadelphia-born athlete and father to the late actress Grace Kelly. But to this day, most of the older blacks still call it East River Drive. In spring on the drives, when the sky remembers winter and remains steel grey, dogwood trees begin to bloom and drip fat white blossoms stained with burgundy edges over park benches and picnic tables. Cherry blossoms shed delicate pink snowflake petals, only to be whisked away by compact cars and SUVs chasing the winding river. Geese inspect fresh sprouting sod with the dauntless pecking of their shoehorned bills while joggers' ponytails impersonate metronomes, maintaining the pace of their owners' hearts. Lovers sprawl across park benches staring at the graceful frames of men and women skimming across the river in crew shells and canoes.

Nilé had agreed to meet her girlfriend Betty at East Falls Bridge to begin their annual spring walk. They would always start walking at an athletic pace, but by the time they reached the Art Museum, they would be strolling slowly, laughing at people and checking out the brothers. Irritated that Betty was late, Nilé phoned her to find out what was wrong.
"Oh Nilé! I'm so sorry! I had a paper to finish, and I've been up all night with it. I'm off today so I wanna' get at least two more hours of sleep in before I go to work tonight."
"Go to work? When did you start working at night?"
"When the landlord upped my rent $50.00 and I found out Kila's room and board wasn't covered this year by her scholarship. That's when!"

"Oh girl, I'm so sorry."
"No, I'm sorry, baby! I forgot to call you."
"Girl, don't sweat it. I'm out here now, I'ma do this myself. Just don't hate when my stuff gets tight, 'cause I **will** be frontin'!"
"Chile, you're gonna' have ta walk the equator to lose that booty, but keep believing!"

Disconnecting from her cell, Nilé felt as the kids would say, "Some type of way" walking alone, but two or three minutes of taking in the breathtaking view lightened her spirits. As she cleared an underpass, she saw a black man at a distance reading a book. Reaching into her pocket, she snatched up some lip-gloss, and quickly yanked away a twisty that held her micro braids in a ponytail. With braids falling around her face, creating a softer look, Nilé sucked in her belly just as she approached the park bench. That's when she recognized him. Brotha' Man! Not knowing whether to slow down or speed up, Nilé's stomach was doing handsprings, and it seemed as if God just turned up the temperature by at least ten degrees. Quickly she decided to act as if she didn't remember him. That way, she would not be embarrassed if he did not notice her. After all, he was engrossed in his book. Looking straight ahead and picking up her pace, Nilé thought time stood still when she stumbled over his foot. It was all she could do to keep from landing flat on her face, and the two huge galloping steps followed by flailing arms every which way eliminated any chance of her looking graceful.

"Oh! Sugga, are you all right?" Nilé thought she was going to implode.
"Uh…yes…uh…I'm OK. Guess I stumbled or something." *I guess I stumbled OR SOMETHING?* she asked herself. *What the hell else could it possibly have been?*

He tried to make her feel better. "No. I've got big feet."
"Was it your foot? I thought I'd hit a rock!"
"Naw, it was my foot, Sugga."

Sugga? *Should I be offended or flattered? It's not quite as bad as Baby, but it is a little early to be calling me...*
"I hope you don't mind my calling you Sugga. It's just the name I've given you since I saw you in the bookstore last year. I mean I never got a chance to ask your name. You just about flew out of the store and..."
Sweet Jesus, my Redeemer! He remembered!
"No, that's OK! My name's Nilé."
"How do you spell that? N-i-e-l-a-y?"
"No, it's N-i-l-e with an accent over the e. My mom just named me Nile, and I got tired of the kids laughing at me so I added an accent by the time I reached junior high school."
"But didn't the kids from grade school remember?"
"Oh I had moved by that time up north, so it was kinda' like a new beginning for me."
"I see. That explains that slight drawl I've been hearing."
"Oh, you have one too, Brotha' Man, just in case you didn't know!"
"Brotha' Man! That's a throwback from the seventies!"
Nilé giggled. "Funny, but that's what I named *you* after the bookstore incident."
"So, you thought about me?"
Little Anthony's song *Day and night! Night and day and night* came to mind.
"Uh, on occasion you would come to mind. What made you name me Sugga?"
Brotha' Man searched the cement path while slowly forming a response. "Your disbelief was so sweet. I mean let's be honest, we're not babies and coy doesn't work anymore. But it seemed like you were so genuinely taken aback that someone would actually flirt with you. And for the life of me I can't imagine why. You're so beautiful. Anyway I named you Sugga 'cause you looked like a sweet little girl on Easter Sunday—eyes all big and smilin'."
Nilé was dizzy. Every physical reaction was kicking in. She had to pee; her knees were weak; she was sweating like a dancing bear. And if there had been a siren attached to her crotch, everyone within a five-mile radius would have heard.

"Ah, do you come here often?" *Oh Lord. Nilé,* ***tell me you didn't just say that!***
Jordan smiled, discerning her embarrassment. "As often as the weather allows. This is my favorite section of the city. There's no other place like it in the world." Nilé sensed it was her turn to speak. "Oh that's nice." ***What did he just say?***
"Where are you heading?" Brotha' Man asked. "Even though it's none of my business."
"Um, I was supposed to be walking with one of my girlfriends. You know, down to the Art Museum and back. A girl's gotta' at least try to knock off a few pounds."
"Why? So she can look good to other sistas? Never got that one. I don't believe there's a brother out there who would say you needed to lose an ounce. Every man likes his steak thick and juicy."
Oh hell, that's it! He's gettin' the drawers! I don't even care if he outright asks for it in the next sentence. The answer will be yes!

"Well! I just don't know what to say!"
"Say, 'Walk with me, Jordan.' That's *MY* name."
It doesn't get any better than this. I'm being paid back for going to church a few times this year. Thank You, Jesus!
"Ah...Walk with me, Jordan?"
"I thought you'd never ask!"

CHAPTER 5

Angie

Since her father's death, Nilé found herself embracing memories of the man she absolutely adored. Though only around dinnertime it seemed, Nilé recalled nights when she and Daddy would howl with laughter while watching a favorite sitcom on TV. Her mother would argue that the only reason why she kept good grades in school was so that she could get to watch TV with her dad.

Mr. Davis was light and easygoing. Both her parents were adamant about homework, studying, and good grades, and Big "D's" wrath was nothing to toy with. If Nilé brought home a C in anything, Big "D" would stare at the grade and mumble, "This doesn't make any sense." Then he would look at Nilé and ask, "Do you know what 'C' means? 'C' means mediocre—do you want to be mediocre?" Nilé would remain silent knowing that the question was purely rhetorical, and if she dared to answer, her head would spin from the blow she would receive.

"Well guess what? Ain't no chile o' mine mediocre. Go get all your books...every one of 'em. Bring 'em right here. I don't care if you have twenty-five subjects this year, we goin' over all yo' subjects tonight!" Sometimes they would be up until 1:00 or 2:00 a.m. Later, Nilé's tears long since dried up, they would find themselves engaged in fascinating discussion in some chapter she was to study that at first was sheer drudgery to learn. Big "D" would always say, "If you don't care about what the teachers are trying to teach you, I better not find out!"

His death came as a terrible blow to Nilé. Somehow, she thought he would live forever. She found out from her sister that "Daddy" passed in his sleep. As far as she and her sister knew, nothing was wrong with him except that he was old. Information such as "medical conditions" her mom and dad kept to themselves. Research would later reveal that Daddy had congestive heart failure. His weight and poor eating habits caught up with him. Eden and Nilé talked for hours the day he died, disregarding the threat of the horrific phone bill that their bicoastal distance presented. After the shock of the news, screaming, tears, and consoling one another, they finally settled down to "remember whens."

Eden reminisced, "I remember when you were born. He introduced you to the couch, the TV, the refrigerator...all the things he liked most! Then he walked you back to Momma stating, 'Now don't get all tight with this here woman just 'cause she's got a sweet tit! That's how she ropes you in!' Everybody hollered but I didn't understand why he didn't want you to like Mom."
"I remember how Daddy would whistle through his teeth silly songs nobody ever heard of. I don't think he knew the song...he was making up notes just to be whistlin'!"

While they mused over memorable occasions, Nilé made mental notes to look into the sketchy aspects of her childhood, but for now, she embraced the moment, enjoying her sister's voice and dismissing a gnawing feeling in the center of her soul.

After her conversation with her big sister, Nilé stretched to reach for her CDs. She was looking for one in particular. Miles Davis' *Kind of Blue*. Big "D" would play it when he came home from work. Closing her eyes, she remembered the smell of Momma's pot roast with carrots and potatoes that stuck to the edges of the old Dutch oven pot. How the collard greens cooked slow all day on the back burner, and how she would steal what Momma called her "pie guts" (wedges of apples soaking in cinnamon and sugar) from a thick white bowl with two turquoise stripes at the top of it.

She could hear Daddy's crisp whistles during catchy musical riffs. She recalled looking over to her sister's room and seeing her sprawled across a bed with eyes fixed on a favorite TV western.

Nilé fast-forwarded the CD player to her favorite tune, the fourth track "All Blues," then sat back and made soft kissing sounds until Patwa appeared. Jumping into her lap, they purred, cooed, and loved each other up until Patwa couldn't take it anymore. He leaped over to a vacant window soaked in sunshine and stretched until the surface of the windowsill disappeared. Dropping his head down to his paws, he swallowed a few times, looked across to Nilé, then he blinked as if to say, "Now *you* go do something productive." Eyes closed, she rocked gently to the sultry sound of Miles' horn until interrupted by a sharp **bam, bam, bam** at the door.

"You knew I was comin' over! Why didn't you leave the door open? Damn! Normals are so inconsiderate." It was Angie Nixon, Nilé's paraplegic neighbor who lived beneath her. Rolling her chair past Nilé and speaking affectionately to the cat, Angie referred to "Normals" as people who think that there is nothing wrong with them. Categorizing them as such simply brought to light that they were the only ones who believed that "Normals" (according to Angie) were the sickest type of people. Real people had enough sense to know that *nobody's* normal, and as a result they were not so hard pressed about becoming one. Outside of a full-blown cuss-out from Angie, being called a "Normal" was a low blow.

"Angie, you never said *when* you were coming."
"Oh, that's right, you need dates and times! Normals operate that way. Sorry...my time is pretty much governed by when I need to take a dump, which is once a day."
"Angie...that's information I don't need!"
"Did ya eat yet?" Dropping a sizable package onto the coffee table, Angie rolled her chair over to her favorite spot next to the fireplace. "I just love this! Knitting needles....colorful

balls of yarn all casually placed by the cozy fireplace in a big fat African basket. You are so creative! I bet you don't even knit—do you?"

"What's in the bag, Ange?"

"Your carrot cake."

"You made it? Oh Angie! I love you, baby!" Nilé commenced to hugging and kissing all over Angie's Bantu knots, which pissed Angie off even more.

"What's with the jazz? You got nigga troubles?"

"No, I was just thinking about my dad and…"

"Turn that mess off! Miles Davis reminds me of that ugly Larry that thought he was doin' me a favor. All I wanted from him was fresh fish! The brother could fish his tail off! He'd get up early in the mornin' and touch the window, talkin' bout, 'Sky's warm, it just rained. That means the fish will be close to the surface today.' I'd roll over and tell 'im, 'Well git yo' ugly butt up and scoop them jernts on out of the river then!' Brother started to even look like a fish. Big lips, bulging eyes, scaly ashy legs….Had the nerve to color his rhiney afro **blond**! He thought it looked good! His black behind and yellow hair made him look like a walkin' cheeseburger! Larry the fish-eyed Hamburger!" Patwa launched himself into Angie's lap.

"Now here's my main nigga!" She whispered into Patwa's ear, "You an' me know sumpin' bout' gettin' off by ourselves, don't we?"

"Don't make my cat nasty like you! Get down, Patwa!"

Angie looked over at the coffee table filled with books and commented, "You got new ones, huh?"

"New what?" By then Nilé was in the kitchen putting on a pot of tea.

"New Afro-books. This one looks good. What's it about?"

"Ah, that's about Marcus Garvey's Universal Negro Improvement Association papers."

"OOOOOh! I seeeeeeee!" Angie's obvious sarcasm forced Nilé to expound.

"Marcus Garvey was a Black Nationalist who led a movement of Black social improvement up in Harlem. Apparently, he was quite charismatic because his reasoning moved many. He believed in the beauty and grandeur of the African race and actually promoted cultural separatism. He urged Blacks in America to build their own nation and was so anti-assimilation that 'Whitey' distributed propaganda stating that he was a con man. The Universal Negro Improvement Association papers attempted to set the record straight. It's a compilation of reports, newsletters, legal records, pamphlets….anything… you name it. The object was to provide a backdrop, picture so to speak, of the evolution and spread of the UNIA. There are about ten volumes. This is just the first one."
"And you gonna read em' all?"
"Eventually."
"Damn baby! *Roots* just ain't deep enough for you, huh?"
"It's not that, Ange. Mom and Daddy always encouraged us to read. Somewhere in my life's journey, I've all but lost touch with what was going on as I grew up, and what is going on now. 'Stick your spoon deep into the bowl of knowledge!' Momma used to say. She said that it was the only meal that should still leave you hungry after eating. I miss sitting up with Daddy late at night and unearthing some of the mysteries of the great stones found on Easter Island. I've decided to look into the history of our people…you know, find out as much as I can about us. For Daddy. For me. I just found out that he passed away on Tuesday. Eden's flying back home next week and we have to help Momma to get him underground. This was his music. I just need to feel him some kinda' way, you know? I am middle aged and I feel like my brain has damn near atrophied! What happened to my caring about the world around me? All I do is work. That media pabulum they feed us on TV is only what the government wants us to hear, and what's going on locally is written to keep us with a defeatist attitude about change and improvement." Nilé knew that she could rattle on and on to Angie. They would often have long, drawn out, and heated

discussions about all topics under the sun. Angie had the time, and though she did not keep her nose in the books, she knew a lot about many things.

"Damn, Nilé! I'm so sorry to hear about your dad. Don't worry 'bout food, I got that, baby....and you know I'll sing."

There was a long silence.

"So why aren't you looking into political stuff? You know, current events and stuff like that?"

"Well...I figured I needed to understand my past before I could intelligently fight for my future..."

"Hmmm, there's an element of BS in that last statement...Was there a brother that you met at the bookstore who's Afrocentric that I'm not hearing about?"

Angela Nixon was beautiful, intelligent, and extremely perceptive. One could wax poetic for hours and hold her captive, but she would pick up the moment a person's agenda changed and quote the very word that changed the weather of the conversation. Born and raised in the Germantown section of Philadelphia, both her parents retired from the Post Office. Government jobs made them lower middle class, which translated to the closest thing to rich as far as East-side Blacks were concerned. Germantown was considered "hoity-toity" back in the day, but Angie always shrugged her shoulders and said it was just a ghetto separated by lawns. The real upper crusts were those who lived on the west side of Germantown Avenue. They were called "West-Siders." Crossing over you could immediately see the difference. In the summer, the temperature dropped about 10 degrees. Single homes, larger lawns, and grand old trees that provided shade and beauty for residents lined the streets. The Mister Softee truck seldom stopped on the West Side, and if it did, it was because the driver had not been advised to move along. The few Blacks who lived there were lawyers, dentists, and doctors. One generation away from the Blacks who "passed" as white, this peculiar group of people formed their own strange "members-only" clan, enrolling their sons and daughters in social groups called "Jack and Jill clubs" which boasted of exclusivity rights to enable their daughters to "come out" yearly, but not before paying exorbitant amounts of money to cotillions to do so. This particular breed of Blacks needed to validate their existence by imitating the white man. They would allow their offspring to socialize with the East-siders, who shared the neighborhood schools. However, no teen could enter their offspring's party door without going through the "brown paper bag" check. This was a ritual whereby a heavily eye-shadowed, red-manicured, high-yalla socialite mother would answer the door, and tap the shoulder of those on her porch who were lighter than a paper bag as a sign that it was OK to enter. Occasionally a nice-looking brown-skinned kid could get in, but they usually were the ones with the "good hair." As they entered, the mother would ask, "Who in your family is Indian, dear?" Those left standing on the porch browner than a paper bag with nappy hair had about ten minutes to get lost or they could expect a police car to patrol by and question them.

Angie Nixon was not a "West-Sider" though she looked like one. She was tall, slender, light as vanilla custard, and pretty as a picture. Angie always had the sharp clothes, but that never made her stuck up. She was the middle child, a textbook representation of a spirit never heard or noticed. She would do outlandish things most of which were harmless yet aggravating to her parents. Her big sister was the social climber who campaigned for political office in high school, entered and won debates, yet remained socially acceptable among her peers. Her little brother could do no wrong. The only male heir of the family, he was treated like a hemophiliac and smothered with protection. No matter what Angie did, her accomplishments were minimized. So Angie hung out with the hippies, most of which were white. Strangely enough, the Black kids did not shun her. She was so funny and pretty, seems like everybody loved her, though she was always described as a "nut." At the tender age of eighteen, Angie packed her bags and ran away. She didn't do it the ghetto way. She left top shelf. Found a way to extract funds from her parents' account (enough to keep her for six months), filed for and received a passport, booked a flight to Europe, and simply flew over the cuckoo's nest! She left a beautiful goodbye letter on the kitchen table. Her dad cried and cried, while her mom ran to the phone to check their bank account status.

Having lived in England, Holland, Spain, and finally settling down in Italy, Angie was not the run-of-the-mill sister. Determined to live life to the fullest, a faulty parachute resulted in her speed fall into a patch of trees that miraculously kept her alive but severed her spinal cord and rendered her motionless from the mid-lumbar section of her spine to her sacrum. By the age of 36, she was back home living with her mom, which she affectionately re-named the "Uber-Nazi." Her father's death was particularly difficult to accept because it was during her later years that she found out that he really loved her but just wasn't the type to show it. It was only during his final months that Angie and her dad became real friends, and tending to his health kept her mind from her disability. After his death, a final argument with her mother resulted in her moving to the small manageable duplex below Nilé, where she remodeled the interior to accommodate her needs. She invested thousands of dollars into her kitchen, and at age 48, she cooks meals for the handicapped and has them delivered steaming hot and delicious to loving clientele five days a week. That's how she met the "Fishman" who, though she would never admit it, broke her heart.

"So who's the brotha'?"
"Ange…why do you always have to go there? Why can't I be **really** trying to improve myself?"
"Beats the sneaks off of me! Who is he?" Smiling coyly, Nilé sat on the edge of the coffee table, handed Angie a cup of Earl Grey and a slice of her own baked cake, sighing, "Oh Ange…his name is Jordan…."

CHAPTER 6

What sistas do best

Nilé told of how she and Jordan met, keeping all the juicy details intact because Angie insisted. She told her of their long walk down the drive, and how they exchanged numbers but agreed that neither of their schedules were ready for anything more than a casual friendship.

"Youze a lie! What else you gotta' do with your life besides build a relationship with a fine brotha'? Whas' wrong with you? Have you lost your mind?"
"Angie! Don't start with me now! You know what's going on with me and how I can't handle any man, let alone a fine intelligent man at this point in time…."
"At this point in time? Just what the hell does that mean? I mean semantically, break it down, Nilé. By the time you finish saying at-this-point-in-time, that point has traveled past the time you verbally had it stuck on! See, Normals don't think before they speak and that really irks me!"
"Oh come on, Angie, I'm not in the mood for your frantic semantic oratory."
"Well, get yourself in the mood to hear that you are a fool."
"Fool? That's just downright mean, Angie."

"F-O-O-L, Fool! A fool to ever think beyond 'this-point-in-time' because…guess what? This point in time is all you get! A fool not to realize that God had enough sense to know we can't handle life unless it's moment by moment. Normals try to clump thoughts and goals into time-shares not even promised to them, and some of which they cleverly try to label as relationships. You shouldn't even say relationship thinking of something in the future. How you know it's gonna' happen? Go ahead and screw up all the potential of what could possibly evolve into a phenomenal moment-by-moment experience. Telling me that both you and he agreed to forfeit **now**…for fear of the future…that you have no control of…because it might possibly hold in it a thing called a 'relationship'…of which you have no idea **how it could be** because you've flagged it! **FOOL!**"

"Oh Angie….please don't be mad."
"I am mad! I'm mad 'cause you hold on to the wrong stuff! Look at me. I once was able to party, run across a street, feel warm sand between my toes. I can't now. Do I cry? No! It's over, Nilé! That 'point in time' is through! Yes, I can still remember, but I'll be damned if I channel all my emotions through some labyrinth called 'the past' retarding my ability to experience the 'now-ness' of my living experience. As for my future, my future is up to Jesus, and He has *never* let me in on it. Before my awakening, I was dumb enough to believe I could control it—my future. Could I possibly walk again? Maybe, but that answer is up to my sweet Savior and a few concerned therapists. Right now, I cook dinners in a wheelchair, and I do that better than most people standing up who took lessons! Right now!"

"Angie, I know that what you're saying is right but…"
"It ain't about right, Nilé, it's about truth. Truth frees you. You cannot move forward because the obstacles of your past are clouding your future. Just check out the contradiction, Nilé. How can the past be part of a future? To me, the phrase 'history repeats itself' is an admission of stupidity! It's this phenomenal looping effect that allows the past to jerk you around because you keep telling yourself 'It won't happen this time,' never realizing that the moment it does, it's because you've simply replaced the 'now' with something that was done in the past instead of being creative and doing something different. Just when will the future get a chance to play itself out? Come on, Nilé, your stinking name means 'the source of all that is living.' Why do you insist on killing that which could keep you alive?"

Nilé was unprepared for that kind of depth of conversation. In an effort to help her friend, Angie touched live-wired emotions within Nilé that rendered her weak. Knowing each other since childhood made it difficult for either of them to camouflage personality flaws, and Nilé was not in the mood.

"Angie...I just wanna' rest for a while" was the only response Nilé could think of, but it became painfully obvious that Angie was not letting go.

"Here's the deal, girlfriend...you are afraid of happiness. You'd rather live in memories of the past where you learned to handle oppression than move toward a future of happiness because you don't know how to function in it. But I'm not even mad at you, Sister-girl, because most Normals act that way. It's a strange thing when you're not in touch with your mortality. That's what Normals believe. They really think they've got a lot of time, and what they end up doing is wasting it and becoming bitter when they're old 'cause that's when their sorry old behinds realize life ain't forever! Yeah, a minute takes much longer when you can't walk around in it! Old folks know that, and are pissed because all they have to look back on is the time they've lost!"

Nilé's buzzer sounded and Angie looked out the window and announced that she saw Betty's car. Up the staircase Betty tipped as light as a feather yelling, "I knew somebody was here 'cause the windows were steamy! How you doin', Angie?"
"I'm sick of your best friend."
"Wha's my buddy doin' now?" Betty bellowed.
"Tell her how you're blowing an opportunity thrown at you by God Himself!"
"Huh?"
"Don't pay no attention to her, Betty. She's got on her philosopher's hat today and she's waxin' with the best of 'em."
"Well at least fill me in."

"I told her how I met this dude.."
"WHAAT?"
"You heard her…" Angie mumbled.
"Calm down! Yes, the day you were supposed to walk with me, wait… actually I met him last winter…"
"Oh hell no! You didn't go meet a guy and not tell me about him 'till SPRING! Now *I'm* sick of ya." Betty and Angie high-fived each other.
"Man! It is a pitiful thing to feel defensive in my own house! First of all, I don't have to tell either one of you heffas anything, and second of all you both for the most part have been blowin' me off, what with all your fancy dinners and you Betty working both day and night…"

Both sisters chimed in, defending and justifying their reasons for not keeping in touch. The volume reached a feverous pitch and was silenced only by the constant ding-donging of a doorbell hardly ever used.
"Who the heck is at my door?" Angie asked. She looked out the window but couldn't recognize any cars. "Who is it?" She hollered down. By this time, all three sisters were peering out the window. Moments later a tall dark brother with okra-wide waist-length salt-and-pepper locks pulled neatly in a ponytail stepped backward toward the street to see if he could see the face attached to the voice that called.
There was silence. Jordan spoke.
"Uh, hello…uh, I'm trying to reach a Nilé Davis?"
Everyone looked at Nilé.
The silence was broken when she cleared her throat, then surprisingly exclaimed, "Oh! Hey Jordan! I'll be right there!"
Though it was quiet enough to hear a mouse pee on cotton, mouths were wide open. Wrists were bent with hands and fingers poised like giant tarantulas frozen across panting chests. Betty broke the silence with a whisper, "Is that who you were talking about?"

"Yes. Yes, and I think I'm gonna' need you guys to disappear because I'm not going to try to embarrass myself…"

"Oh baby, we'll leave, but not till we get a good look. You owe your sister a peek o' dat eye candy!" Glaring at the nerve of Angie, Nilé buzzed Jordan in.

"Ummmm! His footsteps sound sexy!" Everyone was giggling but Nilé.

An incredibly handsome man walked into Nilé's apartment with a book and spray of flowers tucked under his arm. The ladies glanced at his possessions, which prompted his presenting them to Nilé.

"I'm old fashioned and was raised to bring something to the table if I'm gonna' visit…"

"Well far be it from me to contradict yo' momma by saying you shouldn't have!" cried Angie.

"Angie, this is Jordan Beslow, Jordan…Angie Dixon."

"Pleased to meet you."

"The pleasure's all mine!"

"And this is Elizabeth Booker." Nilé remembered that Betty hated being introduced as Betty Booker.

"Elizabeth."

"Call me Betty!" was her response.

"And ah, um…thank you for the book and flowers, what made you decide to stop by?"

"A couple of things. I wanted to bring you that book I was telling you about and I also needed to see if you were being honest about where you lived."

"Thanks, but I could have picked it up at the bookstore…"

"There she go, wreckin' the moment!" With that, Angie wheeled her chair toward the door and announced that she had a pie to take out of the oven. Betty jumped on the cue exclaiming "Pie! You got a pie going? I'm in the wrong place!" Angie and Betty said their goodbyes and privately chitchatted down the stairway and ramp.

"Look, we're getting off to a bad start here. I mean, if your mother went as far as raising you to bring something to the table, she should have told you its impolite not to call before dropping in. Jordan, I'm not a baby, I'm sort of set in my ways and coming over without notice, with or without flowers, is just unacceptable."

"Hmmm, now that you've stated your position and may I say without the least bit of tact, I can comfortably say that my mission has been accomplished. I've seen where you live, and you have the book. Sooooo, keep the flowers—they look so good in this room." Jordan turned toward the door and blew a kiss to the cat, which instantly jumped down and started making figure eights around his leg. "Well at least she likes me."

"It's a he. Look, you're here, you might as well stay."

"And do what? **Visit?**" Then he laughed. "Sorry, I'd rather dine on shark chum! This was a bad idea. I'm sorry. I thought when we were on the drive that you were looking for a friend. I'm not trying to get to 'another level.' I'm not looking for a woman. I too am set in my ways. I am serious about the flowers though; my mom would kill me if I didn't show my manners. Flowers…manners. Manners…flowers. That's it! Sorry you read more into it."

"Read more into it? And just what do you think I've read into your visit? You brought up the *level* business, I just said I didn't want any company!"

"That's why your place was full of people and there are pretty little tea cups and saucers on the table?"

"You know what?"

"No. I don't know what." With that statement, stooping down a little, Jordan gave Nilé a peck on the forehead and walked out the door, nearly knocking Betty over who was standing on the other side.

CHAPTER 7

Introspective

The room rang with silence the moment he walked out. Figuring that it was not a good time to go in, Betty turned and headed back down to Angie's to report that all had gone wrong as far as she could see and hear. Flopping down on a nearby loveseat, Betty sighed, "What's wrong with that woman? Why doesn't she want to at least be friendly to the opposite sex? Every time someone attempts to merely scratch-n-sniff, Nilé arches her back and shows all her teeth. What's up with that?"

"She's scared, Betty. Thas' all, she's just plain scared."
"Scared of what? A meaningful relationship with a fine man? Hell, I'd jump at the opportunity to last at least a year with Boo Boo the Clown! All he needs is a job with some insurance and a $5.00 copay; hell, I ain't gotta like his red nose!"

"Nilé really went through it with FM, you know that. Give her time. She'll come 'round. I've been working on her a little bit, but you can say but so much, then she'll close up on you like one of them fresh clams Larry used to bring in here....damn! I miss that seafood."
"That ain't all you miss 'bout Larry, now go on and say so!"
"Oh I miss Larry all right....but my aim is gettin' better!"
"Girl, shut up and put on some Luther. I feel like havin' a good ol' sing-along. You down?" Angie wheeled over to her CD collection. It looked like a store. Everything was in alphabetical order and sectioned off according to the genre. R&B, classical, country western, you name it, she had it. Strangely enough, she had very little gospel music, but the girl could sing *Great Is Thy Faithfulness* so pretty it would get you saved on the spot! Any funeral that was to be had

would have Angie singing in it. *His Eye Is On The Sparrow, It Is Well With My Soul,* all the classics she knew, and through ruby-red lipstick on full and sensuous lips, each deep unrestricted note would pour out like aged brandy from a crystal chalice. Betty closed her eyes as they harmonized to Luther Vandross's "Because It's Really Love."

Meanwhile upstairs Nilé listened to the sultry base lines and bemoaned the fact that she had sent Jordan away. Smiling as she recognized Betty's pitiful attempt to harmonize, she tried to rationalize all the things she said to Jordan, but her heart was heavy nonetheless. Like her best friends downstairs, she wondered why she ran from love, and just as her breathing began to shorten, her eyes seemed to know the cue, dropping fat salty tears down her face.

"It's FM. Everything is measured against FM. Why?" Feeling her anguish, one by one the ancestors moved closely toward her. It was difficult to get through the obvious spiritual discord, so the sisters of Nilé's life summoned Affia, an ancestor whose personality was beset with similar troubles while on earth. With every "Why?" Nilé posed, Affia recalled moments when her hardheadedness kept her from moving forward. They were so alike with regard to their self-made concept of "order." Affia could not leave her dwelling unless everything was arranged symmetrically. She believed the gods required order in a home before they could properly bless it. This would often result in family conflict because important ceremonial events were delayed because of Affia's obsessive nature. Affia rattled on and on about order until it caught Nilé's attention. Suddenly she thought about how she could never enjoy a cup of tea unless it had a saucer. The thinner the cup, the better, and the saucer had to match. Nilé often said that a large heavy mug made her spirit sad because it reminded her of people without mates. "You see (she'd explain), mugs are thick and heavy like the spirits of single people." She would argue, "They're thick because they have to withstand all trials and tribulations alone and heavy because the weight of such knowledge makes them that way. Now a teacup and saucer although thin and appearing weak with delicate flowers and perhaps scalloped edges boasts of partnership. Though fragile, the cup is still colorful and able to embrace the hottest of liquids, knowing that its mate, the saucer, is nearby. Having separate but equal jobs to do, the teacup and saucer partner and endure all situations together."

Gathering the teacups, napkins, teaspoons, and saucers from nearby tables, Nilé asked herself, "What's that got to do with me and men? Jesus! Why am I thinking about teacups and saucers and crying?" Then, out of nowhere, Nilé felt a biblical scripture verse: *"Wherefore seeing we also are encompassed about with so great a cloud of witnesses, let us lay aside every weight, and sin which so easily beset us, and let us run with patience that race that is set before us..."*

She asked herself, *"What witnesses? What race?"*

CHAPTER 8

"FM"

Jordan's departure left a brooding atmosphere throughout the apartment. As Nilé rinsed soapy teacups and saucers, an awareness of sadder days moved upon her spirit. Though she tried to resist the memories of him, FM kept appearing. His smell, those penetrating eyes, his laugh…his anger. She wondered why she never saw it coming. Was there really such a thing as being caught in a spell?

She was crazy about the man she married. Walking down the aisle, she saw no one but him and he was in her eyes Adonis. In retrospect she realized that there were some who warned her about him, but she didn't take heed. He was funny, ruggedly good looking, intelligent, and had a little thug in him that made the package all too appealing. She felt safe around him, and though at times he displayed somewhat of an imposing jealousy, she rationalized that it was because of his consuming love for her.

He wanted her too. To the locals, she was the "prize" because if you dare go near her, you had better have your act together. Nilé had a reputation of having a razor-sharp wit. Her sarcasm would rip to shreds any foolish "line" that came her way at the owner's expense. Once, a corner boy who did not know her hollered out "Baby, you so sweet I could drink your bath water!" Right about the time when he was wondering why his boys didn't laugh, he heard: "And your belch would be far sexier than that weak line you just threw at me!" That was when everyone fell out in laughter. However, with FM it was different. He never directly pursued her.

They met the first year at Germantown High School. She transferred from Roosevelt Jr. High. FM had transferred from Morris E. Leeds. Strange as it may seem, Leeds was a good school back then, and all the guys who came from it were considered chumps. But not FM.

He was known by many and respected. In FM's high school days, a gang member's honor had to do with how well he could fight. Drug infiltration had not seized the inner cities, and gangs were established for far less lethal territorial reasons. Although FM never hung out with the corner boys, everyone knew he could hold his hands. He could cross territories and only a few fools would challenge him.

On the first day of school, there they were, assigned to the same homeroom. Nilé was sitting alone because she didn't know anyone. FM strolled in with one of his buddies. It was not a stroll per se, more like a swagger. What caught her eye was that his natural was so impeccably maintenanced. Certainly it was a given that the brothers would have fresh cuts the first day of school, but this afro was first of all huge, and second of all just plain pretty. It almost looked like a wig. Nilé studied his walk. He led with his shoulders, and was slightly pigeon-toed. Something inside told her that this person would significantly impact her life. He looked up from his roster and toward her. He was trying to see if he was in the right room. Still unsure, he grabbed the first seat on her row and sat down. Some of the girls sang out "Hey FM!" He looked over and greeted them. Before his eyes returned to the front of the room, he managed to sweep them once more Nilé's way. She, elbow on the desk, with head supported by her palm, received his glance with a blank stare. FM was amused, and got up to sit right next to her.

"You in this class?"
"No… I am an apparition…a figment of your imagination. My *real* body is in the class next door." FM stared at her for a moment. Then chuckled and looked toward the board.

When the advisor walked in the room announcing his name, FM got up and said he wasn't supposed to be there. Several of the girls sighed with disappointment as he walked out.

The first few weeks adjusting to high school was uncomfortable. Only two minutes to get to your next class in a school that seemed to have endless corridors and stairwells was a bit overwhelming for Nilé. In addition, each classroom had a different set of students, and that was hard to get used to. For the most part Nilé was quiet, paying no attention to the come-ons from goofy-looking brothers who thought they had their acts together and ignoring the snide remarks and stare-downs from the what she named "Try-Hard" girls who overdid it. These were the girls who showed a little too much cleavage, laughed, and cracked gum a little too loud and a little too hard. The "Try-Hards" were constantly soliciting FM's attention in the hallways, but he always seemed politely detached. Her heart jumped when she heard a voice say "Hi Nilé." Recognizing the voice as FM's, she casually glanced his way and asked, "How do you know my name?" The question was his perfect excuse to break away from the crowd and he walked casually toward her. His boys hooted and hollered in the background and Nilé tried to maintain composure. FM was obviously anxious and not ashamed.

"I hope you don't try to shoot me down again...that is if I'm talking to the real Nilé and not the apparition." Her smile opened the door to civil conversation.
"What's FM stand for?"
"Promise you won't laugh?"
"No."
"Then you can't know. How'd you come up with the name Nilé?"
"I didn't come up with it—it was given to me."
"Uh oh, there you go again, gettin' smart. You make a person feel like they have to edit every word that comes out of their mouth when they talk to you."

"I'm sorry, I assumed everyone did that since I was taught to think before I speak! So...educate me, people can say anything without thinking about what they say and call it conversation? Interesting!"

"Nilé. Pretty, brown, sweet, and soooo cold. Think I'll rename you Fudgesicle."

"I think this conversation is over."

Looking down at her composition book, FM read her address: "I think I'll come by and pay you a visit."

"I think you're crazy!"

"I am! 'Bout you." The bell rang; he winked at her and walked away. Eight years later, she found herself at the altar feeling as lucky to have him as he felt to have her.

After their divorce, Nilé was too tired to initiate another relationship. She could hardly maintain the routine she established for herself. Overcoming empty-nest syndrome, teaching herself to put a little lipstick on and comb her hair instead of throwing on a baseball hat was a day-to-day ritual. Self-respect was the tall order of each and every one of her days, and Nilé had difficulty with it. Difficulty redefining herself as simply Nilé, not Momma, or FM's wife. Who the heck was Nilé after 50? The last time she was single she wore an Angela Davis afro and some hip-riding-too-tight size 5 jeans with the hems walked out. Now she complained that jeans altogether were a hassle because the seams dug into her hips and crotch. Every other aspect of her life was as awkward and confusing. No, no...she was correct in overriding hormones that reached out to Jordan as if he were the Messiah. But she could not deny her hormones. She could not say that there were no feelings to be near and held by this man, any man for that matter. And, most importantly, (now that all oppression was removed from her life) what was the point of her existence? That was the kicker! She fought for so long to be free, and now it was choking her.

Patwa, either sensing her anguish or realizing his bowl was empty, delicately meowed and broke her trance. Springing

up and feeling grateful that she could fulfill once more her servicing role, Nilé sauntered toward the kitchen cupboard speaking sweetly, "Momma's last baby want his dinner?"
"Arrraaoow!"
"Yessss, him does!" The light conversation broke the spirit of heaviness and the ancestors (that great cloud of witnesses that so encompassed about her) attempted to set the record straight, and lay aside every weight that so easily beset their child, as they softly chanted, "Run the race, Nilé....run the race with patience." Recognizing that she felt them there, they seized the opportunity to call on Nana, Nilé's great-grandmother. It was the voice of Nana, who softly sang to Nilé's heart:

"I don't feel no ways tired!
Come too far from where I started from.
Nobody told me the road would be easy.
I don't believe He brought me this far to leave me."

CHAPTER 9

Nana's Wicker Back

Annie "Nana" Davis was always sort of scary in Nilé's opinion. During the summer months, Eden and Nilé were sent off to Nana's home in Trappe, Maryland, and left to live the "country life" for a few weeks.

Her house was off the road a bit. A large lawn split down the center by a walkway would greet you. Having lived in the city all her life, Nilé was amazed by the country smells. Sweet and pleasant floral aromas of Nana's garden could suddenly be interrupted with frightening and pungent odors that the nearby woods would send, just by taking one step in any given direction. Whenever the car would stop, strange insects would crawl up the doors, forcing Nilé to compromise her fresh air by rolling up the window.

As soon as Daddy turned left, and the highway dissolved into a dirt road, small pebbles would attack the side of the car announcing their arrival, and seemed to voice their distrust of Daddy's foreign northern car with loud clicks and prattles. The old dog down the road would howl for a few minutes, then lumber on back to a porch to host the flies and spiders left scurrying around when he ran off. Two wild cherry trees greeted Eden and Nilé. They imitated identical twins with the only real distinguishing difference being the direction in which their branches leaned. Most of the time the trees would be pregnant with tiny dark cherries and hang wearily over parts of Nana's porch or broken-down fence.

Once Daddy's horn was recognized, Nana would step out onto a white wooden porch flanked by sturdy tall backed swings. Eden and Nilé would scramble to claim the swing that hung evenly as their own, but Eden being the older and stronger of the two always won the straight one. Daddy would fuss, "They ain't no different! All I have to do is pull up one or two of the links and that swing will be straight!" But he never did, hence the battle went on for years.

Nana wasn't one to reach out her arms and beg for hugs. More than likely, she was drying off her hands from cleaning greens or snapping beans and would be anxious to get back to her station, but obligated to come out and talk. "Hey there!" she'd holler. Momma would walk her back to the kitchen, and Daddy would bring in the luggage. After Eden and Nilé had their share of swinging, they would ease into the kitchen to see what Nana had for them. If they arrived in the morning, it was fried corn, cut fresh off the cob, with bacon and fried tomatoes. Homemade biscuits dripping with butter were stacked on a nearby plate, and Nana would bark, "If you're gonna' eat, EAT!" Then she'd push the plates toward her great-grands and try not to smile.

The house she lived in was built by her and her husband. It was huge to Nilé who was used to living in a row house. It had a living room and a parlor. Nilé never understood why only grownups were allowed to go into the parlor. The girl's bedroom was crisp and neat. White eyelet curtains with a sharp crease ironed through the center of each panel adorned the window bottoms while the tops remained free. The wallpaper (tight and brown in the corners of the room, and not very friendly with faded flower buds) greeted the girls with a dry country familiarity. Fresh white linens with a faint smell of the backyard woods were there to offer a little cheer, and though the room was large, smelling of cedar chips, it was always a welcomed sight. The hardwood floors were covered with faded rag rugs and two cast-iron vents in the corners that when opened allowed the heat from the kitchen to flow through the room. The bed stood high with a stool by it. Tall mahogany posts surrounded the girls as they slept. Eden loved the posts, as they made her feel like a princess. Nilé loathed them, saying they made her feel caged in. Across the room, in the center of the dresser, there was a white porcelain bowl with a matching pitcher placed inside. By morning, the pitcher was filled with hot water. A large brown bar of rough textured soap and two white washcloths and towels sat next to the bowl. Because Nana's day would begin around 5:00 a.m., the girls woke up to the smell of fried chicken or pork chops and gravy. Nana would cook dinner early in the morning when the house was cool. By the time they had washed up in the porcelain bowl, hot grits with pancakes and a pork chop or two were being dished out for two little girls, and Nana was hollering upstairs, "If ya gonna eat...come on an' EAT!" Nana worshipped Eden and Nilé but never let on, oftentimes mumbling under her breath, "Them chil'ren just rotten to the core!" Eden and Nilé figured at best that Nana simply tolerated them.

The entire Davis property was theirs to roam, from the cornfield across the road to the woods that they called "the forest" behind the house. Nothing was off limits to the children. Nana knew that they would not venture towards the woods because it had a smell that frightened them. The only thing Nana warned about was the parlor and the "backstairs." Nana was adamant about those backstairs and told them countless times that if she ever caught one of them on them she would "Whup on their tails like they was a mule!" But the threat alone could not keep either of the girls from exploring them. Nana and Pop-Pop Davis built the backstairs as a means of escape. Each floor was designed to have hidden inside its walls an intricate labyrinth with hallways, hidden doors, and stairwells, all of which eventually led to a small cave about 500 feet away from the house. The cave was lined with shelving that held mason jars filled with fruits and vegetables. Jerky wrapped in burlap and tied with twine was stacked neatly in the corner. Eden and Nilé had only seen it once when Daddy took them. It was dark and musty smelling. Neither of them had to be told to stay away from the cave, but the backstairs seemed to call them. One evening when Eden and Nilé out of boredom decided to explore the stairs, Eden came up with the bright idea that they split apart to see if the walls would lead them to each other later on. Young Nilé, not wanting to appear scared, agreed. Eden went left, and she went right.

The walls were cracked and cool. Occasionally, daddy longlegs would scamper across Nilé's fingers but she dare not scream. It seemed like an eternity had gone by when she finally came to a door. Slowly turning the rusted knob, she gave the door a little push, only to find a large piece of furniture blocking it. Instead of turning back, Nilé's curiosity got the best of her. Bearing her shoulder to the door, she pushed with all her might, displacing a rag rug and chest-of-drawers. Her moment of triumph dampened when she looked up and realized that she was standing right inside Nana's bedroom! A switch made of weeping willow reeds braided and wrapped loosely around Nana's fist, with at least a foot-long tail of leaves hanging obediently by her side. It must have been Nilé's big brown eyes (the ones everyone said looked just like Nana's daughter Elsie) that kept her from getting whupped like a mule that night. Nana just said, "Git on outta' hea', gal! An' don't 'cha let me find ya' back on them steps ever a-gin'!" Nilé's only response was a grateful, "Yes ma'am." As Nilé walked past Nana, clad only in a full slip, she couldn't help but notice her great-grandmother's back. What she saw was what looked like large, dead, skin-colored earthworms covering the tiny frame of a woman well over seventy. "NANA! What's that on your back?" Nilé exclaimed.

"They is welts, chile…welts. You disobey the white man an' he'll whup ya fer it. You gals got it easy, y'aint never knowed what is' like to be owned." Not wanting to know any more, Nilé ran out the room, sickened by the sight of her Nana's wicker back. Nilé promised herself that when she grew up, no matter what, she would never be owned by anyone… white or black.

CHAPTER 10

Ironically, time served enslaved

At age fifty, Nilé one day looked in the mirror. It duplicated her voluptuous figure and she stared in disbelief for a few seconds. Just who was that person? The power imprisoned within felt frustrated by an overrated and impotent shell. This particular morning felt heavy. Deep-brown eyes were clouded by tears full of questions that dropped silently on a pillow with no answers.

She felt her life was halfway over and already too full. Full of what she didn't want. It seemed as if the harder she tried to be what she wanted to be, the more life forced her into a role she had no desire or capability of playing. She tried to list mentally all of her accomplishments, in an attempt to lift her spirit. She was a good mother, friendly, funny, a great cook, and artistic. Immediately following came the uninvited shortcomings. Procrastinator, unorganized, scatter brained, nonathletic, distant, unapproachable....hard-headed. She buried her head in the pillow, hoping the list would end. It didn't. What's more, it had a voice. One that sounded like her husband's. The voice that she for years required to define her was now skillfully dismantling her...one fault at a time. She sat up. Rage replaced self-pity and she reached toward her pack of cigarettes. Striking the match and inhaling deeply, she closed her eyes to feel the tears and nicotine create a smoky haze around her pain. Looking at the pack, she spoke softly, "You and Jesus are the only friends I have, and you state clearly on your jacket that you're out to kill me!" Nilé chuckled, then sighed. "I guess it's just you, Jesus."

Closing her eyes, she imagined Jesus sitting on the bed with her. She was embarrassed. The room was a mess, and she was holding a cigarette. Then she whispered apologetically, "It helps the pain go away. Show me, dear Jesus, how to lose this habit." If there was an answer, she didn't hear it, and thoughts of her not being close to her Savior now flooded her mind. A warm and full teardrop splashed on her trembling hand. As she wiped it away, it comforted her, for somehow she knew it belonged to Him, and He after all was there.

She reminisced about days gone by when an effervescent daughter would burst into her bedroom screeching with unnecessary drama: "Momma! I don't understand this part of my homework!" She recalled how the relief of hearing a voice she adored broke prison bars of silence within.
"What don't you understand, baby?" Nilé would whisper.
"I don't…are you OK, Momma?" She noticed the tears.
"Ummmm Hmmm. What don't you get?"
"The teacher's assignment wants me to find this stupid country, and all she gave me is the prime meridian, the equator, and a stupid degree!" Nilé smiled. Her daughter always took the defense, claiming teachers, textbooks, and assignments were ambiguous agents in a conspiracy designed to make her look ignorant.
"That's all you probably need, Sugar. Let me take a look." Nilé purposely assumed the role of one not knowing how to read a map. As she read the instructions aloud, placing one finger on the prime meridian, another on the equator, she drew them together locating a spot on the map.
"Is that the country you're looking for?"
"No."
"Hmmm, then I need to know another point or direction from this point…"
"OH! I think I've got it! You must have to use this degree they gave me. Look 45 degrees northwest." Natalie took the textbook from Nilé and little fingers traced with confidence to the country she was seeking. When she found it (using the stupid degree they gave her), she sheepishly looked up at her mother and said, "Thanks," then disappeared into a bedroom whose walls vibrated with thunderous hip-hop music.

The sound of keys unlocking the living room door initiated panic. "Oh Lord, FM is home and dinner isn't even started!" Whether to make up the bed or dash downstairs to start dinner was an all-too-familiar decision she found herself forced to make. Realizing that she'd be busted either way, she began to indignantly straighten up the bedroom. "Hey FM!" the obligatory greeting spilled from her lips. "Hey" was his response. Listening to his footsteps walk from room to room assessing what she had done with her day, and visually determining not much, she could feel his disgust brewing. Down the basement he went. His lair, sanctuary, haven, whatever…a place that Nilé stayed away from except to do laundry. Looking over the bedroom and determining that it was at least presentable, she turned off the light and found her daughter Natalie close behind her.

"What'cha makin' for dinner, Mom?"
"Ya hungry?"
"Naaa, not really, I just want something that tastes good in my mouth."
"I was thinking about chicken…."
"Oooooh Momma, could you fry it? PLEEEEEZE!"
"Nat, you could eat fried chicken every night if I fixed it, couldn't you?"
"How come you don't?"
"Because you'd be one giant zit! You're blossoming into a beautiful young lady and need healthy food in you. I'm baking the chicken and we'll have a nice tossed salad with it."
"A salad with noodles?"
"OK, a salad with noodles." Feeling she had won the battle, Natalie perched herself up on the kitchen stool and commenced to tell her mother about her day. The chatter comforted Nilé moving about the kitchen as if on automatic pilot. As aromas began to permeate the house, Nilé mustered up a sweet voice and hollered toward the basement, "You hungry?"

"No, I ate a late lunch." More perturbed that she even asked, Nilé rationalized that a good wholesome meal was the point of it all, and she was the one to prepare it for her family, every night, notwithstanding the fact that no one was really hungry. Besides, it validated her. Dinner prepared proved to the world that she had done *something* with her day.

The kitchen door swung open. In walked a husky, lock-wearing, well-dressed, and handsome young man.
"Hey Momma!"
"Hey yourself! How come you home tonight? Fight with your girlfriend?" a teasing smile came across the face of Nilé as she tried not to look so pleased to see her firstborn.
"Naaaa, I figured you'd cook something good tonight since you just threw something together the night before, and the night before that, Dad ordered takeout."
"So you're clockin' my meals is what you're trying to say? Negro, big as you are, you should be fixin' dinner for me!"
"What's my size got to do with it?" By this time, they were pretend slap boxing, and Natalie was practicing the latest teenage dance steps.

It was this time of each day that was good for Nilé. She felt needed and unconditionally loved by two children who unwittingly filled her emptiness with their selfish prate and hip-hop lingo. Attempting to believe her home was not dysfunctional, she ordered Natalie to tell her dad that there was barbecued chicken, rice, and a salad upstairs if he wanted any of it. Natalie danced her way downstairs and delivered the message. Moments later, she returned with a drawn face.
"What's wrong with you?" Nilé asked.
"Daddy said he's not hungry."
"And that makes you sad?"
"No, he asked me if I'd finished my homework, and I told him all I had left to do was math, and he started fussing at me, telling me I shouldn't be in the kitchen playin' around when I know I have homework."

"Go finish your homework, Nat. Daddy's right. I thought you were done."

"All I have is one stupid page…"

"Go do it then!"

Silence fell on the kitchen as Nilé dished out a hefty portion of dinner for her son Dax and handed it to him.

"Glad my homework days are over!" Dax's attempted levity was met with a smile that soon vanished, as did he.

As anticipated, FM came up the steps. "Nilé…" he began, "why is it that I have to become the bad guy every night just to get the kids to do what they know their supposed to do?"

"I thought she had finished her homework, FM…"

"Yeah but did you ask her if it was done?"

"No." Silence filled the room.

"I'm not supposed to ask you a simple question like that, am I?"

"You just did, FM, nobody stopped you."

"Yeah but I'm not supposed to do that, am I? I'm a bad guy again, right?"

"You're not a bad guy; it's just that your timing always stinks."

"Just when is the right time, Nilé? I mean to talk to you. When can I ask you a question without your face turning sour?"

"I don't know."

"Well, if you don't know, I sure don't know either!" He stormed away mumbling to himself something about how he could no longer "live like this."

Nilé sighed and looked at a plate of food for which she no longer had a taste.

It was not always that way. They thought in the beginning that they had a fairly good idea of how to beat the world as a team. But here they were at the bottom of the ninth, bases loaded, and the score was Life 24 years to their nothing. Married too young, kids too soon, and not enough time to get to know each other before getting a crash course in paycheck-to-paycheck financing, parenting, and disappointments in general; life was kicking their butts and she as a pitcher had a dislocated attitude, while he as a catcher couldn't dream of one single signal that the enemy couldn't hit. He worried too much and was insensitive. She paid entirely too much attention to the kids and eventually stopped talking to him altogether. Twenty-four years later, they had no idea of how to enjoy each other's company, let alone hold a conversation. Ironically, it was FM who wanted to talk things out, but Nilé found herself getting nauseous each time he approached her.

Why couldn't she talk to this man? *Her* man. The God-awful answer was locked up in her heart. She was afraid of him. Not so much physically, but of the mean things that he would say to her. When they argued, he would make her feel as if she had no right to disagree with him, that any point he made needed no validation, so if she challenged him, she had better be prepared for the fight of her life. As a result, she picked her fights. Over the years, they became fewer and fewer for she had no energy to battle with him. His manner was rude, passionate, interrupting, and intimidating. Every statement she made was followed by his "What do you mean?" That was so insulting to Nilé as if everything she said required interpretation. Any point made clear was instantly dashed away by his opposing logic, and Nilé could see that he had no room in his heart to hear her point. Therefore, she resolved to be nothing but the face he required to voice his opinions. She would watch him mid-tantrum and wonder to herself how a man could ask for dialog after literally teaching her how not to talk to him.

Realizing that she had not budged from the bed and at least an hour had slipped by, Nilé recalled a song from her youth whose lyrics she out of the blue now understood:

I learned the truth at seventeen
That love was made for beauty queens

Those high school girls with painted smiles
Who married young and then retired...

There she sat, as lonely as a playground swing at midnight. Staring at hands beginning to bulge with veins, she wondered where all the time had gone. When was the last time she was held tightly in someone's arms? She thought of the days when she would spend hours to make herself pretty, just so that she could see FM's gaze the moment he saw her. She had no idea of the concept of pretty anymore, although everyone told her she was "fine" for her age. Realizing that someone had taken control of her self-esteem and enslaved it, rendering her, at best, a lifeless zombie; now at age 50, she looked in the mirror again....and cried.

CHAPTER 11

Two separate worlds

Penn State was a cultural shock for Jordan as a young man. The campus was absolutely breathtaking. Old Main, a building that sat in the center of campus whose grand old bell chimed every hour, surveyed slender young erudite students engaged in intellectual discourse while nibbling brown-bagged sandwiches under sprawling maple trees. Even the squirrels seemed smart to Jordan, as they scampered along, never second-guessing their path as they did on the lethal streets of Philly.

He was not about the business of socializing, although every Black fraternity pursued him. Needless to say, the females, be they independent or sorority T-shirt clad, had an eye out for Jordan. He was quiet but not timid. During classes, he would challenge and argue his point of view aptly to either student or professor, usually winning over both parties with his charismatic charm. His smile was infectious though seldom seen, and once flashed would catch its subject male or female off guard, rendering them captive in a veil of hormonal stickiness, distracting them and allowing Jordan to move in for the kill, thus winning his arguments.

The four years went by quickly at Penn State with Jordan being in it but not of it. He thought of the school as petty for the most part, with professors needing saxophone-shaped pipes hanging from their lips to prove their points, and wearing deliberately unkempt hair to validate their "hipness" and non-conformity. Underneath it all were the reddest of necks masked by liberal pontificating and avant-garde postulating, so much so that Jordan imagined their driving need to prove themselves behind the podium to be an offset to their probable sexual impotence. Nevertheless, he played their game and parroted back the ideas and information buried deep in their treasured self-authored textbooks, receiving the highest awards at graduation.

Working at a high-end pharmaceutical company the first ten years out of college afforded Jordan to move away from his family, invest his money, as well as discover the beauty and mystique of the women that surrounded him and were a part of his profession. They too found him equally desirable as they shamelessly vied for his attention whether at work or during happy hour. Admittedly, he tried hard to fall in love with one or two but found that the culture barrier always seemed to get in the way. Seldom would one find a "sister" in his line of work, and those few who were there sported shrunken heads of men who tried to "take them away from the lab and put them in kitchens" around their waists. He seemed to be particularly contemptible just by virtue of his color, overhearing one of his black contemporaries giggle, "Talk about your proverbial Oreo!"

One day he decided that he had had enough. Being passed over twice with no real practical explanation except the unmentionably obvious one, and tiring of the age-old excuse that a master's degree or more was required for the career path he desired even though many of his Caucasian contemporaries moved up the corporate ladder sans a master's degree, Jordan decided it was time to just go ahead and continue his education, but this time he would go south. Enough of trying to fit in and being a topic of conversation. Enough of the hateful stares. At the tender age of 26, Jordan realized that he needed to be about the business of knowing his own and interacting with them. Twenty-six years of running away and trying to prove that his color had nothing to do with his intellectual competence left him with no reference or cultural base, and though somewhat frightened he made his move.

Graduate school was different. Atlanta, Georgia's Universities had as much of a progressive, state-of-the-art look and feel about them as did the northern so called Ivy League universities, yet held within each building's brick and beam, there was a sense of cultural pride. Students there also chatted 'neath tall old trees, but their conversation was earthier and charged with an intimate energy of unknown relatives, muses of days gone by who broke stereotypes, challenged the status quo, and bled and died for a more accepting society. Nothing…from tuition to a sunny day was taken for granted. Somehow, these students knew why they were there and, like their ancestors, had something to prove to themselves and others.

Jordan's graduate work led him to long days and nights of research. Though he knew hardly anyone beside his project associates, he was well known throughout the campus and neighboring universities and given the name "12:01" because someone described him as a minute blacker than midnight. When he heard of his nickname, he casually laughed it off, while internally his organs twisted. His whole reason for being there was to *connect to* or *disappear within* the masses of his people so that he would no longer hear the slurs about his pigmentation. His goal was to singlehandedly put an end to the age-old belief that one particular race was genetically superior to another by virtue of melanin disbursement. He wanted his name alone to spark images of genius that transcended what man looked like, and arouse universal appreciation of what he would discover and pass on to posterity.

Most of his work was done in labs where he could be found bent over a high-powered microscope or meticulously dropping a chemical through a pipette and documenting numbers on a nearby chart. His concentration was interrupted one day when a fight broke out in the hallway of his lab. Apparently some high-strung neophyte wanted lab rights, and everyone knew that time spent there was based on seniority. You collected squatter's rights based upon the amount of proposals written, approved, and thus funded. Lab time for an undergrad was not allowed outside of the appointed school hours, yet this outspoken and quite irate student felt the need to physically demonstrate her displeasure concerning that rule.

By the time Jordan had arrived on the scene, a nearby trophy case was broken and glass was everywhere. Two guards were holding a 5'2" well-endowed sophomore as if she were a linesman in the football team.
"I don't keer whut the schedule says! My professor said I could use the lab under his name. Call 'im up! I need to finish this experiment before my next class. I'm an 'A' student, I ain't no criminal! I cain't believe y'all treatin' me this way." Seeing Jordan's willowy dark frame, Toni Saunders collapsed and began sobbing, partially out of frustration, and partially to keep Jordan's attention.
"What's goin' on?"
"Oh Mr. Jordan! Sorry to disturb you, a student here wants to break all the rules of the institution just to get a passing grade…"
"I *been had* a passing grade! You the one making just enough to get your uniform out of the cleaners, you minimum-wage-wanna-be-a-cop-so-bad…"
"OK, OK, Miss Lady!" Jordan had his hands up in surrender. He asked the young student who her professor was and smiled when she said "Dr. Gibbs," knowing he was a lover of the ladies and was probably using his title to get to the next phase of his all but subtle means of courtship.
"What do you need to do?"
"All I need to do is check the outcome of a few tests I made, and there are time constraints that have to be taken into consideration. Tha's why Dr. Gibbs said I could come in this evening."
"If I check your tests and give you the numbers, would you leave in peace?" Seizing the opportunity to flirt, Toni interrogated Jordan.

"I don't know. Can I trust you? You a teacher? I've seen you around campus but never in any classes."

"I'm doing graduate work in pharmaceutical chemistry, but with all due respect (flashing a smile), it's not about me right now, is it?" Toni stared into eyes that summoned thoughts not linked to his question, but managed to answer with a weak and pitiful "No."

At that point, the guard knew he could release her. Jordan's presence held her spellbound. The following week Toni left a package at the door of the lab where Jordan did his research. Written on a large brown shopping bag were the words, "Thank you, Mr. Beslow." A warm sweet potato pie was inside that fired up the hallway with cinnamon, nutmeg, and all kinds of delectable spices the moment he pulled it from the bag. At first, he regarded the whole gesture as sweet, until he tasted a slice. There was something about the heavy and firm texture, with its creamy sweet butter blended with the intense warmth of cinnamon, nutmeg, and allspice that awakened the ancient feelings in him as he visualized her once more through more forgiving eyes. Later that week in her bed, she whispered, "You belong to me, Black man," and while in the throws of passionate lovemaking, Jordan knew to be afraid.

CHAPTER 12

Mojo

Toni Sunders was 25 years old and still in undergrad school though she looked to be about eighteen. No one was sure of her major, and many would argue she wasn't even enrolled. However, all considered her fine.

Nothing but curves could be found on her small frame, and when she walked, she bounced. Two deep dimples burrowed in chocolate-brown cheeks and huge amber eyes made her look like the baby doll children wished for underneath their Christmas trees. Her hair was always cropped short in a copper-red afro, and large ethnic earrings playfully dangled from soft-brown lobes. There was something mysterious about Toni. She smelled of oils and spices. Silver handmade bangles hammered and stacked in size order sensuously clinked around both wrists. Toni would rock back and forth whenever she spoke, a habit that was annoying to the women and endearing to the men. Just how she got Dr. Gibbs to give her permission to use the lab was no great mystery, though no one ever saw Toni in any science classes.

Now, seen almost every day on campus walking Jordan to the lab, other women questioned why someone with such intellect and obvious ability to choose anyone he pleased would opt for Toni. None of the overt stares bothered her. She clung to his arm and feigned conversation that at a distance could be interpreted as engaging.

Toni loved being in love. It was the chase, the intrigue, and final conquest that she felt was the very meaning of her existence. Everything else in life was what she regarded as interim moments, disposable time that if allowed to run its course would render a person lifeless. She was also in touch with her ancestors. Raised by a grandmother who held on to ways of the motherland, Grandma Mumbia would teach Toni all that was passed down to her.

"Der's nothing mo' powful' den a woman's desire," she would say, "an' no man alive kin alter whut she sets for ta do!"

Grandma Mumbia's house was crowded, musty, and dark. Large terracotta pots lined her porch filled with herbs and spices. Although the neighborhood was run down, Mumbia's garden had a mystical and magical air to it. A tree on her property with a grand and knotty trunk hunched over with extended arms beckoning passers-by to come closer. Brilliantly colored butterflies would rest on high stems of hollyhocks. Their wings sluggish and hypnotic lured the most subtle of hot Georgia breezes their way. Birds of all kinds fluttered, chirped, and darted in and out of homemade houses of cut up plastic soda bottles half filled with seeds. As a child, Toni loved playing in her grandma's garden. Later she would learn how the fruit of the garden would serve her, bringing to pass the desires of her heart just as she "set for ta do." It was these very herbs and spices that lured Jordan her way, and well after the sexual phase of their relationship died, she was not about to let him go.

One morning while preparing to walk to campus, Toni noticed a smirk on Jordan's face as she grabbed her keys to walk out with him.
"Toni...uh, you don't have to walk me *every day* to the lab. I know my way, baby, besides...don't you have a class to go to?"
"You're mistaking what I have to do with what I want to do, Black man!"
"And that's another thing I need to talk to you about. My name is Jordan, and it is ridiculously obvious that I am a Black man. I need you to stop saying that."
"I will as soon as you come to accept and *love* the fact that you are."

Toni rang a bell so loud in Jordan's heart that he literally vibrated and she knew her truth reached him. He did too. That is what infuriated him. It unnerved him being accurately read by someone considered by most a lightweight and an oddball.

"What do you mean 'accept and love' who I am? You haven't lived long enough to set standards for my life, young lady! How *dare* you?"
"Oh please! A four-year-old can see you're ashamed of your color!"

Having crossed the line, she stayed behind as Jordan stormed out the door. Panic fluttered through her heart for a moment, but she remembered what Mumbia once told her, *"Be keerful, wit feelins. Dey wild and powerful... like de weeds. Don't give um' sanction ta ruin ya garden!"* Therefore, standing still and summoning the strength of mothers before her, Toni presented her fears to the counsel of elders whom she believed were no less real than she was, and listened quietly as they advised.

Mumbia came first. Never looking Toni in the eye, she meandered about, pressing the top soil of plants with her index finger and humming. Upon hearing Toni speak of love, she shook her head. "Don tell me of love no more times chile'...I don heard my fill. Do ya wanna keep de man or show him lesson?" The latter part of the question summoned forth a still dark woman whose back was straight and high. In her hand, she held a walking stick and around her waist was a small red felt bag. "Who's that, Gramma Mumbia?" Mumbia spun around and hollered, "Git! She don't want cha now!" The tall woman flashed blue gums that lined cream-colored teeth the size of corn kernels. The pupils of her eyes glared a brilliant red as she obediently faded at Mumbia's command. *"She be wantin' ta make a fix fer you, but cha don't need dat kind. She mean well, and love ya like you her own, dat why she dangerous. You jus' wanna keep de man still, huh now?"*

"I want him to love me, Gramma Mumbia! This one I want to love me for all of me. What I am, not what I should be. More importantly, I want him to love himself too."

"You ain't seen his heart yet. Sometime dat what inside be so dark it cannot be seen by de naked eye be exactly what nature cover up wit beauty. Come back knowin' his heart. While ya busy... get a lock of haiah from de man. His haiah grow close to his brain; I need his haiah to turn a han." It took years for Jordan to discover the hold Toni had on him was due to a single lock of hair.

CHAPTER 13

Finding self

With newfound freedom that divorce brings, Nilé busied her days with self-help classes from aerobics to Zen meditation. She knew in her heart that this was the time in her life when she needed to realize her full potential. She just had no idea what it was. She also felt a bit unnerved when sitting alone. It would always happen the same way. There'd be a sense of urgency, then once that feeling encompassed her, she'd be left in a vacuum. Upon entering the state of 'nothingness,' fear would often fill the void and there she'd sit in suspended animation listening to frightening concepts build upon themselves until she could do nothing else but weep.

What was she here for? Was her sole purpose to raise children and then fade into darkness? If that was so…what dismal future was in store for the children born of a mother whose lifetime agenda was to simply raise them? Nilé knew better than to think her life was merely half over. She was approaching fifty for crying out loud! She could feel the sand beneath her feet hollow and race downward toward the neck of her life's hourglass. Those cruel and unmerciful ideas sped through her brain, insisting that she be urgent….urgent….act on something…..but what it was always remained beyond her grasp.

One evening while reading a book on slave narratives, Nilé felt compelled to draw a picture of one of the people she had read about. Yanking a piece of paper from her printer, she dug through a nearby junk drawer for a pencil. The first strokes were difficult. Thoughts that she was not thinking rationally ran through her head. Why was she doing this? How was she supposed to know if the face she drew really existed? Why was it so important to draw it? Nevertheless, she pressed on. Through clouds of dark and untamed graphite strokes she transferred the sorrow of an unknown spirit onto paper. It was quiet and all she could hear was the hurried movements of her hand. As she began to detail features, her mind would steer her toward pencil strokes she would never have imagined herself. Slowly, the dark mass of shadows transformed into the face of a woman whom she never knew, yet her heart knew existed. Looking at soulful eyes, the face seemed to express thankfulness to its creator for having persevered and found her amidst the shadows. Quietly she stared back and said, "You're welcome," to a picture formed by her hands yet was ancient as the soil of Africa. Soon her small study was filled with these enslaved souls. Nilé in obedience would draw each member, detailing characteristic smiles, remembering moles, and oftentimes omitting eyebrows completely. Each completed face freed Nilé as she felt that releasing them from the pages of a book and creating actual portraits gave them honor, even though their lives were beset with degradation. Oftentimes she'd find herself talking to the images asking them what they wanted her to show. Other times her hand knowingly moved by the dictates of creative energy beyond her own understanding.

"Sweet Jesus! Nilé!" Angie hollered one day while rolling through her rooms.
"Who the hell are these people?"
"What people, Angie?"
"These people in your back room! Don't none of 'em look like family, and to be honest they're downright spooky."
"Oh, I'm uh…I guess you could say giving myself therapy. I've been reading so many books about our history particularly slavery and the individual accounts of how this barbaric phenomenon shaped lives and influenced mindsets that are still in place today. Angie, it blows my mind when I read about men and women who were innately brilliant and forced to suppress genius for fear it would cost them their lives. Take this woman for example…." She pointed to a

heavyset strong-jawed woman whose nose was keen and flared. "She volunteered to be her slave master's wife's nanny only because she knew it would allow her to continue to lactate. Her teen-aged daughter who was raped and carrying the master's child was due any day, and this woman knew her daughter would be too weak to breast feed properly after having worked the field. Each night after her grandson was born, she'd wait for her daughter to fall off to sleep with newborn baby at her nipple. The moment the child began to cry, Nessa, that's what I named her, would grab her grandson and place her ample bosom to his lips. Later she bragged that her grandson grew up so strong that he could till a field even with a swayback ox. She convinced her mistress to 'come up pregnant' each time one of the slave women did to insure that her husband wouldn't forget his true Caucasian bloodline. By doing so, Nessa managed to breast feed many a hungry black child and continued to lactate well into her fifties."

"Thas' deep! I don't know if I could do that. Would you?"

"Don't know what I could do until put to the test."

"That's no lie! I didn't know you could draw! Look at these pictures! I mean they seem to be staring right through you. You should do something with them, Nilé. I'm serious."

"I want to make them more real. Paper and pencil is not enough. I want to buy clay or plaster or paper-mâché or something…they need dimension…"

"Well les' get some!" Angie boomed. "You're on to something, Miss Thang, and I like it. I may not like the way these slaves is lookin' at me but I'm diggin' on your drive and the talent that's surfacing as a result of it. Come on, let's get some clay."

"But I don't even know how to sculpt!"

"Did you know how to draw before you picked up a pencil and started doing this?"

"Well…not really."

"Thas' what I'm talkin' 'bout! Let them butt-ugly people tell you what they look like. Just find them in the clay. OOOOOh! I'm getting chills just thinking about it. Les' go!"

CHAPTER 14

The heart of Jordan

Hearing that his mother Mamie Beslow died, Jordan dashed the next day to Philly without telling a soul where he was going. His brother met him at the door.
"You too busy splittin' atoms to bother with Momma—why you botherin' to come by now? Ain't nothing here but a carcass that once held a broken heart. There ain't no will, so don't look for money. What the hell you come back for wit' your black ass?"

Not thinking, Jordan found himself moments later standing over a short stout man sprawled out on the floor holding a busted lip. Relatives from everywhere were yelling and someone hollered, "Call the cops," but a tall, slim woman in her late sixties calmed the mob scene down.
"It's all right, it's all right! Y'all just cool out for a minute! Dang! Everybody in the whole family so full of drama! That's my little brother Jordan, and he and Darnell ain't never liked each other. I'm surprised he ain't kicked his butt sooner!" Darnell was mumbling something about getting his gun and Gina called him on it.

"Don't even try it, Darnell! You ain't gettin' no gun 'cause you ain't got no gun. Who you frontin' for? Whatever you said, you had it comin'. He ain't no little boy you can push around no more. Now get up and get over it." Darnell continued to spew threats while folks Jordan had never laid eyes on stared at him.

"Hey Baby! You got some way of comin' back and makin' a big scene!" Gina stood on tippy toes and beckoned her little brother to hug and give her a kiss.

"I'm real sorry about what just happened, Gina; it's just that I can't hear that ignorance anymore. All I want is to see Momma…to say goodbye and I'll get out of everybody's hair."

"You ain't in nobody's hair, little brotha'! Now come meet your kinfolk like you s'posed to. I'm tired of explaining who the hell that little darkie is in all the pictures on the mantle!"

As Jordan and Gina made their way through the small and crowded house, some relatives' eyes were kind and gentle. Others gazed at Jordan as if he were a freak on display. Some old folks whispered as he walked by confirming how he looked just like "Thompson," then they'd shake their heads. The whole experience became overwhelming to Jordan who felt as if he was suffocating in pools of judgment.

"Look Geen…I gotta go…when is the funeral and burial?"

"Day after tomorrow at 10:00 and we're burying Momma right after, Baby, you comin'?"

"I'll be there."

"Good, Sweetie. I'll harness Darnell for ya, OK?"

Saturday morning was cold and rainy. To Jordan it seemed appropriate that the whole world cry for his mother that day. Folks from everywhere poured into the small church where Mamie Beslow lay. Jordan followed the crowd. As he entered, he had to tilt his head to clear the low arched doorway. Approaching the casket, thoughts of his mother and the personification of unconditional love flooded his heart and mind. Though she worked two jobs throughout most of his childhood, somehow she would find time to spend with her "Sweet Chocolate Baby." It seemed as if all of his worries and cares were soothed to a state of tranquility when she walked through his bedroom door. Darnell would go out of his way to distract her. His tactics lacked shame, but most of the time they were met with a flat-lined tolerance at best. Once the turmoil created by Jordan's sibling was addressed, she'd turn toward a young man whose voice was being distorted by vocal cords in the process of an explosive growth spurt, and he'd witness an adoring but tired woman crack a smile that equaled the break in his timid hello. He recalled how she would quietly listen to Jordan as he'd attempt to explain the mysteries of DNA (God's code as Jordan would often call it) to an attentive yet primitively discerning ear. His love for Mamie consumed him with each step he took toward the coffin, so much so that the moment he touched her silvery-gray skin he wept openly with no concern of the strangers who looked on. No one but Mamie seemed to care about his passion for science. No one but Mamie would spend hours pouring over newspaper articles, chronicling, clipping, and pasting every step of his academic accomplishments into a battered leather-bound scrapbook. And no one but Mamie understood her son's need to unearth the nature of this thing called "color." Why he was obsessed to prove to himself that he was not a freak of nature simply because his skin was as black as pitch. As they lowered his mother into a well-manicured plot, he winced at the sight of a puddle forming at the bottom. His instinct was to cry out, "Wait! Please don't lower my momma into muddy water!" but his better judgment restrained him. Instead, he jerked away from the crowd as they sang her favorite hymn "In The Cross."

Walking slowly toward his car while fumbling for keys, he couldn't help but feel a set of eyes that followed him. Looking abruptly toward the stare, he saw a tall thin man with a wide-brimmed hat yielding to the pressure of the rain that was coming down heavy now. They locked gazes for what seemed to be an eternity to Jordan, but he was determined not to break the stare. Then, as if prompted by some unheard cue, the old man began to slowly bend his knees, then stand straight never breaking the gaze. The standstill dance grew rhythmic and steady as Jordan in a trancelike state could do nothing but watch.

CHAPTER 15

The power of pain

Nilé tried to tuck her feet under a heavy patch of blanket so that she wouldn't feel the sharp bites of a playful cat's attempt to wake her. "Come on, Patwaaaaaaaaaaaa! It's Saturday!" As she protested, Patwa hunched low. His focus was on a particular lump of bedding that suggested it might be the source of movement underneath. With pupils as wide as saucers, he wiggled his rump then pounced. "Ouch! Patwa! That hurts!" She tried to hit him with a pillow, but to no avail as he was midway down the hall. Struggling to rationalize why she shouldn't pack the cat up and take him for a long ride, she reluctantly swung her feet over the bed and searched for nearby slippers. Reaching for her robe, Nilé wrapped and scuffed down the hall only to meet her furry companion sitting upright greeting her with a hungry "Bllllerrrrooooowww!"
"OK man, you win. But I'm gonna' make a cup of tea first. That's what you get for making me wake up. You gotta' wait!" As the teapot filled with water, Nilé looked out of her kitchen window. Drops of rain pooled and found their way down the pane the same way tributaries meet rivers, growing wider and stronger as they raced toward an overflowing sill. Each water strip warped the image of the park across the street until it looked like an impressionist painting. Nilé's teapot whistle blew and condensation created opaque curtains causing the landscape in the park to grow faint.

Usually Nilé enjoyed rainy days. The random sprays of automobile tires broadcasting their presence on the street that could be heard at a distance usually brought a sense of comfort, yet today Nilé's spirit was melancholy and the sounds only darkened her mood.
She reached toward a book on the coffee table and began leafing through its pages. Old Negro spirituals came to mind

while reviewing photographs of men and women who once in Africa had irrigated soil and erected obelisks were now bent over fields of cotton in servitude. Pulling away from one picture to keep from crying she looked out the window. To her surprise and relief, her weary eyes rested on Jordan Beslow. It had been several months since he "dropped by." The need in his eyes was almost visceral, yet while motioning him to come up she couldn't help but notice his hesitance. Once in, he timidly initiated conversation.

"I knew you were in because the windows were all steamed up."
"How long were you out there? You're soaked!"
"Uh, not long, I uh just came from a funeral and…" After a long pause and staring at the end of Nilé's couch, he sighed. Nilé noticed tears forming then splashing onto large hands that quivered as they held a hat whose usefulness had long since run out.
"Oh my God, Jordan…I'm so sorry. Who passed?"
"My umm mother, and I…" without hesitation she threw her arms around him and held him close as she guided his broken spirit toward a nearby chair. Her arms were soft and warm, and although her robe was worn to a thread, it held a subtle bath oil fragrance that smelled like Jordan's momma. Nilé's mind raced for ways to comfort her friend, but all she could do was hold him. She knew to reject some of the more carnal thoughts even though she couldn't deny the raw beauty of the man in her arms. Then one by one she could feel her ancestors enter the room. They all seemed to make way for Nana the matriarch whose spirit always resonated with Nilé's.
"What should I do?"
"What de Lawd say do?"
"Oh Lord, I don't know, I haven't been to church in so long I…"
"De Lawd not always in church, chile."
"I don't know how to talk to Him. Ask him for me, Nana. I know you know God way better than I do. Be my spokesperson…pleeeeeease!"

"You weren't there for me when I wuz in need." Then she chuckled. *"I ain't knowed how to talk either, but I sho' nuff talked anyhow! B'sides…yo fren's talkin' to Him right now he just don' knows he is."* Frustrated with all of Nana's seemingly doubletalk, Nilé looked at Jordan whose eyes were now closed. Not knowing what else to do she asked, "Want some tea?"

"Yeah, that would be nice." Awkwardly they shifted to allow Nilé to get up. He watched soft rounded hips navigate their way toward the kitchen while a playful cat swiped furiously at her robe sash. While in the kitchen she prayed that God would give her an idea of what to say and do. She hardly knew the man. He seemed so despondent. Moments later, she appeared with a tray and two hot mugs filled with tea, along with buttered muffins. As she placed the tray on the table Jordan's hand reached for her shoulder. Turning, she met eyes pleading her not to ask questions. Instinctively she submitted to his embrace. The warmth of her body thawed his fingers and melted a heart barely beating. He buried his head into her bosom and sobbed as she gently kissed and pulled damp locks away from his face. The rain outside was pounding harder now as if to hide them from the world. She began to hum to him the way a mother would soothe her baby creating the melody as she went along. It was a familiar peaceful tune. She cooed the way Nana used to when she rocked in her chair and mended torn sweaters. Jordan stopped weeping, yet held on. She shifted her hip to allow him more room on the couch, and felt his hand begin to slip. Deliberately trapping it with the back of her calf by pulling her leg back and close to her thigh, she continued the serenade. With one thumb free, Jordan began to stroke her calf. She hummed and kissed his forehead, feigning not to notice. Moments later, he was kissing her ample breast tenderly. Soon they discovered and uncovered primal pleasures as the heaviness in both their hearts evaporated like the steam in their cups on their way to cling to nearby windows.

CHAPTER 16

When He hears

Hours later as he slept, Nilé, for the first time, lay in bed holding a private and intimate one-way conversation with God.
"I know this is the worst way to come to you, Lord, with a man I hardly know only a foot away from me in my bed. But I've gotta speak with somebody and right now seems like you're the only one who would understand what I'm going through without going into a whole lot of history. I need to know what's going on with my life, Lord. What are you doing with me...or...are you doing anything with me at all? Is all of this just me here reacting to whatever life brings me? I'd like to think I'm subliminally following some elaborate plan of yours but to be honest with you, Lord, I don't know if I would even know if you were leading me or not. I've trusted you with the lives of my babies, never once doubting that you were there with me in times of trouble. Why is it that I can't feel you orchestrating **my** *life?"* A big hot tear found its way past damp lashes and spilled quietly into a crevice created by her nose. She could feel her sinuses swelling, but she dare not sniffle for fear of waking Jordan. Instead, she allowed the teardrop to follow its course, and as it neared her lips, she caught the warm saltiness with her tongue. *"Am I not worth the bother, Lord? Oh Jesus, I need to know you're here with me. I don't care if you see this man! Let me know that you see me! ME! Who am I? What have I become? Help me, Father!"*

While Jordan lay beside her sleeping, Nilé felt an old voice chuckling in her spirit.

"Oh the Lawd done caught you wit'cha pants down, huh!"
Nilé turned her attention to her grandmother. Somewhere in a realm between certainty and uncertainty, her soul found its

way to Nana. Nana, neither sitting nor standing, met Nilé in trancelike ambiguity and there they exchanged thoughts.

"Grandma Nana, what do I do? I don't even love him; at least I don't think I do."

"*What you know 'bout love, gal? Is love what ya felt wit' that FM boy? That's what you call love, eh?*"

"That's the only love I've known. And to be honest, I don't think I could ever love that way again…I've emptied out, Nana."

"*Good! That kinda love needs to be emptied out. Besides, ya love fuh' him was designed fuh' that man only. Crazy as a roach under a flashlight, but it was complete. That's why you empty. The FM boy got all the love you had custom made fer him…so be done wit it! Ya need to learn ta love some otha' way now.*"

"What do you mean, Nana?" Nilé sensed she was pushing it. Nana was never one to talk much, and the more you pressed for conversation, the more irritated she would become.

"*Listen gal…each love ya feel should be as different as the fingerprint of the man you lovin! Decide!! You gonna love him or no?*" Nilé glanced at Jordan's hands. Long slender fingers with creamy palms slashed with near-purple lines lie limp on a floral sheet.

"Oh Nana, I'm so embarrassed. I know nothing about his fingerprints! Yet I've SLEPT with him! I don't even want him to wake up for fear of an awkward conversation."

"*Did yeh talk to the Lawd?*"

"Yes! Nana, I did! Honest I did just what you said."

"*An' what He say?*"

"Nothing. At least I didn't hear Him say anything."

Nana chuckled. "*Den I know yeh talked ta Him!*"

"What do you mean, Nana?"

"*He nebber say nuttin! But believe me, chile, He heard yeh loud an' clear. He knowed yeh wuz sincere. He knowed ya <u>had</u> to be…talkin' ta Him wit a new man in ya bed!*" Nana chuckled again. She seemed to delight in the fix Nilé was in.

"Well, what happens now, Nana?"

Nana's presence began to dissipate. Inside the mist of uncertainty, Nilé could see faint images of other beautiful Black women catering to or calling Nana. As she faded, a light in the distance appeared to be pulling all of the women toward some obscure place. A place where Nana now resided in peace. No more snapping beans, no more scrubbing marble staircases. A place where her very being inhaled and exhaled rays of light and her heart was in sync with the rhythm of millions of hummingbirds and her consciousness had adjusted to planets orbiting around other faraway suns. Just then, Jordan shifted and coughed. The sound woke him up. For a moment, he seemed startled, not remembering where he was, then reality forced him to slowly open his eyes and deal with the fact that he was in Nilé's bed.

The rain had subsided. Jordan's eyes wandered around the bedroom. An antique chest of drawers adorned with tattered black baby dolls and a silver jewelry box stood beside a wing-backed chair upholstered in soft yellow and red stripes. A satin pillow was tossed in its corner resembling a large pat of butter. Jordan's soul felt at home, as he examined the details of her room, concluding that everything in it looked creamy. He glanced toward Nilé and saw that she was deep in thought. Ineptly he moved his hand toward her. A tear splashed from her chin as she looked helplessly toward the ceiling struggling for words to say.
"Hey....Sugga....don't cry!" is all he could think of. He grabbed and held her close as she sobbed.
"I...I don't..."
"Shhhhhh, neither do I, Sugga, it's OK."
"What *is* this?"
"I don't know. I don't know."
They lay there in silence. Then Nilé spoke. "I didn't know what to do. You seemed so sad. I mean...I don't usually console people like this..."
"I'm glad to hear that!" They both laughed.

"You want some tea?"

"Ahhhh! Tea! The ultimate cure-all!" He smiled and looked deeply into her eyes.

"Tell you what. Why don't you let me make *you* a pot of tea? After all, I crashed your Saturday, the least I could do is wait on you."

"But you don't know where anything is…"

"What's to know, tea is usually kept in the cabinet near the spices, right? The sugar I'm sure is in a pretty little flowered bowl, probably near or on a matching tray and let's see…the cream or lemon is in the refrigerator, right?"

Nilé stared and smiled as Jordan described the elements in a kitchen he'd barely seen. She slipped into her robe, then hesitated.

"Oh wait…you'd better wear this I have other.…" before she could finish, Jordan had wrapped the top sheet around one shoulder then twisted the remainder around his waist.

Throwing his hair behind huge muscular shoulders, he assumed the position of some great pharaoh and whispered to Patwa, "Toga party!"

CHAPTER 17

Mixed signals

Nilé's kitchen began to change colors as the evening announced the end of day. Bright orange streaks and brilliant purples drenched white eyelet café curtains and forced their way onto walls and cabinets. They talked about everything under the sun—the books she was reading, his research, her marriage and children, and briefly about an affair that he deemed took too long and was all but ridiculous. Almost a gallon of tea had been consumed, when Jordan finally asked, "Where's your bathroom?"
"Down the hall, turn left. Hey, you've been here all day, you want some dinner?"
"I don't want to impose, Sugga....you've already been so good to me, I can't ask for dinner on top of that."
"It's nothing, besides, I gotta' eat, I could use the company."
"That sounds good...real good. OK, you've twisted my arm. Hey, do you mind if I shower?"
"Not at all. You'll find fresh linens...never mind, use your sixth sense. You seem to know where everything is in this place!"
When Jordan returned, he was dressed and acting strange. An obvious change of mood had infiltrated his persona, as he was rushed and impatient.
"Look Sugga...I know you started, but I gotta' run. I forgot I had something to do and I'm already late."
"But..."
"I know...I shouldn't have said OK on dinner, but look at it this way, you'll have enough for tomorrow." His raincoat was on and he was looking for his hat. Nilé, realizing that she could do nothing to change his mind, motioned that his hat was sitting on a nearby radiator. Tucking stray locks underneath a wide brim, he was asking himself the same

thing Nilé's eyes were…"Why do you have to go?" Nothing was said. He simply reached for her hand and kissed her forehead goodbye.

CHAPTER 18

Love's the crutch

Weeks had gone by before anyone had heard from Nilé. The only outside contact she made was to a few agencies advising them of her availability for work. Her contractors forwarded stacks of documents, and as the phone rang and rang she'd sigh and praise God for the invention of caller ID, then bury herself in her work, allowing the rings to trip over into her message machine. One morning the doorbell rang and Nilé though sleepy stumbled out of bed expecting to sign off on another manuscript delivered. As she opened the door with pen in hand, there was Angie who immediately jammed the door with the wheel of her chair so that it could not be shut.
"Angie…it's early…."
"Save it! I'm in here now. I see it's not too early to receive a package, or do you always walk around with a pen in your hand at 9:00 a.m.?"
"I was expecting a package. I've got a lot of work to complete. I'm sorry I didn't answer your calls, but my deadlines…"
"Deadlines, shmedlines! What's goin' on with you to make you hermitize yourself? This place is nice but Lord! It's all closed in and smells like a week of B.O.!"
"Ange….pleeeeease! I don't have time for this now."
"Make the time. Here, I made you a quiche. Heat it up; I'm hungry. And put a pot of tea on. Heeeeeey Patwaaaaaaa! How's my best buddy?" Nilé realizing defeat slumped toward the kitchen and turned on the oven. Angie was on her heels prattling about all of the things that had happened to her while Nilé had gone "Off the air." Finally, after an awkward lull, Angie spoke softly, "Look buddy, there ain't much that passes me by. After all, I'm stuck here in my own particular hellhole but at least I make the most of it. I saw

"Dark Shadows" come by last Saturday. I saw when he left. I never was great at math but I can add two and two together. Truth be told, I was sayin' a little prayer for you and I thought it was answered. By Wednesday of this week when you didn't answer my calls, I figured something terribly wrong had happened with the Saturday hookup and, dammit, I gave you a week to git over it! Now yo' ass is trippin' and I needs to kick it back in place. Sometimes things don't work out the way we plan, baby...."

"Oh Ange....I don't even know what went wrong! I mean everything went right all day! Then when I started to prepare dinner, Jordan asked if he could shower up, and when he came back, he had on his coat and was lookin' for his hat! I'm too old for this. I deserve better or nothing at all!"

"Listen to what you just said. You just contradicted yourself in less than ten words. Damn! You now hold the stupidity world record for Normals! You deserve better or you deserve nothing, which is it?"

"I'm leaning toward nothing. It's easier."

"Well, most the people I've seen leanin' needed a crutch. An' if you're leanin' on NOTHIN' you sho' nuff gonna fall so that's not an option, sista girl."

"What happened, Angie?"

"Chile, thas' what I've been tryin' all week trying to find out. All you told me thus far was that he came and then he left."

Nilé told Angie about everything. Two hours and a half a quiche later, Betty came by too. While Nilé cried and moped around, Betty picked up the place fluffing pillows and opening windows. Everything she touched she asked, "Do you want this?" Each time Nilé would shrug then Angie would bark, "Put the thang down! You cleanin' or shoppin'?" By the time the vacuum cleaner had been pulled out, music found its way out of the speakers with Angie as self-appointed DJ of the day. With "Bootylicious" booming, the living room was filled with gyrating women imitating Beyoncé and swearing in their own minds that they were sexier. Betty took Nilé's yellow chenille throw and placed it on her head throwing it around as if it was hair. Angie was wiggling and bumping into furniture so much that the cat ran down the hall. Nilé knew what they were doing and didn't mind. Finally she was laughing. When all had agreed that they were past their prime, they fell on sofas and overstuffed chairs panting and reluctantly giving homage to Beyoncé.

"Hey Nilé! How's the artwork comin'?"
"Uh OK, I guess. The last few pieces I've done are kind of dark, but that's what I was feeling at the time."
"Let's see it. Let us be the judges." Moving single file down a long hallway, Nilé opened the door to her back room. Quietly they entered. The walls were papered with sketches. Some complete, some struggling to break free of thin lines suggesting anatomical elements yet to be defined. As their eyes traveled, they noticed a progression from left to right of mood change. The earlier portraits were somewhat mindless staring vacuously at their viewers. Later drawings revealed subtle personalities while the more recent ones screamed with emotions. In the center of the room was a small table with a lazy Suzan that held a sculpture in progression. It was carefully covered with a cellophane dry cleaning bag. Underneath was a damp cloth covering what looked like a bust. Carefully Nilé removed the coverings. Betty and Angie gasped at the reveal.

There it stood, the head and shoulders of a Black child in her early adolescence. The face was round and soft. Her hair was nappy...disheveled. And then there were her eyes. Eyes that were wide, crazed, yet innocent. Eyes that evoked a sick numbness through each woman in the room. They were haunting, questioning eyes that reflected a child's inability to process the act of violence forced upon her seemingly moments ago. They cried out for an explanation, begged for comfort, yet found no solace. After a few moments, Betty turned her head placing her hands over her eyes and wept.

Angie quietly looked up at Nilé, and while shaking her head she smiled.

"I couldn't stop even though I wanted to." Nilé whispered.
"I'm glad you didn't. You've freed this little chile's spirit and honored her in the process. It's good, Nilé. You're good. Damn good." Betty had by then composed herself then began to speak.
"I'm sorry. I wasn't ready for that. I….I thought that years of therapy had healed…."
Both women looked at each other with surprise. With arms outreached, they huddled around Betty and held her tight as she collapsed on a nearby chair convulsing with sobs.
Nilé whispered, "Oh God, Betty…I didn't know….I didn't know!"

CHAPTER 19

An answered request

November in Georgia this year was cold and damp. Blustery winds blew resisting wet leaves that had lost their color weeks ago into huddles of pasty piles along the edges of sidewalk curbs. Tree branches now naked quivered and pointed at passers-by, imitating the gnarly fingers of old ladies reprimanding children who picked their flowers.

Toni Saunders walked home from work briskly pressing against winds angry that she would not yield and walk in their direction. She was tired. The weight she picked up over the years made it difficult to maintain that light and bubbly bounce once seen in her signature stride as a young lady. She now passed male pedestrians on the street without exchanging a dimpled smile to their flirtatious winks. She realized years ago that no one was winking anymore, and for the most part she didn't care. It had been too many years since Gramma Mumbia passed away and Toni's personality changed. She was raised by her grandmother as an only child, and though she knew she had older siblings, she never pursued a relationship with them. They too knew of her but thought that both she and their crazy grandmother were physical manifestations of witches from some old island storybook found in an attic.

As Toni reached her grandmother's porch, she stopped to pick up shards of pottery that had blown away from a cracked pot holding rain-soaked soil and a bulb hidden in its center. She glanced for a moment at a rundown yard seized and overthrown by weeds and recalled happier times when Mumbia had planted herbs and she chased butterflies. Then turning slowly toward a door with a giant black wrought-iron knocker she fumbled through her pocket searching for keys.

The living room hadn't changed much except it now held a 27-inch TV on an IKEA stand, and an answering machine that was now blinking in the dark. Reaching for a nearby lamp, she dropped her keys on a semi-circled table that held a cut-glass dish filled with wrapped candy and a picture of a beautiful chocolate-brown little girl with long fat braids framing her face like giant parentheses. She too had dimples and her smile held the sparkle that her mother once owned. Draped over the frame was a crocheted cross. A dated program that read "In Loving Memory" was folded neatly and anchored by the picture. The picture, cross, program, and table were now shrouded in a thin layer of dust that vibrated a little as Toni walked by.

After hanging her coat on the back of the closet door, Toni flopped down near the phone to listen to her messages. Most were canned solicitations offering home refinancing offers or great deals on aluminum siding. As she deleted one at a time, not even listening to hear the entire message, she almost deleted a message that simply stated: "We found eem." A chill ran down her spine, as she rewound the recording and listened again to an all but familiar voice that she hadn't heard in years. She waited. All that followed was the hissing of the recorder.

"Oh my God! Oh my God! What do I do?" Realizing that one night's seriously powerful summoning of ancestors finally yielded results sixteen years later, Toni didn't know what to do with the information she was receiving. She had no friends with whom she could talk about matters such as this, simply co-workers who tolerated her weirdness because she was a dependable employee. Hunching over, holding her head, and circling around in the same spot on the floor didn't seem to help. Ever since that fateful day, she had made an oath never to conjure again. She now remembered that she failed to pull back one of her requests sent out prior to her daughter's death. Desperately she cried out. She ran over to the machine and pushed "Delete All." Then, just to make sure, she played back the tape. There was silence. Toni sighed. Then, a few moments later, she heard…"We found eem." The moment that message was uttered, somewhere in that realm of uncertainty where Nana dwelled, a large wavelike tremor swept through an energy field which instantly necessitated a meeting of the ancestors.

CHAPTER 20

Gathering

One by one, the others felt the ripple and, without hesitation, moved swiftly toward the place where Nana instinctively knew to go.

As they moved they individually requested the guidance of their Creator thanking Him in advance for His Sovereign wisdom. The tremor was not new. They had encountered it before, for many, centuries ago. The manner and speed in which they responded indicated that it was a force to be reckoned with in utmost urgency. This tremor was serious. Something grave was about to enter into Nilé's world, and the dynasty of women who had paved the way for her existence were profoundly aware of its significance. Their spirits were in tune with that of the Creator. No longer was their wisdom amassed linearly on a trial and error basis as when they dwelled inside flesh and blood. They were all on one accord, respecting the wisdom gained through each individual walk with their Creator and knowing that their cumulative experiences would be the foundational force of energy from which they would need to draw.

Since Nana had felt the first ripple of energy penetrating their realm, and Nana had personally walked the earth with Nilé for a brief period, it was a unanimous decision to allow Nana to lead Nilé through the crisis that was about to take place. Though Nana was the youngest ancestor, her wisdom rivaled even the eldest of ancients who lived, loved, and prayed to one God and followed His spiritual guidance even long before the Bible announced the birth of Jesus. As they moved, they summoned others and the mass grew. This time they knew it was a matter of numbers. Numbers and will. The will of their God.

"*This wave is not like the ones before,*" whispered Batu, Nilé's grandmother who preceded her by sixteen generations. "*It is governed by a personal and vengeful agenda outside of the one we know, and it believes this time it will win.*"

"*It always believes it will win. It always fails. What we must insure is that our lineage is not corrupted in the process,*" interrupted Simone the great granddaughter of Batu who inherited the fighting nature of her father.

Nana spoke next.

"*Nilé's still searching. She avoidin' the spiritual because she afraid of it. The only time she ebber reached out toward de Lawd was when her babies wuz in need. Now dey knows Him an' she don't!*"

"*To fight widdout the Lion of Judah is a war doomed from de start,*" whispered Batu.

Simone cried out impatiently, "*Den we make her lub de Lawd!*"

"*Cain' nobody make ya lub de Lawd an' you know it! We gotta try ta git her ta wanna know. Dat's de first step.*"

"*But we ain't got time!*"

"*De Fadda do. We ask im fo' de time ta do our job for' Him. He gibbet to us!*"

In unison, their arms reached upward and heads lifted. Long mahogany necks stretched upward. With full lips smiling and eyes closed, they petitioned the One they adored, pouring out love and receiving strength and power with every moan and wail. Finally, after much prayer and petition, they knew what to do.

Sunday morning was crisp and clear. Angie dialed Nilé early and snapped, "Don't question me, don't resist me, get up, get dressed, you're going to church!"

"Uh…OK…why? Somebody die?"

"No, but somebody 'bout to. You! The only time you go to church is when somebody dies! Now thas' a dang shame!"

"A DANG shame? When did you get prissy with the profanities?"

"I don't cuss on Sunday. That day belongs to the Lord and it's holy."

"Now get yo' stankin' behind up and wash it. I'll be up in about 45 minutes. I'm waitin' on the corn bread to brown."

"What you bringing with the corn bread? I'm hungry and church goes on forever you know."

"I got some eggs and home fries goin' too, don't you worry 'bout that. Just get up."

"Betty goin'?"

"Betty go every week. You know she don't play. I'll see ya in a few. Oh....thanks for not resisting!"

Nilé hung up the phone with a silly grin on her face. She was glad she was going to church, but truth be told, it was strange that she didn't resist the invitation. About an hour and a half later, her living room was crowded with mindless chatter about tissues, offering, mints, and whose car is clean enough to pull up in front of the church. Finally, Patwa watched as Nilé jiggled the doorknob a few times to make sure the lock was set then closed it. The room was quiet, heavy with the scent of perfume and sausage.

Holy Redeemer Church was packed with regulars as Nilé and her crew filed in. Angie favored this church because it accommodated seating for not only "Normals" but also what she liked to refer to herself as a "Holy Roller." The usher's smiling white-gloved hospitality directed them to the far left where Angie pulled up close to the end seat and parked her chair. The house was rocking with six rows of choir members swaying and clapping their hands to "We'll Understand It Better By and By." The lead singer poured memories of occasions when her Savior's grace saw her through, while the hands of members in the congregation were lifted and swaying, imitating thick and thin branches of trees in dark forests and woodlands who also knew of God's great love. Nilé sat still and smiled taking it all in for a moment. Closing her eyes she could hear Angie's red-lipped voice extracting delicious and rich harmonic tones to enhance the spiritual moment being drawn out through song. The song was over. Hallelujahs and shouts of praise filled the room. Then a small thin woman advanced to the microphone. With gray hair swept back and neatly pinned in a French twist, pearl earrings, and a thin cross dangling around the neck of her purple and yellow robe, she waited for the room to still. Then, slowly she began to sing a song that was vaguely familiar to Nilé. It wasn't until the choir chimed at the chorus *"Ahhh, don't...feel...noways tired....come too far from where I started from"*.....that she recognized the tune. She stood up immediately as if some one had cattle prodded her from her seat. Tears rolling down her cheeks she sang softly, *"Nobody told me the road would be easy and I don't believe He brought me this far to leave me."*

Soon, everyone settled down and the pastor began his sermon. Nilé, still moved by the song, allowed her mind to wander. She felt an awareness of a presence surrounding her. It seemed to beckon her toward a corridor inside of her mind promising her that she would not lose the message brought forth by the pastor even though she'd be taken away. At first, she resisted. Then the visual impressions she received grew stronger, and Nilé found herself traveling back in time to a place where life was rural and harsh. The "amens" she heard around her began to transform to wails and moans of people in distress. She jumped in her seat when she heard the crack of a whip and the blood-curdling cry of a young woman bound to a tree. The whip cracked again and she heard herself pleading, "Just kill me, please just kill me, Massa, please, no more!" She looked closely and saw that she was the woman tied to the tree and remembered the scripture verse "Cursed is everyone who hangs on a tree" wondering what she could have possibly done to be so cursed. She wept openly and found her friends' arms around her, rubbing her back and handing her tissues. She heard the pastor reminding the congregation that they were heirs to the Lord God and that they should act, walk, and talk like royalty. Then something strange took place. A voice like that of Nana replaced the voice of the pastor. Everything he said, she was now saying, speaking with the same power and authority. As soon as Nana realized that she had Nilé's attention, she then instructed her with a fading voice:

"You'll have to go against your name to find your freedom, chile. Look hard and never faint. We and the Lord your God will be here to guide ya." Not understanding what was said, Nilé was frightened. A sudden sense of fatigue consumed her and she longed for peace. She heard the pastor beckon souls who needed comfort to come forward and surrender their lives to Christ, and Nilé found herself at the foot of the altar with Betty and Angie by her side, all of them sobbing through tears of sorrow, relief. Surrounding her in the spiritual realm were Nana, her great-great-great-great Aunt Affia, along with a host of other sisters of her lineage hooting and howling with triumphant joy.

CHAPTER 21

Traveling against her name

Betty took everyone home, and both Nilé and Angie agreed that a good nap was necessary after today's sermon. Closing the door, Nilé began to strip down to her underwear while walking toward the bedroom. Sitting on the bed, she pulled off her stockings and threw them across a nearby chair. Patwa seized the moment and pounced on the one foot dangling and in moments he was delightfully entangled. Nilé sighed and made a mental note to purchase pantyhose from the corner store before the day was through.

Drifting off to sleep was easy. Thoughts raced through her head in a dreamlike state. Deeper and deeper, she was being pulled into a surreal backdrop of impressions she had read from slave narratives. People from as far back as the Dogon civilization were mixed with memories of her childhood in Maryland. As she lay there, she could clearly hear her faucet dripping from the bathroom sink and her clock ticking. She was also keenly aware of smells and textures brought to her attention in this enactment of a dream. The whole journey seemed to race her backward in time. The travel was not linear in that she could both experience the deep past along with more recent events and process the events logically. The people she met were distant but all seemed to know her. Just as she was about to get spooked, she saw Nana standing there drying her hands with her white apron. With head tilted, she spoke with authority, "You gonna' come or not?"
"Come where, Nana?"
"Wit me, gal! We got a lot to do. Some things you need to know I gotta show you."
Nilé was amazed because all of the conversation she was having was being done without she and Nana moving their lips. She could hear voices urging Nana to speak on things

and Nana spouting, "Not so fast, the chile done just got here." As this was happening, Nana and Nilé were both moving forward while standing still.

The first stop was Nana's house. Nilé felt relief as the images of her unknown past faded, and she was brought into familiar surroundings. Nothing had changed. The only difference was that Nana seemed younger, stronger, and more vibrant. Her hair was no longer thin and gray. Instead of being brushed and rolled under in what used to look like an endless bang in the front and back of her head, it was thick and nappy, with traces of braids formed days earlier that had been sweated out and were overrun with a coarse thicket of undergrowth. Her face was fuller but still strong featured. As she swung the porch door open, she was met by Pop-Pop who was tall, thin, and strikingly handsome. Nilé knew in her heart that she had never met him. She remembered his picture hung on a wall near the potbellied stove. *So that's what he looks like* was the thought that raced through her head. He greeted her with a sharp and barking, "Hello Rascal!" Nilé found his playfulness a refreshing counterpoint to the otherwise somberness of her new environment.

She was allowed to revisit the house room by room. Memories of a simpler past raced through her mind as she ran her hand across worn-out armchairs of no particular color and stubbed her toe on the heavy iron that was used as a doorstop. She found Nana in the kitchen. For the first time she wasn't busy cooking. She was sitting there on an overturned aluminum washbasin waiting for Nilé. As Nilé timidly approached her great grandmother, she witnessed a gentleness never before shown in her eyes.
"Chile, you need to find out some things and I'm here ta show ya."
"What things, Nana?"
"Things that'll make ya understand why it is that you here, chile. Why it is that you struggling so hard, and why it is that

youse' special. You alone hold de key ta closure fo' a lot of us heah…you alone!"

Nana took Nilé's hand leading her up the stairs to her bedroom. Fear rushed through her as she recalled the time when she was caught exploring the backstairs and inner hallway which led to Nana's room.

"Ain't no sense gettin' scared of what'cha never got a whuppin' for! Youse grown! Now you kin see what de eyes of a free chile wasn't ready for!" As she opened the small wooden door that led to the inner passageway, she let go of Nilé's hand and without invitation began to proceed down the tiny hallway toward another door. Nilé wondered why at age 50 and 170 lbs she could fit through the narrow tunnel as she struggled to keep up with her ancestor now nimble and free from arthritis. Beyond the second door, there were no paneled walls, only cold hard earth and cobwebbed walls that seized Nilé's nostrils with an almost prehistoric stench. The farther they descended, the smaller and colder the corridor became. Nilé noticed other passageways branching out from the one they traveled. Each one was as worn as theirs. Occasionally she'd notice small holes that were dug out in the sides of the walls that held metal tins of burned-out wax.

After about ten minutes of silent walking, Nilé sensed that she had traveled at least six or seven feet underground and she guessed at least an eighth of a mile from the house. Finally, they reached another wooden door that protested and creaked open when Nana's shoulder pushed against it. There with eyes wide open in amazement Nilé took it all in.

It was a great room whose walls were tall and smooth. A ridge of packed-in earth about two feet from the ground was sculpted around the walls that was almost as wide as a cot. Three feet above the man-made seat were planks of wood held in place by nearly petrified stakes of wood or tree branches driven into the mud-packed walls. Each shelf held old dusty mason jars halfway filled with dark liquids or what looked like tree bark and leaves exhumed from the woods. Just as Nilé's eyes became accustomed to the darkness, Nana dug into her apron pocket, pulled out a candle, and struck a match. She delicately placed it on one of the old tins on the wall. The sound of the match startled Nilé but not as much as what she would witness next. The sight was too much to process. Nilé curled over and covered her eyes and ran into Nana's arms. She sobbed and begged Nana to allow her to leave. Nana now sitting on the edge of the man-made seat stroked Nilé's braids and began to sing, *"Ah don't believe He brought me this far to leave me."*

There they sat for a while until Nilé was able to compose herself. She knew that she couldn't physically fit on Nana's lap, but it seemed as though she was curled up with knees tucked under her chin and feet pressing against an old apron. Nana beseeched the kindred spirits to handle the matter delicately. As Nana rocked Nilé, the old grandmother discussed with her fellow ancestors the most appropriate way to be made discernible for no one knew how Nilé would take it. As Nana rocked, one woman began to hum in a low and comforting tone. Another chimed in adding sweet as honey harmony and balance to a tune that sounded of distant hopes unfulfilled yet sought after. One by one, the voices within the room found their place and produced a rich soothing melody that permeated the very essence of Nilé's soul, all in cadence to the beat of her Nana's gentle rock. Nilé dare not open her eyes. The sound was too beautiful. She felt that, although the experience was all too overwhelming, she wanted to be there for a while.

Slowly she opened her eyes. The room had transformed into an earlier time. The walls were no longer dark and gloomy but vibrant and alive with colors of brilliant yellow ochre, bright oranges, and the deepest of purples. Figures painted on the walls twisted in hues of sienna, midnight browns, and blacks that seemed as dark as their grief. Colors extracted from the earth and birthed by berries whose skins begrudgingly split from the pressure of hardened hands were blended together, yielding tones that depicted the sinews of a people who like their ligaments had been twisted and stretched into thin monstrous physiques. Each motion, each outstretched hand cried out its personal and painful story. Nilé tried to figure out how the color indigo could have possibly been made as she gazed at the sorrowful wall paintings depicting scenes of the escapees and hopes of fugitives who chronicled events in their lives. Every square inch swirled and echoed messages much more significant than the words that their new and ugly world could ever express. Nilé gazed in awestruck disbelief at what she would later discover was the greatest underground sanctuary of all time.

CHAPTER 22

Ten circles, plus two

"Are you ready to meet some o' yo' kinfolk?" Nana whispered. Nilé did not answer but as a child allowed her great-great-grandmother to shift and turn her to face the rest of the members now quietly sitting and standing in the great room.

"Now les see...Ah s'pose we should start from dis end..." Pointing to a short stout woman who was smiling from ear to ear, Nana announced, "Dis is Mabel. Miss Mabel to you of course. She not blood family but she knowed how to make peoples well don't cha' know. Miss Mabel come from de Carter plantation. Mr. Carter wuz one o' de meanest Massa's in de South. 'Specially when he found out dere wasn't no law dat could keep colored peoples slaves. Tried to whup de black off ol' Mabel but Mabel 'membered from her momma how ta use the tree bark you sees up on dem dere walls to heal her wounds. Seem like the more the Massa whup her, the better her potions got. She wasn't bout to miss a day away from her sweet Nate who tol' her dat dey should stay put 'cause they wuz gettin' fed by workin' in de fields. So she hurried up and made herself well through dem' dere tree bark potions, and wuz back in the fields the next day! One day when Massa Carter wuz in his evilest of moods, he took ol' Nate and whupped him pretty good. Dang near kilt 'im. Das when Nate decided to leave. Well, Mabel got wind of Nate's leavin' and round nightfall when Nate was runnin' as fast as he could, he heard footsteps comin' right up on 'im. Jes as sure as he figured himself lynched an' dead, he seed ol' Mabel through de thicket. Liked ta scared the patched up pants right off his hind, it did! Dey gots here first. Me an' yo Pop-Pop hid 'em behind the stairwell an' they promised to pay us back some way. At first, we didn't want no paybacks but den I gots ta thinking. I tol' ol Pop-Pop of an idea that was swimmin' round in my head and he wuz the one who got thangs started."

Nana told of how one night they (having been free legally two years before the Emancipation Proclamation) journeyed north to find a less hostile place to settle down. They happened upon a young white couple by the name of Lester and Frieda Shelby who befriended them and helped them build a home not far from theirs. All the while Nana and Pop-Pop were afraid that though they had papers, someone would come along and deny them their freedom. There were occasions when just that almost happened, but the Shelbys would come to their defense stating that they belonged to them. It seemed as though the townsfolk needed to be assured by the Shelbys that they weren't sharing the same land that God gave to them with Blacks. Once the Shelbys did that, no one overtly bothered Nana and Pop-Pop.

The house they built at first was simple. One room afforded the necessities of life, but as time went by and the town folk grew to know them as their white friends' "slaves," they added on without anyone noticing or even caring much. Pop-Pop knew to build near the woods for at any given time they could run into the arms of a dark and terrifying thicket for solace. It was Nana's idea to build hidden passageways behind the walls, and even the white folks they befriended weren't aware of them.

One night, when Nana and Pop-Pop lie in bed tired and sore, Nana began to weep as she felt the hands of the man she loved gently caressing her. She desperately wished that she didn't have so many welts on her back. It seemed as if there was not one square inch of smooth skin she could offer her man's hands to rest upon. Angrily she sat up and asked her husband, "How far kin you count?"
"Not past ten, I figure," Pop-Pop answered. "Why?"

"I want you ta count de amount of stripes you figure is on my back." Pop-Pop counted ten at a time as Nana made a circle on the dirt floor for every ten he counted. After they had ten plus two circles, Nana proclaimed, "I gotta do somethin' wit dat number. I don't know what it is, but that number gotta be reckoned with in my lifetime."

Nana recounted the days when she was whipped for not yielding enough cotton. She remembered the whippings she suffered from her overseer's lash. Some of those were so severe that the master of the estate allowed her to stay home for a day or two to recover. One of those days, when lying face down on a dusty floor, young Annie at age 14 couldn't do anything but stare ahead at a nearby wall. There, in the corner, she noticed a spider weaving a web. She watched as it spun its threaded silvery quilt from one corner of a wall to the other. She marveled at the thought that the spider needed no help and dauntlessly worked for hours using only the materials that God had endowed it with. From what she could determine, those tools were merely saliva, determination, and the innate genius of swift and dexterous hands. While attempting to crawl closer to the spider to get a better look, Annie's hand swept across a mound of dirt close by. Soon she found her hands being attacked by an army of zealous ants protecting territory that had been dismantled by the innocent swoosh of her fingers. Brushing them off she noticed that twice as many ants came from below, and because she knocked off the top, she could see that they came from a radius that almost tripled the size of the hole. Annie, forgetting her pain, studied the spider and ants as they restructured their fortress, never understanding at the time why she was so captivated.

Years later and now free, the Emancipation Proclamation seemed to make the souls of evil white men more wicked than before. Though the Negroes were free, they were still being hunted, and this time with a vengeance. When Mabel and Nate happened by the house and Nana and Pop-Pop gave them shelter, Nana got the idea to ask that they stay long enough to dig a tunnel that led to the edge of the woods. Nate and Mabel happily obliged as Nana and Pop-Pop kept them safe by day and fed them what meager food rations they had.

CHAPTER 23

The mortar of men

Nana told how she, Pop-Pop, Mabel, and Nate took turns digging that tunnel. In the beginning, the attempt seemed futile as the soft earth collapsed above them and they would spend half of the day repacking vulnerable walls. One night when Nana had to get up and relieve herself, she noticed that her menstrual cycle had begun. Grabbing a pail of cold water nearby, she dipped a handmade rag into the water and began to cleanse her body. She was so sleepy that she failed to harness her rag close to her body, and when she awoke, she found the bed a bloody mess. Pop-Pop assured her that it was no big deal but Nana was mortified. Grabbing the one piece of material that they claimed as a sheet, she immersed it into a bucket of cold water and began to scrub vigorously. The edges faded with the scrubbing, but she found that the center of the sheet had become stiff. Holding the sheet close to her face, she examined it closely. The dirt from the ground they slept on and her menstrual fluids had mixed and formed a stiffening agent so strong that even her hardest rubbing would not compromise it. She sat for a moment. Then she thought, *Dis is the stuff I needs ta mix wit de earth! Dis is what de Lawd is tellin' me!* Quickly she gathered a handful of dirt and mixed it in with her blood. She added her own saliva, remembering how the spider had done it and pasted the material on a small patch of material. Several hours later, the "formula" had enmeshed itself into the material and dried to a rock-hard patch. Elated, she reported her scientific findings to her husband who though proud of her accomplishment asked, "How you gonna get enough blood to pack a tunnel wall?"

"Jus' like God showed me dis, He'll show me dat!" she barked at him.

The next day she timidly asked Mabel when her "nature" was going to start. Startled, Mabel asked why. When Nana told her of her discovery, Mabel hollered so loud that a flock of sparrows perched close by broke camp at the sound of her voice.

"De Lawd done showed you that the wretched filth of your body kin be a tool fo' good use! Shoot! Why wait fo' our nature? Whuts wrong wit our dung? I sho' nuff kicked enough rock-hard turds dat near broke off my toe on mah way up heah!" Nana and Mabel began to laugh hysterically then secretly agreed to work on the "formula" night after night until eventually the best mortar known to man was developed. The four men and women would take turns, starting at dawn, and secretly dig a tunnel until noon. Then they would break for supper and within an hour form a small room that Nana called a "pod" at the end of the tunnel. On the opposite side of the entrance, they would begin again digging further north into the woods. Soon it was easy to construct an underground pod in the boundaries of a full day.

Nilé awakened gradually, realizing that something significant happened to her. She lay in bed staring at the walls around her trying to sift real thoughts away from the ones in her recent dream. Strangely enough, she wasn't afraid, just curious. She wondered why all of this was happening to her yet was certain that her recent zeal for information about the past and slavery tied into it all.

She was almost ashamed of her beautifully decorated surroundings. Having spent what seemed like an eternity underground in small podlike rooms, Nilé's room seemed to sprawl out as far as the eye could see. Patwa jumped up onto the bed and immediately turned his back to her, looking up the hallway toward the kitchen. This was an indication that she was to get up, refresh his water bowl, and fill up his tray with kitty nibbles. Stretching and praying that Angie wouldn't own up to her promise to "Check on her later," Nilé moved toward the bathroom much to Patwa's chagrin.

Feeling the need to recapture the wonderful feeling at church, she wondered if she had any gospel music around. As she moved toward the kitchen, Nilé began to hum what little she remembered of the tune that greeted her when entering the church. Her voice became louder and louder as she recalled certain verses and incorporated them into the song. By the time she fed the cat, and a fresh pot of tea was brewing, Nilé found herself clapping her hands and dancing in the middle of the kitchen singing:

Trials dark on every hand
And we cannot understand
All the ways that God would lead us
To that blessed Promised Land
But He guides us with His eye
And we'll follow 'till we die
For we'll understand it better by and by.

As she sang, she felt others in the room helping her along. She imagined her relatives, links to her past, raising their hands to certain key phrases that they personally could testify to. She sensed her grandma, Nana, standing there, hands patting a fresh white apron nodding her head in approval to all of the ruckus going on, and suddenly she was overwhelmed as the visitors in her kitchen continued singing without her in resounding harmony:

By and By!...When the mornin' comes
When all the saints of God gather home we'll
Tell the story of how we overcome
And we'll understand it better by and by!

With hands in the air, she wept openly and thanked God for answering her prayer. She realized by the song she had sung and the dream she dreamed that God was answering the very question she raised to Him weeks ago, *"Why is it that I can't feel you orchestrating **my** life?"* She understood that He was using her great-grandmother Nana to arrange this completely incredible journey. But what did Nana mean when she said,

"You'll have to go against your name to find your freedom, chile."

"What's my name got to do with it? *Nilé* is just the name of a river!"

CHAPTER 24

Toni's conjure

The entities of Toni's conjure felt the power of their rival rumble throughout the spiritual realm. A meeting was called. At first they spoke quietly, and their concerns were laced with a modicum of fear.

"We have come up against dis body before and failed, ja' know. Deese women are one, and although dey claims to simply protect der lineage, dey represent and are backed by de Ancient One whom has thwarted de plans of our master for ages." This truth was whispered by Dom, the oldest of the spiritual entities.

"De stakes are too high to meet Toni's request! Besides, all we promised ta do is find eem…dat's all she aks. We found eem…we finished!" The feeble black fist of Clara (a wise but paranoid spirit) met the old wooden table with a thud where everyone assembled. Some argued that previous bouts with Nana and her band were met under unfair circumstances, and that if anything was to be done on Toni's behalf, strict guidelines should be established prior to the onset of the battle for a soul. Bantering among the entities went on for at least an hour until a cold dark heaviness slipped through the cracks of the walls. The chill was unnoticed at first, and the spirits grumbled and argued their points grabbing and repositioning shawls around shoulders. Eventually frost was billowing from their mouths and their ability to articulate was stifled by the cold heavy presence. Finally, the old ones found themselves huddled together more frightened than before, knowing that they were being held captive by their own fears and that which lorded over them was present. Then the presence spoke.

"Look atchew! Sapposed ta be powerful and unafred…but look atchew!" The voice speaking walked through the door.

Its face was hard and deeply creviced. Black sparkling eyes with no whites to them glinted behind a veil of heavily wrinkled skin that pulled downward with every muscular opportunity. A small wide stumpy nose glistened at the nostrils as mucus found its way to the speaker's lips. Each word was punctuated with lisping moisture flying through jagged and blackened teeth.

"Ya **NEBBA** stats a fight wit worries! **NEBBA!** T'aint no sense in de battle if ja gots fear! Das how de sistas won de firs' fight, cause de wasn't skeerd and dey trusted deer leader! Das how WEEEEEZ ta win DIS fight now mind ja." Silence enveloped the room. A hand that held a black crooked cane hit the side of the table.

"Who here is afraid?" Silence.

"Who here trusts deer leader?" Slowly the hands of all at the meeting were raised. As each hand lifted, warmth began to radiate throughout the room. With the warmth came a sense of empowerment as the entities with their timeless leader began to develop strategies for an attack on Jordan Beslow.

CHAPTER 25

Betty

As Nilé began to prepare dinner, she realized that she didn't want to eat Sunday dinner alone this night, so she decided to invite her two best friends over. The first phone call was to Angie, who answered the phone with her usual salutation, "Yeah!"
"Hey Ange?..."
"Yeah!" (This time with a slight tone of annoyance.)
"Uh...you wanna eat up here? I mean...you start dinner yet?"
"I started dinner over an hour ago! But hell, I'm tired of my cooking. Besides, my macaroni an' cheese ain't cooperatin' with me. What got into you?"
"Oh, I don't know, I just want to share a meal with my friends, I guess."
"Lyin' on a Sunday! Well maybe not, I take that back, the sweet love of Jesus got into you, I reckon. I'd be a fool not to cash in on a free meal, so count me in! You call Bet yet?"
"No, I'm getting ready to. Do you think it's too late?"
"Heck no! Les, she done gone up to Mickey D's already. You know she don't cook!"
"Oh, I hope I can catch her...let me go!"

The phone rang and rang. Just as Nilé was about to hang up Betty answered.
"Hey Bets! You eat dinner yet?" There was a long hesitation followed by a flat "No, Nilé, not yet."
"What's wrong? You OK?"
"No, not really, Nilé, let me call you back."
Nilé and Angie ate dinner in relative silence. They were both moved by the morning service, and although they enjoyed each other's company, they still needed to be wrapped around individual thoughts that required answers.

"Ange... I've been having dreams..." Nilé began.

"Dreams about what?"

"I dunno. Dreams that take me back to when I was a young girl in Maryland. I had a great-grandmother who would keep me and Eden for the summer down there, and she seems to want to tell me something. I mean I've been meeting her in my dreams lately. Does that sound strange?"

"Nope. The way I figure it, dreams are the only tools we really have to sort out reality. A dream can either drive you insane or pull together what little sense you have left. What you think your granny wants with you?"

"That's just it! I don't know. I know she has something to do with my need to draw all these pictures because I swear some of the faces I've drawn I saw in this dream. When I go into the back room to sculpt or paint, it feels like they are with me, telling me who to portray next. I mean, really Angie, I'll hear thoughts like 'No...she had a dimple in the left cheek, not right.' Or 'I was never that fat!' When I make the adjustment, I feel relieved, or I'm sure that the correction is right, even though I have no real point of reference but my thoughts!"

"Deep! So Granny is bringin' out the artist in you, eh?"

"Not just that, Ange...seems she wants me to understand that I am the key to some sort of closure needed in the family, but I can't for the life of me imagine what it could be."

"Funny you should mention all this 'cause although I haven't been havin' no dreams or nothin', I do feel a presence around me tellin' me that my wisdom ain't all mine! Hell, at first when I felt that idea, I barked back aloud: 'Neither is yours 'cause you would know that I ain't got a lick of sense!' Soon as I said it, I felt like more of the fool than I was arguing since there wasn't anybody there in that room but me! I never had that thought cross my mind again, but I have been prompted to call you or encourage you to do more with yourself lately. Girl, you stay on my mind and that bothers me!"

"Why Angie?"

"'Cause I ain't tryin' ta be no damn lesbian that's why!"

Nilé jumped up and ran around the table to give Angie a big fat sloppy kiss on her cheek while hugging her.

"You know you want me!" She screamed.

"I want you 'bout as much as I want a plate of cold grits, girl, get your big knockers outta my face!" Their bantering was interrupted by the ringing of the phone.

"Hey Nilé? It's me, Betty."

"Oh, hey girl, you wanna stop by for some dessert?"

"Yeah...I think I need to."

About an hour after the phone call, Betty showed up at the door with fresh baked cinnamon rolls and a gallon of ice cream. They assembled in the living room plopping down on favorite chairs. Nilé grabbed the remote assuming they'd watch something on cable, but Betty interrupted her move by blurting out, "Oh Nilé, let's just talk, OK?...I mean...I wanna talk...I need to talk about...something." Sensing the urgency in her voice, Nilé placed the remote down onto the coffee table and sat on the edge of Betty's chair.

"What is it, baby? What's going on with you?" Betty tried to establish a story "setup" but her words and thoughts were jumbled.

"Does what you want to say have something to do with you being raped as a child?"

"Angie! Why you so ignorant?"

"Well damn! We all skirtin' round the issue. We know that church will bring out the best and the worst of you. We all stated that today's sermon did a number on us. I mean church has a way of shakin' out the crumbs of your life and making you take inventory. Maybe that's what needs to happen to Betty. Maybe that's what she wants to talk about. Maybe you and your tactful behind would never get to the point and maybe God is usin' my ignorant behind to get Bets to do some real soul searchin'."

"Don't get mad, Nilé. Angie is right on point. She usually is. True, her behind is ignorant, but it's on point. Today's sermon really hit home for me. Seemed like nobody else in the room needed to hear it but me, and for that I was embarrassed and ashamed. Truth be told, I thought you were

going up to the altar just to get me to move, but then when I saw you completely immersed in your own pain and need, I realized how God can slam dunk more than one person at a time. Listen you guys, I need to let you know that most of my what you call 'quirks' are directly related to that horrible incident and the way it was handled. I still believe that I'm not worthy of love, especially the love of God, because I lured the guy who accosted me. He kept saying it over and over again while ripping into my insides. He kept saying…"
At that time, her words were inaudible. She was convulsing and rocking back and forth in her chair. Angie spun her wheelchair around and backed toward Betty's.
"Listen to me! No, no…let her go, Nilé!" Then at the top of her lungs, Angie bellowed, "Dammit to hell you better look up and listen to me right now or so help me I'ma slap the taste outta you!" The room rang on Angie's last word then fell silent. Desperate yet quiet energy flurried through the room at seemingly breakneck speed, much like the power of a silent winter storm. Betty looked up at Angie, and Angie then spoke delivering to Betty's ears words that were typical to Angie's vernacular yet held a spiritual authority that was not her own.
"I don't give a damn what the fool said! He said nothing, NOTHING that belonged to what is right and good and TRUE about you. Do you hear me? NOTHING! Now you can keep playin' that broken record of his lie in your ear, but I tellin' you now, until you pick up that needle diggin' into your psyche and LIFT that scratched-up evil lie out of your head, you will never be good to no one, man or woman, much less yourself! You did not lure him; LUST suggested and then DEMANDED that he take your innocence, and he tried to free his shame by accusing you. As long as you buy the lie, he will be free! Decide right now who's guilty and free yourself right now! In the name of Jesus!" Angie without thinking placed her palm smartly on the forehead of Betty who slid down her chair like a marionette whose strings were suddenly cut. Nilé watched in amazement the events that were taking place so very quickly. She watched

how her friend buckled at the touch of her other angry yet loving friend. She watched as the bowl of melted ice cream dropped from Betty's hand onto her floor. She watched as the energy flowing from Angie's hand not only rendered her friend limp but also jolted through her own limbs, as momentarily Angie lifted her hips from her chair then slammed down…all while Nilé watched.

CHAPTER 26

Pharaoh's army wears hoods

Now Nana and Pop-Pop had established a level of comfort within the little town they resided in. The neighbors believed that they were still owned by Mr. and Mrs. Shelby and for the most part were hospitable toward them as far as the boundaries of Black/White relationships would allow. Occasionally the neighbors would request their housekeeping services and Nana would respectfully oblige. After a while, they became indispensable so the Shelbys devised a plan where they literally rented Nana and Pop-Pop out, arguing that all of the work being done for the neighbors was cutting in on their regular household obligations. The system worked out to be quite profitable for the Shelbys, and every once in a while they would give a dime or even fifty cents to Nana and Pop-Pop when a service was rendered properly. The quarters were saved and the dimes were used to buy everyday necessities at the general store.

Pop-Pop would never frequent the general store because it was owned and operated by James T. Brokes who firmly believed that Blacks were merely farm animals who could walk upright and speak. Now that the Negroes were free, Jim Brokes thought the world was going to come to an end.
"How the hell you jes' let farm animals run free and live right next te' yeh? Next thang ye know, they gonna want te' eat wit ya, an' have a say in gov'ment policy!"

Most of the men in the town felt the same way but weren't as vocal as Jim. Jim had an ugly spark in his eye, and would often deliberately knock a product over when Nana came in, just to order her to pick it up. Next thing you know he was squealing and hooting about her breaking up his store just so the few consumers would take his side and glare at Nana as if she were a dog.

"Jes' 'cause they talk don't mean they's 'telligent! What you want, gal?"

Nana would hand her paper over listing the things she had money to buy. She'd purposely omit some necessities because she knew old man Brokes would add "interest" to the cost and she didn't want to come up short. She'd stand perfectly still and watch Mr. Brokes fumble around for her products even though she knew exactly where they were located and could have acquired them far more quickly.

"Thas' thirty-nine cents, Missy. Last time you came up short an' I let it go! Won't be happenin' this time, you kin be sure!" Nana handed Mr. Brokes four dimes knowing that her list only required thirty-two cents. He shoved the bag into her arms, and she walked away never expecting her penny change. Sometimes she'd ask Mrs. Shelby to purchase a few groceries for her when she only had the exact amount of money needed. Mrs. Shelby understood, but didn't want Nana to make a habit of her "running her to the store."

Nana would choose bright sunny days when Mrs. Shelby was in a particularly good mood and wanted to go in town to shop. Those were usually the days after Nana and Pop-Pop had broken their backs and worked for every neighbor within a four-mile radius. As a result, the weeks' rental fees they had drummed up were good and Mrs. Shelby would be itching to get her hands on some new material for a dress or curtains. When those days would come, Nana would gather the runaways early in the morning to the first holding pod that was tunneled underground by her and Mabel. They'd inform them that the only way to earn their keep was to dig until Pop-Pop said stop. The digging was always the same. First Pop-Pop would count off five steps from the center of the pod. Pop-Pop always knew the direction to dig, saying that God told him where north is no matter where he stands, and the rest of the map to freedom was either on the back of the woman he loved or in his head. Once they marked their place, they'd use stones and sticks and scratch like dogs, throwing the dirt behind them through their legs. Nana, Mabel, and whatever other women and children were there would gather the fresh soil in their dresses and quickly scurry it out and up to the outhouse behind Nana's back porch. There, Nana would lift the seat and gently deposit about one pound of new soil to the sludge of manure, ammonia, and urine that was bubbling below. The smell was horrible, but Nana had grown accustomed to it. Then she'd scoop about five pounds of tarry black pitch into an old barrel and roll it down to the first underground pod. The tarry mortar was used to tighten and plug the walls of the tunnel being built. The children at first would gag and vomit at the smell. Mabel would tell the kids to mix their vomit in with the rest of the sludge and keep on packing. The little boys were instructed to dig fist-sized tunnels upward toward the earth's surface to allow for the passage and flow of air. At the top of the tunnels, the little girls created nets by braiding the center veins of leaves together. They then gently anchored them over the tunnel openings with rocks and camouflaged the openings with nearby leaves. This way when it rained, the openings would not collapse inward and obstruct the only available means of air circulation. The rainwater was routed down the sides of each tunnel through what looked like an irrigation pipe made of the branches of a tree similar to bamboo whose limbs were loosely veined and virtually hollow.

The children invented games. As the boys' fingers reached the top of the soil, the girls would grab those fingers claiming them as their personal future husbands. Some of the boys who didn't want to be claimed would hold a nasty black water bug in their fists. When the girls grabbed their hands, they'd open them to find a dizzied black bug frantically racing up their arms. Word traveled, and because more and more young men and women found out about Nana and Pop-Pop's pods, they opted to go north via the tunnel. As a result, the tunnel extended quickly. Usually by the time the Shelbys returned from town, a new pod was created exactly one-eighth mile north, east, or west of the last pod.

At night, Nana and Pop-Pop would retire, leaving their runaway families still busy at work. Nana would cook yams and loaves of corn bread until late at night. The Shelbys loved the smell of sweet aromas that wafted from Nana's kitchen late into the night. Nana was careful to bake a loaf for her neighbors, just to keep their attitudes as sweet as her corn bread. Pop-Pop would make the last walk down to the tunnel. He'd knock once, then hesitate, then knock twice to let them know it was him. Sometimes he would sit and fellowship with those who were known as the "Stayers." Nana would worry until Pop-Pop came home, and then light into him when he walked through the door, accusing him of "flirtin' 'round with one of the new gals."

CHAPTER 27

The Stayers

Ordinarily it would take about one or two weeks depending on the age and physical abilities of the runaways to create several new pods. Then they would rest, receive directions of where to go when they surfaced, and then move on. Pop-Pop would hear of a new posse of runaways coming through when he would go into town. An old Black ex-slave kept by the Robinsons for handy work would always be in or nearby the grocery store. He was almost bent in half because of years of pulling a plow that should have been drawn by an ox. A blow to the right eye by the butt end of a rifle rendered him blind and a cataract formed over it. All the white children in town were deathly afraid of him, nicknaming him "Ol' Ghosteye." Ghosteye bragged of his freedom and how nobody owned him but de Lawd Jesus. Truth be told, he was no good to anyone, and the Robinsons, a family once dirt poor in England and struggling to make ends meet in America, decided to take him in for odds-and-ends jobs around the house. Their having Ghosteye around made them feel a sense of status and they treated him as if he were a retarded child. Ghosteye was Pop-Pop's alert to the new band of runaways. He'd always act beholding to the Robinsons letting all who had the patience to listen to his babbling know that if it weren't "fo' de Robinsons, he'd be one dead nigga boy." He'd tell the story over and over about how a band of white folks gathered around him and had a noose around his neck ready to string him up when Tom Robinson out of "de kindness of his Christian heart claim him dat day as his lost nigga' and he wanted him alive so he could whup him good." The fact that Ghosteye had his freedom papers meant nothing to the blood-hungry mob. The ringleader took ol' Ghosteye's freedom paper, crumbled it up, and lit his pipe with it.

"Dat dere minute was de minute dat took me off de free man's list...'till Tom Robinson took me in. Dat day he tolt me dat in his *mind* I was always gonna be free, but I hadda act like his slave, or he'd have me kilt. Seemed like a pretty good deal ta me, since I nebba knewed whut exactly it 'twas dat a free Black man did anyways, all I wanted was ta be **called** free. Shoot, a nigga ain't sposed ta do nuttin but werk fo' white folk, 'cause dey's da ones dat's smart!"

Ol' Ghosteye would go on and on building up the ego of all white men merchants or customers who had the time to listen. As he spoke, Pop-Pop would bow his head and agree.

"See, I nebba undastood a nigga who'd wanna run away. Dey's lookin' fer sho nuff death! You ain't sposed ta run away. Youse sposed to wait, do right by yo massa, and den by God's grace he'll gib you freedom. Wait on de Lawd! Dat whut da' Good Book say! Dat's whut happened ta me. God's grace gib me my freedom, an' God's grace kept me free wit or wittout papers. But deese heah niggas runnin' away, dey different! Every week I heah 'bout some foolhearted slaves tryin ta run from a good man's home. 'Specially since de President don shot off at de mouth an' tol' de Massa's dey had to lose what was rightfully theirs. Stands ta reason any sensible businessman wouldn't wanna do dat. I tell ya right now, if I git wind of any of that there foolishness, Ize ganna be the first ta tell! Dat's right! I tell Mr. Tom Robinson for protection sake. Protection of his fam'bly! Take Massa Winslow's plantation fer instance. (Pop-Pop's ear would perk up.) Massa Wndslow done tolt Tom Robinson dat two a his prize nigga's done run off! Not only did they leave but they had the gall ta up an' take dey brides an sebben chilren' wit em! Sebben! Do ya believe dat?"

At that moment, the townsmen would look to Tom for confirmation. Tom would then verify Ol' Ghosteye's story and the men of the town would huddle together to decide on a secret "town meeting." About that time, Pop-Pop would gather the cornmeal and yams and various other things Nana sent him to town for and bring them to the counter. That's when out of sheer meanness the owner of the general store would double the price, rationalizing that he wasn't about to take the good food God made out of the mouths of white men and sell it to Pop-Pop and Nana for a mere pittance. Later that evening Pop-Pop would advise Nana to be ready to take in eleven runaways—two men, two women, and seven children. Nana would tell the Stayers to mix a batch of healing salve and to boil certain roots and leaves together because she heard that one of the women running was pregnant.

The Stayers were runaways that did not want to move north for freedom. They considered themselves free living underground and enjoyed the idea of aiding fellow Blacks in their flight. Some of the runaways at first would try to be a Stayer, but after time, the closed-in environment and tireless workday and night would break their spirits, and the desire to be free up north took precedence over the seemingly glamour and wisdom of being called a Stayer. Stayers were indeed different. Timeless wisdom and quiet patience resonated within each of them. Notions and potions of a world left behind remained ingrained in their minds, and though they could not articulate how or why they did what they did, they knew without ever having done it before that their remedy would work.

Once a child about the age of five was found strapped on the back of a runaway slave. When taken down to the pod, Nana said she watched the father of the child lie down carefully as the mother unwrapped the young lad. The child lay limp from the waist down. One of the Stayers exclaimed, "Git up boy!" but the child through pleading eyes spoke of his inability to move. That moment, as if assigned to the fate of the young man, the Stayer who commanded that the boy stand grabbed the baby boy by the waist threw him over her shoulder and disappeared into the tunnels. Weeks went by before the parents were able to see him, then months. When the father stated that he was ready to move on, his wife said, "Not widdout ma chile. Dey done took im' away...I couldda had dat done by de Massa. I gon' stay here till dey show me he either dead or libe, but I ain't gone nowhere til I know." Moments later, the child was seen by the eyes of his mother walking down the dark hallway from where he was snatched months ago. His back was upright, and his legs were strong. He smiled sheepishly as both his mother and father embraced him weeping and praising the Lord. The Stayers watched for a moment, then disappeared into the dark hallways.

Nana asked years later what it was that they did to the boy. This is what was revealed:

> M'dabe, the head Stayer embarrassed that she had given a command to a lame child, took it upon herself to heal the boy. She sent Nana weekly to the general store requesting three boxes of Argo starch. Now starch was considered a luxury item for Blacks, and the need for three boxes every week raised enough eyebrows to start a town commotion. How she and Pop-Pop managed to ease the paranoia and queries of ignorant whites looking for a reason to string anyone Black up was the genius of Nana and Pop-Pop alone. M'dabe was not concerned how they do it. All she insisted was that they do it.

> Each morning, before the boy had awakened, M'dabe would boil water and rags soaking in the Argo starch. Then she'd lift the boy and sit him on a makeshift table. She and Sara, another Stayer, would begin to wrap the boy from the waist down with the steaming hot rags. The young boy could not feel a thing because he was paralyzed. When his waist was wrapped, they'd each wrap one leg. Through the course of the day, both M'dabe and Sara would take turns carrying the young boy around while gathering leaves and berries for their potions. As the rags dried, they would form a casing around the young boy until his waist and legs would be as hard as rock. The boy would remain in the cast all day until it was time for bed. During the day, they'd sing and tell the boy stories about a place called Africa where children played freely and never had to work. A place where their mothers' baked yams filled the air with a sense of comfort and their fathers' nimble fingers twisted thatched roofs to make homes for newlyweds.

Weeks went by and the boy learned much. He never whimpered when thickets smacked against his delicate face as the Stayers walked through the woods. He simply loved being with them.

One morning after M'dabe lifted the boy onto the table to place a hot rag around his waist, the young boy screamed in agonizing pain. Both of the Stayers were startled and removed the rag immediately. After a moment of silence, M'dabe and Sara began to grin at each other. The grins brought on chuckles, then laughter, then rejoicing! Immediately they realized that their potion had healed the young boy. Something in the starch potion revived the nerves of his back and strengthened his back and limbs! Something in their potion revitalized deadened nerve endings so much so that a five-year-old boy screamed in agonizing pain as any normal child would when touched by a scalding hot rag. Now all they had to do was teach him how to use those working limbs! That wasn't difficult; for the boy was more than eager to learn. M'dabe later told Nana how she'd watch the young man making walking motions while sleeping, and at daybreak, he was never startled to see her because he was always awake and waiting for her. Through the unforgiving thicket the five-year-old boy learned to walk, using branches from bushes to support him until his legs regained their muscular strength. Though thin, his limbs grew strong until the day that he walked back to his mother's pod camp, beaming.

The Stayers could communicate at times without saying a word, knowing what was to be done when presented with a challenge. Many had roots in medicine from the old country. Many remembered potions, and at night would risk running out into the woods to gather tree bark, berries, and roots. They claimed that the night animals would warn them of impending danger, and they would never stray far from the refuge of a nearby pod. Before every venture, Nana would insist that they pray to the Lord Jesus for cover and safety. Many Stayers also, like Nana, were raised or converted to Christianity. Those who were not had better not mention anything else to Nana, or she'd send them on their way. What they all had in common was a notion and deep devotion to a higher Being. Some called that Being "Amma" and argued that it was the Motherland's name for the Creator of Jesus. Nana would quip, "You kin' call 'im anything ya wants while you 'lone, but in my presence de Savior's name dat I'm gonna heah 'round here is Jesus!"

The Stayers seemed to take all of their clues (from the mixing potions to knowing when Pharaoh's army was going to come riding through) from nature. They claimed berries would not ripen quickly when the energy level of evil was high. At least ninety percent of the time when the berries harvested were either sour or bitter, the clansmen would ride through the following day. Based on the texture of the bark of a tree, and whether it was plucked from the tree or picked up off of the ground, would determine the potency of a potion. The ones that were bitter were crushed and boiled down to a deep-blue brine that was used to color cloth and paint walls. Sometimes animal dung would be gathered and smeared around the portals of the pods that they were in to ward off evil spirits, as they would gather late into the night giving credit always to the wisdom of their ancestors and the blessings of God for their healing accuracy. They believed that the particular animal that dropped a deposit of feces was a messenger of God. Using the animal's dung around their pod was a protective shield, and all that was evil would regard the scent as repulsing, and move away from the site.

The Stayers would warn Nana and Pop-Pop of weather conditions, stating that they could determine how hot it would be the next day by the number of times the crickets chirped combined with the length of silence before another interval of chirping. This information would be used to orchestrate them meeting runaways at the edge of the woods, and that information would be conveyed to Ol' Ghosteye who would articulate a clear and concise message to the slaves planning to run that night. All of the wisdom of the Stayers was a mystery to Nana and Pop, but they believed it as God's ability to enable his children with the knowledge of the universe, which after all…belonged to Him.

CHAPTER 28

The first meeting

Nana and her band sensed that the war had begun. Simone (a noble warrior in her own right, and the daughter of Batu who preceded Nilé's grandmother by 15 generations) out of deference to the others knew to temper her eagerness and desire to attack the ones who placed Thompson's spirit into Nilé and Jordan's life. She spoke softly, always looking to her mother with immeasurable respect. "Momma Batu..." she began. "Momma, you know that my love for you runs as deep as the Creator's first river. You also know that the fire I hold inside is a warrior's fire." Batu nodded.
"All of us realize that a root was prepared for this new man in our daughter's life and we know well the source of de conjure." The women in the room lifted their heads in agreement. "We also know that the spirit of Thompson is so strong and holds much evil, so much so that his name throughout the years has never changed. The old ones kept it from generation to generation for fear of his ego." Nana's patience was wearing thin.
"Where are you going with this? What do you propose? Thompson is only a tool of the old ones. He is as old as time, but younger than a newborn. He is the very source of our tribulation throughout and even before slavery. He's not black or white yet can be both. He can manifest himself in the loins of every man living! What you proposin' ta do? Kill 'im? Ya caint! Ya caint kill dat which de Fadda created. Eben when it's used in an evil way! Be keerful, Simone...your fire could turn 'round and burn us all!"
Simone stiffened her back, then smiled at Nana.
"Seems like de fire be in you too great, great-great-great-great-great-great-great-great-great-granddaughter." With each "great" spoken, Nana could feel the subliminal charge made against her. She had overstepped her bounds and in

doing so disrespected Simone. Then Batu, mother of Simone, spoke.

"Once de life of flesh is over, all knowledge come tagedder in de form of either good or evil. We…only by de grace of God have been chosen to work fa' good. Let us not fall prey to splinters while we's tryin' ta break de rod of evil! Granddaughter Nana speaks wisdom from firs' han' knowledge of our dear chile Nilé. She de one who remember her touch, smell, and innocence. Simone, howebba, know de evil of Thompson long befo' slavery! She also rememba' how he wuz defeated by witnessing firs' han' my personal battle wit 'im. Dis battle must be fought wit de tools God gib us, not Thompson's. Dis battle clearly fo' all us womens! An' all us womens must stand tagedder in mind and spirit! Das where Thompson's weakness lie!" Just then, old Henny, Simone's great-great-granddaughter, noted for her promiscuity while living on earth crashed the meeting.
"How much did I miss?"
"'Bout de same as you always miss, chile! Best you sit an' listen ta ketch up!"
"Ah would but I have news. News dat could be a help fo us all." She looked to Batu who nodded her on.
Sliding wide sensuous hips into a nearby chair and savoring every moment that all eyes were on her, she began.
"Well….Ah just came back from Georgia, weather's lovely there around dis' time…"
"Git on wit it!" Nana snapped.
Henny's wide eyes and full lips froze and stared at her grandchild. Then she slowly hissed, "We's all de same hea' in de spirit world, but we should nebba fo'get how we was taught ta respect dose dat brought us by de flesh into the living world. You'd a knowed better not ta use dat tone wit me when we wuz in de flesh!" Batu, oldest of the band of women, was the only one who seemed to be able to keep Henny and Nana in check. "Come on chile…everybody here knows how fine you look and how you enjoy runnin' 'round. We's all anxious ta hear whut ya gotta say!"

Rolling her eyes at Nana, she slowly continued.

"Seems like a pretty young girl named Toni pulled da root on dis Jordan fella years ago when dey wuz' fooling 'round wit each udder. Anyway's her intent was jest a hold on ta him til he came 'round ta really feelin' love fer her but she went and got knocked fo' the root could take holt! She called off in her mind all bets of bein' wit him 'cause she figgered he'd love her outta' pity, but fo'got ta take him off de root. Meanwhile, he jes up and disappeared from her life. Well you know de old ones…dey won't quit till dey make good on a promise an' ol Thompson fount Jordan at his momma's funeral a few months back. Das' how all dis mess heia' started!" The room was silent. Angenna, a distant cousin who was gentle in spirit, asked: "Kin' we get dem ta call it off?" Henny hollered. "Call it off? Baby, once you gits ol Thompson sniffin' round potential do-daddin', ain't no callin' it off! Look at Nilé! She beautiful! She lonely. She confused. Frum whut ah hears 'bout Toni …she da same way. Das de perfect soil fo' Thompson ta plant his evil seed. Ah personally don't unnerstand why y'all fight 'im so much. He ain't dat bad…jes want his way, das all! Whuts wrong wit gibbin' 'im his way? If ya gots any sense, ya figger out a way ta make it werk fa ya!" She tapped Simone on the leg and winked at her. Simone drew back her leg in disgust.

Suddenly a small and timid personality entered the room. No one from Nana's band knew her, but there was a sense of propriety and purpose in her demeanor. She was a beautiful chocolate-brown little girl with long fat braids framing her face like giant parentheses. She had dimples and a smile that held the sparkle her mother once owned. She simply stood at the door unmoving as if someone had dropped her off and offered no instructions as to what to do once she got there.
"Now ain't that a pretty lil' thang!" Henny quipped after seeing the child. "Who is you, sweet darlin'?"

"Exactly! Who is she? An' who sent huh?" was the next remark made by Simone who by this time had abandoned her chair to approach the child.

Batu rocked back and forth in her seat and closed her eyes. Her thick dark lips curled to the side forcing a mischievous smile to disrupt the deep crevices etched in a normally stoic expression. "Do it make any difference who sent huh? She hea', ain't she? An' seems ta me she hea' fo' a reason." Simone recognized the look in her mother's eyes. She adored every memory of their brief yet wonderful life together and held tight to all of the marvelous words of wisdom Batu bestowed upon her while she was young. She recalled the smile her mother was now directing toward the young child as the smile that tucked her to bed and hummed lullabies to her when she was little. She was all too familiar with the rocking motion that meant that Momma Batu was partaking in the most intimate nature of dialogue with her Creator, and it seemed at those times when Simone noticed that her mother was happiest.
"Momma, what is it?" Simone whispered.
"Everything belong ta da' Creator. Everything. We's ta use de tools He gib' us. Dis be one of de tools He done sent!" Simone turned quickly to the child, but before she could speak, Nana asked the little girl: "Who you belong to, chile? I kin' still smell the breath of life on ya." The little girl looked up at Nana with eyes that seemed to hold the wisdom of eternity within their sparkle.

"My mother is alone." Each member's heart in the room was torn with sadness. They all imagined incredible scenarios that could have possibly prematurely torn the child away from the expected years she was to dwell on earth with her mother as a living soul. They all privately mourned and felt the loss that the child's mother must be feeling each and every waking moment of her life now without her. Simone, Nana, and the others looked to Batu who unlike the rest of the mothers was simply smiling and rocking…

Nana asked, "Who yo' motha be, chile?"

"Her name is Tonia, but everybody calls her Toni." The crowd of women looked in silence at each other while Batu rocked.

Henny then spoke: "How you come to such a pass?"

"I took ill with the flu one winter. Mommy couldn't pay for all the medicine an' doctorin' needed to get me my strength back so I jus' faded away. I tried ta hold on for Mommy's sake...she prayed an' prayed for me to hold on, but it was so hard. Besides, everything I dreamed of was so much better than when I was woke. One day I jes' decided ta let go of Mommy's hand...jes' for a moment. Next thing I knew we were so far apart I couldn't reach her no more. I saw her standin' all alone. I wanted ta go back but I couldn't."

"Sweet chile, you know now that yer Mammy is not alone don't 'cha?"

"Yessum...but she don't!"

"Ah knows dat but in time she'll come ta realizin'...jes wait an' see!"

Then with the wisdom of ages, the little girl spun around and spoke to Batu.

"We gotta do somthin' 'bout Thompson!"

"I knows, chile. What do you propose?" Nana was somewhat perturbed that an ancient ancestor would pose such a question to such a youth. Not only was she new as a spirit, but she had only experienced twelve years as a living soul on earth. Nana kept silent waiting for the child's response.

"He's found my papa, but he don't know how ta 'proach him. He knows that my papa is a smart man, an' wants ta use him not only for the conjure assigned, but to settle a score wit' y'all." The room was silent and dense with concern.

"Why you sidin' wit the enemy? Ain't you kin to da ones dat made up da conjure?" asked Simone.

"Half me is but half me ain't! Him who called me home is the same Creator you serve!" Some of the members of the meeting chuckled. Simone bristled having been put in her place by a child.

"What do de Creator send you for ta tell us?" asked Batu.
"He tell me ta tell you ta trust the wisdom of His which is timeless, steady, and present, neither giving power nor preference to strategies used in the past anymore than ideas believed to come in the future." Batu knew that the message was from God. No child could think a thought so profound, and no spirit that new could grasp a concept that vast.
"I needs ta turn over in my mind all dat de Lord has delivered." At that moment, she stood up, tapped her walking stick three times, and vanished from the room. Like heavy wet vapors of steam, the others disappeared as well, leaving Nana and the little girl alone.
"Come wit me, gal! We got some talkin' ta do!"

CHAPTER 29

Accidental exposure

Jordan and Nilé grew closer as weeks passed. They shared a common interest in African-American history but for totally different reasons. Jordan argued that his thirst for understanding the culture was scientifically based. Blacks in America as a whole, he argued, were the only race that hadn't excelled as other races. He was convinced that skin pigmentation was directly related to one's zeal (or lack of) to acquiring the finer things in life. He would bombard Nilé with statistics proving how melanin is a substance that is not simply responsible for skin pigmentation, but also plays a significant role in the brain as it aids in controlling emotional stress, acting as a neuro-stimulator in many instances. Jordan was hell bent on proving the theory that so-called laziness in Blacks had to do with their having an excessive amount of melanin in the brain, and that there was scientific fact to prove that they were lazy not because they wanted to be but were genetically predisposed with this mindset. To chemically alter or manage melanin was Jordan's dream. If he could calculate the disparity of melanin between the two major races, then surgically remove or implant the appropriate amount into either, he was convinced that this twisted mindset known as racism would disappear. He argued that it was the energy of one and lack of energy in the other that sparked and eventually fanned the flames of hatred that now exists today.

To Nilé his argument seemed far-fetched to say the least, but impressive. She dare not mention that he must have lacked the typical amount of melanin found in the brain based on the passion he was exuding! She wondered what event in his life triggered his desire to research such a bizarre concept and defend what whites had been shoving down the throats of Black men for years, particularly since he was a living breathing antithesis of his own theory! A part of her was enraged and outraged as he waxed philosophic for hours on end, scientifically apologizing for a race of people whom he believed brought no significant value to humanity in general by virtue of their emotional detachment. Sure, there were a few exceptions to the rule who Black historians held in high esteem and boasted of, but few in comparison to the achievements spurred by passion-oriented minds of men with white skin. He argued that too much emotional stabilizing produces laziness and gets in the way of achievement, clouding the thinking process. An abundance of melanin in the brain was a curse given to men and women of color. He even suggested that innately the white man must have known of this.

"I suppose I'm boring you to death with all of this theory, huh?"
"I wouldn't say that your theory was boring."
"What would you say it was?"
"Confusing. Not in an 'I-don't-understand-what-you-mean' way, but in an 'I-can't-for-the-life-of-me-understand-why-you-would-want-to-prove-such-a-theory' way."

"Sugga, don't you understand? We as a people have been struggling to be something that we are not! We are not emotionally cut out to be power mongers! We are quick to fight and just as quick to forgive, whatever is easier…and because of that we have never gained respect or power or land or anything for that matter that would enable us as a people to negotiate our way to the top!"
"Sounds to me like you were injected with a stiff dose of self-hatred."
"No Babe! It's just the opposite! It's because I love my people so much that I'm going through such great lengths to get them off the hook so to speak. Didn't you ever wonder why we could never get on top? Didn't you ever ask yourself why is ours a race that for centuries remained downtrodden?

There has to be a reason for that! Moreover, I've stumbled upon a genetic reason that was staring us in the face for years! Black people are lazy because they are BLACK!"

Nilé's heart was racing. She wanted to dispute every word he said, but she had been trained in her former marriage not to argue. She felt sick inside that she could not stand up to him, and at the same time proud to know such a brilliant man who did in fact spend years and years in research labs and libraries trying to prove his theory. Part of her hadn't an ounce of fight left. Part was never inclined to partake of such an outrageous subject. Part of her was guarded, reminding her to protect her love interest; for outside of his wacky obsession, he had the potential of being a wonderful companion.

Jordan's conversation was interrupted by a knock on the door. Nilé excused herself from the table to see who was there.
"Hey Baby!"
"Hey Ange! Come on in! Jordan and I were engaged in deep conversation in the kitchen. This is the kind of subject matter that you can sink your teeth into. Come on back, I'm interested in what you'd have to say about one of Jordan's theories."
It took about fifteen minutes for Jordan to bring Angie up to date with all that he had explained to Nilé. Angie listened intently.
"Well....waddaya think?" Nilé prodded.
Angie reached over the table using a knife to hook the corner of the butter dish and pull it near her. She began spreading the butter slowly, being ever so careful not to miss a corner of her raisin muffin.
"Ange! Talk to us!"
"About what?"
"About what you think of Jordan's research and theory about Black people—that's what!"

"All I have to say to you, my brother, is the next time you want to spend 'bout fifty, sixty, seventy thousand dollars in tuition and fifteen, twenty years of your life on somethin' that smells to me like a sack of horse crap, call me first. I'll take your money, make monster love to you for all them years, and in the end deliver you the finest bag of crap you ever wanted to see!"

Jordan dismissed her with a shake of his head and a smile. He didn't want her to know that he was profoundly hurt by her comment. Nilé, feeling the tension growing, asked sweetly, "Now Ange...since we are in fact speaking on a scientific basis, it would be nice of you to back your theory with some…"
"I ain't got to use no science! Look at me! I'm as yallah as the backside of a Chinaman an' I'm also as emotionally tricked up as the rest of the niggas he done grouped us all to bein' like. My Blackness ain't got nothin' ta do with melanin. Sorry ta bust years and years of research 'Mr. I Got The Definitive Answer' but ya gonna have ta change your name or change your game!"
"You're not seeing my point! It's not the melanin dispersed throughout the skin; it's the melanin harbored within the pituitary gland that I'm talking about."
"Well, did your pituitary gland spring a leak? I sure do feel a lot of passion comin' from your Black behind! Or were you just one of the 'lucky ones' who got just the right amount?"

Jordan and Angie went on for what seemed like hours before Nilé conjured up the nerve to suggest that the conversation end. She was tired. Tired of hearing both sides of an all-too-ridiculous argument. Jordan was relieved that Nilé broke up the meeting of minds and used the occasion to remove himself from the premises. Determined to prove his point, he moved toward Angie, bent over and gently kissed her forehead, indicating his total control of emotions. Angie mumbled, "You may act like the cold-blooded white man you place on a pedestal, but yo' behind is still black as pitch! Come 'Shoot Nigga Day,' you gonna be the first ta die!"

Inwardly shaken by her comment, Jordan hesitated. Then a strange and distant smile, one that curled his lips at the corner with foul and malicious intent whispered, "Ordinarily an insult like that would warrant a serious ass kicking, but then…why waste my time? You wouldn't feel it, would you?" Before walking out the door, he picked up his hat and tipped it over one eye, winking with the other…the same way Thompson always did.

CHAPTER 30

Thompson

The slam of the door punctuated what Jordan felt momentarily. A combination of anger, triumph, and embarrassment. He walked quickly toward his car trying to snap the invisible bungee cord attached to his heart, which still remained pounding at Nilé's place. As he drove away, he could feel himself at war with his emotions. It seemed as if everything good in him was ashamed of what he said, while a strange desire to rationalize and praise his behavior took over.

The hell with Nilé and her miserable old maid coffee clutch! he thought. Why would he even try to explain something he held so dear to him to such backward-thinking closed-minded people? His rationalization evolved to rage as he sped closer to home. Soon he began thinking of even more clever putdowns he could have, *should* have, said. With each thought, Thompson grew stronger inside of him experiencing the clench of Jordan's teeth, and the pulse of his heart. He enjoyed racing through old corridors of anguish unleashing grudges and memories of Darnell. He captured every side-glance and "Lord have mercy" utterance that Jordan thought he had silenced. Each hurt, each glance of condemnation Thompson found and hurled across Jordan's mind like old worn-out clothes until they lay in a heap exposed, musty, and out of season, screaming for a place to be. When rage turned to despair, Thompson's strength was almost completed within Jordan. Jordan sat parked in front of his house still holding on to the steering wheel staring at hate. At that moment, Thompson spoke to his heart. *"Nuttin' is more important dan' power. Not understanding, not love…nuttin'. That's what you really want, boy, ain't it? Den get it! Stay focused, I'se here now…I know de way ta power!*

Ahhhh...you got a beautiful machine of a body heah, Jordan mon! I like what I feel! We be gettin' along real good you an' me...jes' wait an' see!"

Jordan felt uneasy and instinctively cried out to his mother. He had no idea that her attempts to reach him were thwarted by Mumbai and Clara, the spirits determined to honor their beloved Toni's conjure, and as he crawled out of his vehicle he became nauseous. Entering his house, he found mail on the floor. Shuffling through expected bills, he stopped at an envelope whose return address read "Inner Faith University." Curiously, he opened it, and it read:

Dear Mr. Beslow:

Upon thorough review of your research documenting the role and genetic disposition of melanin in Caucasians and Blacks, the faculty and administrators of Inner Faith University would be honored to provide $1,500,000.00 in funding toward the completion of said research.

In addition, we wish to offer an opportunity for you to interview as a candidate of our esteemed faculty upon completion of your study.

IFU has always been an advocate of cutting-edge theory and investigation. You'll find that our university can provide state-of-the-art technology conducive to meeting your needs.

Sincerely,

Graham M. Stapely
Chairman, Inner Faith University
Science & Research Endowment Committee

Dumbfounded, Jordan dropped the letter. He reached for the phone to call Nilé, then paused. Remembering his recent incident, he picked up the letter and placed it back into the envelope. Feeling vindicated from all that had happened, by one simple and timely letter, his sense of hunger kicked in as he marched like a peacock toward the kitchen.

CHAPTER 31

Destiny in design

Days passed before Nilé could even approach Angie. Jordan's horrible remark left an ache that throbbed within her gut. Angie, sensing her pain, phoned her stating mail that belonged to Nilé was sent to her, and she wasn't physically up to rolling uphill to deliver it. Nilé sheepishly agreed to come down.
"Ange…" Nilé began.

"Don't even start. It's gonna' take more than a fine (but ignorant) Black man to separate us! I read your mind all week. An' there you go tryin' ta fix what you didn't even break."

"I can't believe he said that! It's not like him…"
"How do you know what's like him? How long have you known him? How long have you known me? In defense of the brotha', I can say some things to Normals that rattle the bones. He had a right to retort. What got me was not so much what he said, but how he said it. How could such a cold and caustic statement be made by someone who was so passionately engrossed in conversation with me only moments ago? Thas' what scares me! That a brotha' could change up on you like that so quick. Nilé, you got to be careful with this one…"
"You need not go there. I've already decided to chalk him up. He scared me too. Not because of what he said, but that he would dare say it to my closest friend! Ain't that much fine in the world! Besides, I was never enthused about his scientific findings. Jordan seems to be chasing or running away from some sort of demon, and I am not up to unraveling or healing the neuroses of anybody until I at least get mine healed." They glanced at each other exchanging

intangible love that only time understood, then blew kisses toward the air.

"Hey, what's this letter about? Says it's from Trappe Municipal Court in Maryland. You know anybody there?"

"I had a great-grandmother who used to live in Trappe, Maryland...but I don't know anybody there now." Opening the letter, Nilé first read quietly. Then with a look of curiosity, she read aloud a sentence that was too mind blowing to contain within her head:

Therefore, the county of Trappe, Maryland, is offering $ 1,500,000.00 to serve as a closing cost to the owner of said property.

"What said property?" Angie boomed. "You never told me you owned property! Why the hell you livin' in a....."

"Shhhh Angie! I don't understand this. They're trying to get me to sell my grandmomma Nana's house. That shack ain't worth fifty thousand, let alone one million five hundred! What's up with this? I wonder if Eden knows about this offer. Did they send her a letter? Why me?"

"Maybe they trying ta get around your grandmomma's back. Maybe she ain't sellin'!"

"My great-grandmomma's been dead for decades now! I had no idea the property was still standing, or that she would even think to put my name on anything having to do with ownership."

"Well, $1,500,000.00 seems like a hell of an incentive to investigate! You need an assistant? Damn baby, you gonna' be rich! Now don't get hincty on me. I knew you from way back, and I'll kick yo' behind from this wheelchair to Trap Flavor Georgia if you get new on me!"

"Trappe Station, Maryland, Angie, that's what my folks called it at least…"

"You know what I'm talkin' about!"

Nilé called her sister Eden who stated that she knew through Daddy of Nana's desire to leave the house to Nilé. She even expressed relief in her voice when she heard Daddy say that the choice was made for Nilé because Eden had no interest in it whatsoever."

"It was Daddy's choice ultimately to sign the papers over into your name."

"Why didn't he tell me?"

"'Cause he was sure you wouldn't want it either, and he had already 'bombed out' in his appeal for my interest."

"So you knew and didn't say anything?"

"Nilé...at the time it wasn't that big a deal. Besides you and FM were engaged in your usual drama, and I thought if I brought it up it would cause one more spark to fly. You gonna look into this, aren't you?"

"One million five hundred thousand bucks??? You kiddin'? You dang skippy I'm looking into it. Only one thing..." There was a pause.

"Only one thing? What Nilé?"

"I'm scared."

"Oh don't be silly. Just make a call to find out first of all if all of this is legitimate. Then work from there. You're an intelligent woman, Nilé; there's no danger in placing a call. You want me to do it for you?"

"No, I'll do it. Eden, you have such a take-charge personality. Where was I when they were handing out confidence?"

"You were there, you just used it all up being a little fresh behind as a child! Now you hesitate too much. Just go for it, lil' sis! This is big money! When everything is cleared, call me and I'll help you spend it!"

"Laugh if you want but you know I'll do just that. I don't know what to do with that kind of money!"

"Chile....I done spent half of it right now just thinking about it! This is gonna' be fun!"

Nilé hung up the phone, relieved and excited. She thanked God for her sister who always managed to present a positive perspective to situations. She missed her dearly and imagined how the newfound money would bring them closer together. A million bucks can fly you back and forth like

131

most folks ride the bus! Shoot, for that matter, she could buy her own plane! She smiled thinking about what she'd name her private jet. *Nilé High* or maybe *Nilé's Bliss* or perhaps *Nana's Dream*. Soon Nilé had dozed off with Patwa snuggled up on her warm soft lap.

CHAPTER 32

Composure compromised

"Hello, Mr. Stapely? Yes...this is Jordan Beslow. I just received your letter, and I was wondering... yes? Yes! No, this Saturday will be fine. Now I do need some particulars on...oh, OK, let me give you my email address and your secretary can contact me." Jordan and Mr. Stapely spoke a few minutes more. Once he hung up the phone, he clapped his hands and leaped into the air. He wanted to tell someone, anyone, but whom? He had no friends to speak of, and he knew in his heart he had severed any possible ties with Nilé as a result of their last encounter. A sense of melancholy was quickly dashed by an overriding thought that people in power are usually lonely. Lonely because no one can see or understand their vision. Lonely because those affiliated with them are usually parasites, so he'd better get used to the idea of lonely because it came along, part and parcel, with the position of success and power. Jordan turned toward the bedroom deciding that he should pack for the trip that was only a few days away. He smiled thinking of Mr. Stapely's statement that he needn't bother with the details of travel, that his secretary would FedEx him roundtrip airfare, and hotel accommodations had already been set up. The lilt in Mr. Stapely's voice fanned Jordan's ego as he described the itinerary for the day, all being established to woo Jordan into staying with their university. He thought, *Now there's someone who has intelligence enough to think outside the box! These are the kind of people I need to be around...people with intellectual competencies that match mine. These people and only these are the ones I choose to befriend!*

"I hope your trip was satisfactory, Mr. Beslow. God forbid we lose you because of a poor flight!" Mr. Stapely's tone was that of a man of confidence. His comment while extending his hand for the first time to Jordan was understood as purely rhetorical, and seemed to almost require a positive response from Jordan. Soon, Jordan found himself among officials and high-ranking honchos, all of which cooed and purred at him while uniformed attendants scurried about catering to their every whim. After a full day of touring the facility, they dined and, by invitation of the university president, adjourned to his personal lounge and library where Jordan was offered a Cuban cigar from a most exquisite humidor. Jordan paused and for the first time beheld the silence of the group of men surrounding him.

"As a rule I don't smoke, and on those few occasions when I do, Nicaraguans are my choice. However…since I see that such great care has been taken to offer only the very best, I think I'll indulge myself this once!" The group released an appropriate chuckle, one of obvious relief that Jordan was indeed their man. His observation was keen, and his response was favorably appropriate. They all lit up and puffed silently for a moment.

"Now that we've fattened you for the kill, so to speak, Jordan, are there any questions that you may have?" Jordan hesitated feeling all eyes on him.
"Uh yes, perhaps one." The silence was almost visceral as they waited for his next sentence.
"Actually the question is embarrassingly simple. Why me? Why so much attention to my particular project? I'm sure there are fellow colleagues as passionate as myself who have approached you with projects just as intriguing. What was the thing that set my project apart from all of the others…so much so that I'm being offered a position to teach, not to mention carte blanche entitlement to complete my research. In some ways, gentlemen, this is too good to be true!" Several eyes shifted, but as a group they maintained a calm air about them, much like that which a leopard maintains, a sort of tense steadiness and unwavering focus necessary to

execute the calculated slaughter of unsuspecting prey. Finally, Mr. Stapely broke out in laughter.

"My dear Mr. Beslow! You had us worried! If the motive to your question is to simply ease your mind about our appreciation of your intellectual prowess and how it compares to your fellow constituents, rest assured (and I dare say I can speak on the behalf of the entire group here) that your particular project far exceeds any presented to us in the past few years...perhaps even decades! As you know, our university has been in the process of an ongoing expansion project. We're knee-deep in property acquisitions, foreclosure investigations, etc., none of which would interest you I'm sure. However, you would play a small role in an ongoing picky and quite arduous dispute we've been having with a neighboring township about sixty miles away known as Trappe. Apparently the townsfolk stubbornly refuse to relinquish a small piece of land that we'd like to purchase because of some property they claim is of landmark significance."

"Oh? As much as your offer entices me... I certainly don't want to enter into any political dispute...exactly how would I play a role?"

"Trust me, Mr. Beslow, your energies will be spent solely on research. Let our big guns handle the political stuff. That's why we have lawyers!" Mr. Stapely smiled and quickly moved on to close the deal. "Now without further ado, I have in my hand a simple contract delineating all that we talked about....except in legal-schmegal terminology (the group chuckled nervously) and all I ask is that you oblige us with your signature."

"Would it be OK if I looked over everything tonight and signed in the morning?"

The group hesitated, then again (as the days ahead would prove) Mr. Stapely spoke, "Certainly my boy...and mind you, I'm only saying boy as it relates to age. Because of the aches and pains in this stiff and now thoroughly drowsy body reminding me that I'm too old for night-time negotiations, and you....well look at you, you probably haven't even hit your stride tonight!"

"No offense taken. In my opinion, to take offense to an age-old prejudice is the same as placing speed bumps on the highway designed to be driven at 70 mph. Feelings serve no purpose when one wishes to progress. Don't you agree?"

Jordan felt the group lift a simultaneous eyebrow of approval to his statement. Smiles appeared, feet shuffled, and torsos moved forward in their chairs as if to anxiously await the next profound statement he would make.

"Poignant observation, my friend! Morally and metaphorically!" Stapely bellowed. "And on that note I believe we can retire to our quarters...Madeline has provided you with your key?"

"Yes! Yes, she has. Your secretary is amazing. So professional and timely. Please thank her again when you see her for all she's done." As the men gathered together shaking hands, snuffing out cigars, and fine-tuning their corporate witticisms, they one by one thanked him for coming. Their eyes resembled the eyes he saw and dismantled as a child in his big sister's doll babies. Vacant blue crystal balls that opened and shut because of a small hinge and rubber band attached behind them. The eyes that blinked as a response to how they were mechanically, as opposed to emotionally, moved. Eyes that seemed genuinely happy to have him there but for the wrong reasons, and while saying good-night and shaking hands, Jordan felt his two-ness, as an American, and a Negro—two souls, two thoughts, two unreconciled strivings; two warring ideals in one dark body, whose dogged strength alone kept him from being torn asunder.

Months had passed since Jordan signed on to the university and he had done a wonderful job of impressing everyone involved in his project from undergrad assistants to major investment stakeholders. He welcomed the new accommodations and surroundings. His manner of charm and gentle persuasion had a magnetic effect to novice scientists. Even though the concept of the research was to most young African-American scientists totally convoluted, they signed on, if for no other reason than to see his hypothesis evaporate through research. Some peers made dismal attempts to befriend him, as he was quite charismatic. Yet he remained antiseptically distant, gracefully declining invitations to dinners and social events that most newcomers would leap at the opportunity to attend. Although he presented as warm and charming, his heart grew colder and colder.

Each night Jordan would be greeted at his doorstep by his loyal companion, loneliness. She'd acquaint him with the familiar smells of leather chairs and then drone the all-too-haunting melody of footsteps climbing a hardwood staircase. As he'd prepare for bed, he'd oftentimes turn on the TV and unconsciously listen to the news, stale commentaries about painfully uninteresting events going on locally and around the world. Occasionally he'd allow his thoughts to drift to a better time. He'd recall a time when he could feel the colors of Nilé's apartment warming his being. When her subtle fragrances of lotions and primal essences embraced and teased him, as he'd gaze at voluptuous hips moving toward an awaiting teapot. He wondered if the relationship could have gone anywhere and secretly ached for the journey, as long as it was with her. Instinctively he knew her love was right for him. Nilé's love could walk comfortably within the boundaries of the nurturing love of his mother, and then playfully entice him past those boundaries to where no mother should rightfully be. Those were the nights when Jordan would squeeze his pillow and rock silently, as loneliness watched.

One morning while hunched over a microscope, Jordan was startled by the aggravated voice or Mr. Stapely in a nearby corridor.

"This is preposterous! That smalltime crop of backwoods coons think they can pull a fast one on me? And who the hell is this...this Nilé Davis character? Who does he think he is coming down from the great northeast to reclaim territory he doesn't even have a clue about?"

"Now Mr. Stapely, please sit down. Remember your pressure." Mr. Stapely's secretary, Madeline, was hysterically trying to calm him down and it seemed as if all attempts were resulting in futility. Jordan stepped out of the lab and calmly walked toward Mr. Stapely. His curiosity was multifaceted. Did he just hear Mr. Stapely say "backwoods coons"? Did he just hear the name Nilé Davis? Was that actually the beet-red face of the man who epitomized corporate composure?

"What seems to be the problem?" Jordan asked.
"Problem? Problem? My dear son, there is no problem here. Not one that I can't fix with a little ol' midnight township meeting!"
"Excuse me?" The immediate response that came from a feisty young Black undergrad that was ready to engage in a bout of serious verbal butt kicking and had already argued in her mind that her expulsion would be worth it all. That squeaking tone of audacity brought Mr. Stapely back into focus as he quickly regained his composure. Deliberately dismissing the hip-holding rubbernecked stare of the young reprobate, Mr. Stapely walked hurriedly toward Jordan grabbing his lab coat to suggest they speak in private. Madeline puttered behind, reaching for her cell phone and canceling scheduled appointments for the day.

Once inside Mr. Stapely's office, Jordan once again repeated: "What seems to be the problem?"
"I...uh...I'm extremely frustrated with the outcome of a battle for a piece of property that should have been acquired years ago. We have been more than generous with these townspeople but they just won't let go. They have no idea,

nor are they remotely inclined to care about the intricacies of their decision not to sell. But dammit, if need be, I'll go all the way to the Supreme Court for this! It's a matter of principle!"

"Is this the little town you were talking to me about before I signed on?" Mr. Stapely answered yes but was not really up to unearthing all the details about his ongoing battle with the town of Trappe. He was being consumed by his emotion, that inadequacy Jordan was so convinced Mr. Stapely lacked was escaping out of every orifice of his body, and as it grew it awakened Thompson who saw Mr. Stapely as a perfect candidate for his move toward power and the ultimate destruction of the authority now held by Nilé's lineage.

"Mr. Stapely, I'm not understanding…"
"That Davis person! Look at the letter! Some cretin named Davis wants to keep his land. This little piece of land that I WANT!" Jordan looked at the letter of apparent denial. Skimming through legal terminology he desperately searched for the name Nilé Davis. And there he found it. His heart pounded with mixed emotions of joy in seeing her name and fear, knowing the fight she had on her hands.
"Why won't she let go?"
"It's a SHE??? Oh my God! You mean to tell me my legal team can't beat a woman?"
Grabbing for the phone, Mr. Stapely barked out several demands to Madeline that were to be taken care of immediately if not sooner. Watching Madeline through the glass-paned window of Mr. Stapely's office, Jordan was taken into a realm of surreal tranquility where he saw all things happening, yet there was no means by which he could access or interact with anything. All Jordan could hear or feel was the beating of his heart and his thoughts asking questions, piecing parts of a puzzle that was impossible to imagine.

CHAPTER 33

Coincidence

"Hello Nilé." A studied pause of disbelief was followed by a cool "Hello Jordan."
"It's been almost a year—how have you been?"
"Why would you care?" Jordan's heart sank but he pressed.
"Crazy as it may seem, I missed hearing those sarcastic remarks. You're really quick... and good!"
"Why did you call me, Jordan?"
He wanted to go on with light banter, but her tone and question wouldn't allow it.
"The purpose of my call is twofold. First to see how you are doing…..which I guess I've found out and secondly…well, just to say that I've noticed that you've been causing quite a stir here in Salisbury, Maryland, where I've relocated. Seems like you and my boss are butting heads over a piece of land?" Rage raced through Nilé's soul. Through flaring nostrils, she quipped, "And you've been sent by Massa to sweep me off my feet and turn it over to him?"
"Oh Nilé, that was a low blow."
"No lower than your casual call to me after ten months of noncommunication. Not to mention your grand exit that day. Just what the hell was that all about? Low blow? Why you didn't even talk long enough to weasel an apology for your despicable behavior—no, you just opened up with the weakest of small talk and then plowed right into your boss's agenda. What does my holding on to my property have to do with *you* anyway? Will you lose your job if I don't sell? Well that concept just strengthens my resolve!" SLAM! Nilé stared at the phone still ringing from the impact of her hanging up. Grabbing a dishcloth, she squeezed dishwashing liquid into a pot in the sink and began running water while talking to the imaginary Jordan in front of her. "Just who the hell do you think you are, lover boy? You come waltzing

into my life, deliberately dismantling all of my plans to live a calm and peaceful sedentary life ALONE…. What did you think? Your pretty black skin and pearly whites would sweep me off my feet? What was your motive? Just what did you want with me anyway? A few nights together and a fight with my best friend? That's what you wanted? That's what could drive you away from me? NIGGA PLEEEEEZE!" Patwa raced into the dining room where it seemed safer. Moments later Nilé found herself sobbing over a pot overflowing with soapy water. Then the phone rang again. She stared at it and decided not to answer. Then she heard a thumping from the floor below, a pause, then the phone rang again.

"Hello Angie."

"You know…you are one hot mess! Here we are in the twentieth century and the end of my broom handle is caller ID for you. We may as well put two tomato cans together with a string and call each other!"

"This is a bad time, Ange…"

"OK, it's a bad time to talk; all I'm calling for is to ask you for a stick o' butter. We ain't got to talk. Just open the door and throw it down the flight of steps if you want. We doin' everything else primitively, I can deal with bent-up butter."

"I'll be down, Angie."

"How 'bout I come up? You sound really bad."

Although Nilé hated to admit it, it was times like this when Angie proved to be a dear friend. No judgment, no "if-I-were-you," and no body language came from Angie as Nilé laid her heart, fears, and emotions out in the next few hours. She only asked questions to piece together parts of a story that was all too clear in Nilé's mind, but when spoken presented themselves as ambiguous bits of a puzzle that could have served as a breakthrough. Finally after having talked her heart dry, Nilé asked, "So what do you make of all of this drama?"

Angie traced her fingers across a pattern in the tablecloth to buy time. Then she spoke slowly as if to edit each word before it came from her mouth.

"You know...it amazes me how scientists and physicians can dismantle the heart and even mend it when the physical aspect of it is in need of repair. Yet no one has the ability to fix that intangible aspect. That part of the heart that when it hurts, hurts real bad. Nobody has a pill or shot for the heart that hurts. Hell, for that matter, nobody even knows exactly where the *feeling* heart lies within a man or woman. Nobody but our Creator." She looked up at Nilé and smiled. "I can feel in *my* heart that *yours* is hurting, but I don't know where that piece of hurting heart is, nor do I have the tools to fix it. Words seem somehow inadequate, yet they're all I have to reach out to you. So as a desperate friend trying to play surgeon and save a heart from dying, I will at least try, Nilé...but know that that's all I can do, try...

"I badmouth 'Normals' every chance I get only because of an unfortunate chain of events that forced me out of the club of normal people. I can observe now how people take for granted all that God gave to them, and it makes me so angry when they don't appreciate it. Yet I find myself being turned and twisted through a labyrinth of emotions, none of which move me any closer to discovering how the heart works, or should work. What I can say is that I know emotions are a symptom of something that's happened to the heart, and that 'Normals' have a tendency to react very quickly to them. Because I can't move like I used to, I've had to learn how to control them....my emotions. See, everything that's happening is a setup. You can't afford to move fast right now 'cause the situation hasn't gelled. This is where you must trust in God. It's no coincidence that you rededicated your life to Jesus, Nilé, no coincidence that you've been haunted by some sort of ancestral force lately. You... Jordan...that place, Trappe, Maryland... and the potential destruction of it is all interrelated, but I don't know how."

"Oh Angie...that's ridiculous! Nana's property has nothing to do with Jordan outside of the fact that his boss wants it, but that's simply coincidence! What I'm mad about is that he called only to speak on his boss's behalf. If it weren't for that, I'd still not know where his tired behind was!"

"Yeah! Coincidence! Coincidence is a word used casually by 'Normals' as a slap-on bandage linking the unexplainable to reality. Reality we can handle, but that which cannot be explained...well it has something to do with intangible forces. Now that's moving in the realm of the unknown. Funny that that's where God would allow our hearts to reside. 'Normals' can't deal with that, myself included! That's why I have to trust in what I know is out there controlling it, even though I can't. I'm only influenced by it. To me, coincidence has something to do with the past, the present, and the future all banging into each other at the same time. We think linearly, but God thinks eternally. There is no past, present, or future in His realm. It's all there and it's all good! Sometimes He throws us a bone of intuition, and we trust our inner gut, but not often. Nilé, all I can say now is trust your inner gut. It's connected to God. Your gut knows where your heart is. Your gut can find its way to God. It's the instrument used by your ancestors who have been reaching you through your desire to read about them, draw them, and sculpt them. Develop your gut. Ask God to reveal the other spiritual parts of your body too. Ask for spiritual ears, spiritual eyes, and an appetite to hang out in His world!"

"That's too scary, Ange. I'm not ready for all of that."

"Apparently you are. You've been prepared for what looks like a glorious journey. What's the Bible say? 'If God is for you who can be against you?' "

"Angie, I'm..."

"Don't be afraid, sweets. I'll be by your side all the way. I ain't got nuthin' else ta do! Besides, I've been prayin' and askin' God for wisdom ever since that run-in with Jordan. I wanted to like him, but that statement he made turned me

around. I want to know if the brother is right for my best friend. So I've been askin' my Savior."
"What has He said?"
"HE AIN'T SAID SQUAT! Don't think you can get easy answers! Shoot, if that was the case, I'd know if I was ever gonna' get up from this chair or if them dang doctors was just blowin' smoke up my behind to make me try harder."
"Angie, I love you. I really love you!"
"No more than I love you, sista girl. Not half as much as the One who knows where our hearts live." The phone rang again. This time Nilé reached for it staring at Angie.
"Hello? Yes, this is she speaking." Angie could tell from her tone that it was someone Nilé didn't know. Then she watched Nilé try to remain as polite as possible as anger wrapped its fingers around her throat and nearly strangled her final response to the caller.

"Mr. Stapely, you've caught me at a very bad time. Perhaps later on in the week I can contact you so that we can discuss *your* concerns about *my* property in depth. Oh, it is indeed my property, Mr. Stapely; I can assure you of that, and the longer we stay on this phone, the more you convince me that it will stay MY property. Try to have a good day, Mr. Stapely." Angie could hear the voice in the receiver still talking as she witnessed Nilé's hanging up with detached repose. There was a smug grin on Nilé's face as she stared past the kitchen window to a place where dusk and dawn met. For the first time Nilé was not afraid, and even though she had no idea of her next move, she knew that every decision and every ounce of energy she had within her was lining up to fight for her Nana's home.

CHAPTER 34

Rebirth

Inner Faith University's campus though small was beautiful in the autumn. Chubby oak and maple trees vied for the students' attention by dropping nuts and crimson leaves in their paths. Squirrels raced toward unknown destinations with the determined senility of going nowhere. The air was crisp and heavy with the aromas of fall, and Jordan kept himself busy to keep from going crazy. There was a war raging inside of him, and he knew that he had no more control of it than a young private sent on a tour of duty torn between two voices. One voice he served was a force that was driving him with the fuel of ambition and another voice deeper inside questioned his every move. It was a voice that seemed to dismantle every aspiration he had ever dreamed of. That was the voice that longed to scrap it all and run back to Nilé and ask for her forgiveness. This voice he'd hear late at night when he could not sleep. This was the voice that he'd dismiss with haughtiness when the morning would greet him with renewed determination.

Nilé was busy with her own battles as well. She'd wax and wane for weeks on end about the necessity of dealing with what she considered one moment a pain-in-the-rear inheritance, then the next moment everything her life, family, and history stood upon.

One afternoon, while editing a brochure sent to her about the history of Gettysburg, her attention was drawn to a quote, which stated, "Though the past has passed, it should never be forgotten." To her chagrin, it brought her own personal anguish to mind. Pushing her laptop away, she ran her fingers through her hair and closed her eyes. "All I have to do is sign a piece of paper and I could have a million bucks!

Why can't I go through with it? Is it because I don't like this guy Stapely? I've never even laid eyes on him! He's trying to give me money for crying out loud! Is it because I'm trying to lash out at Jordan? I'm supposed to be over him. What's this hold he has on me? Why can't I make one single decision? It's not as if my life depended on it!" Then in the midst of her anguish, she cried out the most guttural sound that came from the depths of her soul. She couldn't tear herself away from the mental writhing and through it all moaned as if giving birth to a child that lived within her for over fifty years. As the midwives of her past circled around her, they knew that this pain was necessary for that which was pent up inside of Nilé for so long was going to be born today.

CHAPTER 35

Round one

"Shhhhh…" Nana ordered the hundreds of souls around her. "Dis where we must hea' from de Lawd whut ta do."
"Shoot! It be so easy ta jes git inside her and make her do da' right thang! Caint we jes do dat?"
"If we did, we'd be interferin' wit' her free will, an' das not whut de good Lawd want."
"But look at her. She so mizible!"
"From the cup o' pain flows the sweetest wine. Let her call on de Lawd." An hour or so of Nilé's tears brought no relief.
"Oh Father in heaven! Why am I so afraid to do your will? Set me on the right path, no matter how hard it is, I want to do what's right." Her prayer was immediately snatched and lifted high above as Nana and the family held hands high, praising, rejoicing, and beseeching their Creator for instruction. Then swiftly and in harmony with the universe they poured into Nilé's being a macrocosmic picture of all things past and present as it related to their individual struggles, triumphs, responsibilities, and accomplishments. They insisted and persisted until every cell within her was forced to recall moments of her life and how they had to relate to her present situation. Every bone, every muscle in Nilé cried out "Remember!" while her heart raced through passageways of history lying dormant within. Pictures of her great-grandmother's house, memories of the back wooded area, and recollections of Nana's contained tenacity poured into her mind along with her daddy repeating, "Ain't no chile o' mine mediocre." Somehow, she could feel her father lifting her up even though she was only two days old and walking her through each and every room in their house. Thoughts mixed with memories of her and her mother and sister pouring over books on Saturday mornings lulled her. The songs her mother would sing, every word, every verse,

every chorus...she remembered. Her heart's memory held her hand and proceeded to guide her back to a place that she'd never seen, yet it resonated with familiarity. Somewhere distant and warm and altogether lovely, where there was no fear and family members worked, cooked, played, and slept together. There was order in that place. Then her heart braced her for the passage she was to experience next. A sudden jolt, a horrible cry, and images blurred and bloody sped past her. Babies crying, Black skin smoking, then blistering from brands while women silently wept as their breasts and thighs were squeezed and lifted in inspection. Burlap sacks wrapped around the limbs of children's legs huddled together for warmth and the sound of branches cracking and hounds howling in the night frightened her, yet her heart continued pounding rage and fear along with hope and courage until it rested in a place of refuge that Nilé would come to realize as Trappe, Maryland. The montage was surreal. Sensations of a people who claimed her as their own breathed their essence through her, raising the hairs of her skin on end, as adrenaline pumped in obedience to its ancestors on high an enormous dosage of dignity, and pride. Nilé's life force at long last had given birth to a new awareness of her unique self-worth.

Nilé lifted herself from her chair, dazed. With a new sense of purpose, she called Mr. Stapely. As if on automatic pilot, she advised him that she would be in town the following week and would love to discuss the particulars of the land that she owned which he deemed so necessary to purchase. Mr. Stapely was delighted to hear the news and offered to pay for her accommodations. Nilé respectfully declined.

"Patwa...you're gonna have to stay with Aunt Angie for a while, OK?" Patwa's response was a momentary look up toward Nilé and then he resumed cleaning himself. The night before she set off to Trappe, Maryland, Angie and Betty stayed with her. They chattered and fussed about what she should pack and how she should react to Mr. Stapely. They advised her of all the possible pitfalls she might encounter, and warned her not to be sidetracked by Jordan. They also noticed that she was not herself. She smiled with an inner peace and laughed with assurance. She never once mentioned that she was afraid, and they were pleased. In the morning, they kissed her goodbye, gave last-minute advice, then silently prayed as she drove away.

CHAPTER 36

Round two

"Good afternoon. I have a two o'clock appointment with a Mr. Stapely." Madeline looked up from her massive desk and posh surroundings. She greeted Nilé with a professional smile and asked her to have a seat. Moments later Nilé witnessed a large heavy well-groomed man with a receding hairline of over-gelled salt-and-pepper gray. His eyes were as cold as ice and of the color of dirty dishwater. She studied him closely as he adjusted his tie and smiled while extending a hand toward her.

"I thought this moment would never come, uh…Nelly, is it?"
"Ms. Davis."
"Yes of course. I'm pleased to have you here at IFU. Please come with me into my office." Nilé was cordial and calm, expecting that his office would hold the typical accoutrements found in a high-ranking official's office such as his. She figured that he'd hold light conversation for a while before he moved toward business. Her visual expectations were met; however, instead of an audience of one, she was greeted by what looked like a band of Colonel Sanders look-alikes.
"I hope the number of people here to meet you won't cause any duress on your part." Mr. Stapely lied. He wanted to intimidate Nilé in every way possible and the party of grey-flannelled suits parked in his office was part of the plan.
"Not at all." Nilé responded casually as she pulled kid-skinned leather gloves from impeccably manicured fingers. "In fact, I'm more at ease knowing that I have witnesses. After all, I can't imagine that many ladies manage to survive your charm negotiating with you one on one!" The group chuckled and Mr. Stapely was genuinely flattered.

During the meeting, Mr. Stapely boasted of the university's cutting-edge research program, and their desire to acquire land in the nearby counties to expand their campus.

"Ms. Davis, we're at a time in history where modern technology can practically accommodate every scientific imagination. Theories can be proven scientifically; ideas can be played out through the miracle of three-dimensional holograms for crying out loud! It boggles my mind when I walk through these halls and watch young men and women setting the standard bar so high and actually achieving their goals! But we need more laboratories. We need more lecture rooms, more land, Ms. Davis… And that's where you come into play. Our offer to you should indicate that we are quite serious about the acquisition of your property and, personally, I can't imagine any sentiment outweighing such a generous offer! Would I be stepping beyond the boundaries of appropriate behavior if I asked why you choose to hold on to such a modest piece of land?"

Nilé smiled as she composed herself. She watched the group move forward slightly, and she could feel the tension in the air was thick and sweaty.

"Hold on, sweet baby…" Nana whispered. "Dey kin hear the chickens cluckin' in yo' barn but only you kin tell 'im how many is in there!"

Nilé sat up in the leather wing-backed chair. She smoothed a wrinkle from her skirt and checked her nails, knowing that every second she delayed bought her control. She was also aware that the wrong response could yield devastation. Finally she spoke.

"Yes…yes, I believe your question has indeed stepped beyond the boundaries of appropriate behavior, Mr. Stapely, as well as your assumption that my personal sentiments can be purchased." At that moment, Nilé slowly lifted her eyes to meet Mr. Stapely's. She watched as rage surged through him and revealed itself through a heaving chest and the hatred of hundreds of hooded nightriders. A small vein surfaced in the middle of his forehead and the hand that was once perfectly posed in tripod fashion on his desk had now become a clenched fist. The stares they exchanged were interrupted by the buzz of an intercom.

"Mr. Stapely, Mr. Beslow is here for your three o'clock." Somehow, the call brought back his composure. He had planned to use Jordan as a pawn. He surmised that Nilé would be swept off her feet by his charm and good looks. He figured the fact that both were Black would dispel any resistance and the deal could be closed by day's end.

"Oh that's right! I almost forgot! Send him in, Madeline, send him in!" Nilé's heart raced. Immediately she prayed that God would be by her side. This one she was not prepared for. The door opened. Jordan's and Nilé's eyes met.

"Ms. Davis, I want you to meet one of our finest and newest members of our distinguished faculty. He is also involved in a project so incredible that we are keeping it under wraps until he reaches a breakthrough. Dr. Beslow, this is Ms. Davis, the owner of the property that we wish to acquire for your research." Nilé felt relieved that Jordan hadn't told Mr. Stapely that they knew each other. Her eyes searched Jordan's, begging him not to let on. Meanwhile, Thompson through the eyes of Jordan was devouring her body. Though Jordan was dizzied and saddened by her familiar fragrance, Thompson was titillated.

"Hello Nilé."

Eyebrows raised, "You know Ms. Davis?"

"As a matter of fact, I do." Jordan was devastated at his response. Nothing in him wanted to hurt her, yet the part of him of which he had no control kept on. He told Mr. Stapely and the group of their mutual interest in Black History and how they met in a bookstore in Philadelphia. Nilé stared at him in disbelief, as Nana whispered, "It's begun."

CHAPTER 37

The Sisterhood

"Your hours will be scheduled one week in advance. There will be times when you'll have to pull some evening hours...our fiscal year is coming to an end...will that be a problem?"
"No, ma'am."
"You will be paid biweekly, and you have a three-month probationary period. Do you have a place to stay?"
"I'm looking now."
"May I suggest Morgan Park Place? It's a nice apartment complex near campus, three blocks away to be exact. The rent is reasonable and much quieter than the places in town."
Writing the phone number and address on a memo pad, Madeline tore off the page and handed it to her newly hired assistant Tonia Saunders.
"Thank you so much, Ms. Madeline. I really appreciate all of your kindness."
"Call me Madeline."
"Yes, ma'am." Madeline smiled and watched the plump yet attractive woman walk out the door. She made a mental note to mentor her, as she saw potential in the woman, but something obviously had stripped her of her zeal for life and this university prided themselves in producing and employing aggressive and passionate people.

Toni rented a one-bedroom unit at Morgan Park Place, handing over all but twenty-four dollars in her checking account. She wondered how she would get her belongings from Atlanta to Maryland, but reasoned she'd be able to move a little at a time as her salary came in. She dropped her handbag and suitcase at the door and looked around. The living room was clean and friendly with recently polished hardwood floors. Opening windows to let weeks of stale air out, she looked over across the street and saw a playground. Tears welled up in her eyes as she thought about how her daughter could be swinging on one of those swings. The thought made her move away from the window and change the subject by looking around. The bathroom was around the corner at the end of a short hallway. Mint-green tiles greeted her with a promise that they could be made attractive if the right accessories were placed around them. The bedroom was small. Probably only her bed could fit in it, certainly not the big antique chest of drawers that Grandma Mumbia left her. Walking back up the hallway, she decided to take a second look at the kitchen. It wasn't really a kitchen, just a wall with a mini oven, sink, and refrigerator at the end of it. Old wooden cabinets with mismatched knobs lined the top of the wall, and a small framed picture of a fat black woman with a red polka-dot dress holding a spoon and grinning from ear to ear quoting: "I ain't ja Mamma, but I can cook!" was on the wall perpendicular to the cabinets. Toni saw no humor in the poster and removed it immediately. She sighed as she asked herself how she would sleep tonight. No bed, no TV, just a shell with a promise. Then she began taking out her clothes. She threw a soft yellow cardigan over the shower curtain and turned on the hot water. As steam began to accumulate, it assured her that it would knock out most of the wrinkles if she closed the door. Then, with the twenty-four dollars she had left, she set out to find a nearby supermarket.

The first few days on the job were difficult. Toni was sore from sleeping on the floor, and she found the instructions given to her confusing. Eventually she, through trial and error, improved and even took on more responsibilities without being assigned them. Madeline was extremely happy and found Toni to be very cooperative and conscientious. Every once in a while she'd flash a dimpled smile Madeline's way that would warm her heart.

One morning as Toni was preparing coffee, Madeline asked: "Toni, do you have any children?" There was a pause and finally Toni replied, "Yes, I have one."
"Boy or girl?"
"Girl."
"Is she of school age? We have a wonderful school not far from here."
"She passed away, ma'am. She doesn't need to go to school anymore."
"Oh Tonia, I'm so sorry! Please forgive my indiscretion. I thought that because you said you had a child..."
"It's OK, Ms. Madeline, I understand. It's probably my fault 'cause I just can't say that I *had* a child yet. Past tense just doesn't seem to fit in my mouth. You see, she'll always be my child, and I feel like she's still with me at times, you know? I feel her, but I just can't see her." Madeline sensed her pain and dropped her papers to wrap her arms around Toni. They stood there for a few moments as Toni sobbed. Then Madeline cheerfully stated, "Let's put a picture of her in your cubicle! Do you have a picture of your daughter?"
"Yes, ma'am." Toni rifled through her wallet and Madeline noticed that there was absolutely no money in it, just business cards and receipts. Finally, she retrieved a snapshot of her baby girl and bashfully handed it over to Madeline.
"Well, that's just too small! We'll have to enlarge it." Taking the photo over to her PC, she scanned it and produced a lovely color reproduction of a chocolate-brown dimpled girl with thick braids in 5x7 proportion. Proudly looking at it, she said, "I have a few frames in my cabinet, let's see....this one looks nice." Taking scissors and carefully cutting out the picture to fit the frame, the procedure took only about five minutes as Toni watched. "There!" she said proudly.
"OH...what's her name?"
"Monnie...I mean Monica."
"Well Monnie, welcome to our humble office! Now, you sit right here and watch your momma. Make sure she remembers everything I taught her. You can do that, can't you?"

Toni smiled and sat by the picture. Turning to Madeline she whispered, "Why are you so nice to me?" Madeline's eyes welled up as she replied, "Nice isn't a thing that you find much around here. Nice gets in the way of progress, and should only be used as a means to a greater end…at least that's what the subliminal message has been. I miss being nice. You deserve nice. Seems like you haven't had a good dose of nice in your life for quite some time! Now…anymore 'nice' questions?" At that moment, Toni knew she had a friend.

After work Madeline offered to take Toni to dinner stating, "Unless you have fifty dollars folded up in your brassiere, don't tell me you have plans to eat tonight!" They went to an Italian spot that was modest and charming. Stuffed and relaxed, the two women began to unravel their life stories.
"I'm from the Bible belt. Straight out of Memphis, Tennessee! My father was a self-proclaimed minister of the Word and my mother stayed at home raising seven kids. Dad said he wouldn't stop giving Mother babies until he reached the number seven…God's perfect number. I was the fourth of those seven and kind of got lost in the shuffle. That was fine with me because I didn't really care for any of my brothers and sisters. They all seemed like mindless drones, quoting the Bible when it was appropriate to meeting their needs, yet carrying on like hoodlums from hell the rest of the time. I was closest to my mom. She was quiet, but I'd see a spark of defiance in her eyes every once in a while. As I got older, I'd see it more often…along with bruises and swellings around and about her cheeks and lip. Mother did what Dad told her to do, but when the baby of the family turned about eight or nine, she just up and left us all! Dad was devastated, and all of his sermons turned to fire and brimstone. In his mind, every woman on the planet earth was going to hell. I dug deep into my schoolwork promising myself that a good education was the ticket out. Scholarships got me through college, and I'm a half-year shy of my master's degree, not that it makes a bit of difference here.

Most of the administrators see women the same way my dad sees them, about as useful as background music. Some day I'm gonna get up the nerve to get out of here, but the pay is good, and for the most part, I get my revenge by being so indispensable to Mr. Stapely. He couldn't tie his shoes if I wasn't there to assist him."

"Why don't you leave now? I mean you have a degree and I'm sure anyone would take you with all of your skills, not to mention that you've practically completed your master's requirements." There was a long pause. Then Madeline presented Toni with a most peculiar smile.

"I'm addicted to the power."

"The power?"

"Yeah. Strange as it may seem, this place has a way of taking you in, enslaving you to the need to become powerful. I saw it happen to Stapely. When he first came in, he was such an advocate for the pursuit of higher education. He'd lobby the old stogy administrators, beseeching them to look beyond the statistics and fiscal year financial reports of enrollment to see young eager scientists with the highest of hopes and outrageous dreams. He really stood up for them ya know. As time went by, and they lavished him with bonuses, incentives, a cushier office, and most importantly inclusion, he began to turn a blind eye to the needs of the students. Oh yeah, he talks the talk, but they all know that he won't do a thing without the approval and guidance of the good ol' boys behind him. And the good ol' boys have a hidden agenda. They aren't the least bit interested in cutting-edge technology and scientific breakthroughs. All they want is an opportunity to acquire more land. You see, land is the final frontier. The more you own, the more power you have."

"What's that got to do with you?"

"I've become just like Stapely. Having come from a poor family, money became my drug of choice, and he knew it. I hated it when he began to change, but as he changed, he stuffed my pockets too! Oh…and he let me in on secrets, secrets that would give me just the amount of edge I needed to negotiate unwanted meetings with reluctant stakeholders.

It's the knowledge of secrets that's all too consuming ya know. Yeah, anyway I'm consumed. My status as Mr. Stapely's personal secretary has become quite a prestigious position. I've come to love it and find myself selling out my integrity each year I stay with him. Each year it gets a little easier. Each year, power becomes more important. Now how's that for self-assessment?"

"Wow! I hope I don't catch that bug!"
"Ya can't help but! It's in the hallways and corridors of this institution. It's like a virus. Even the students show symptoms of it. IFU has a consuming spirit." Then as quickly as she turned mysterious, Madeline playfully changed the subject. Searching through her purse, she found her wallet and presented the waiter with a card. He disappeared long enough for Madeline to slip into Toni's hand a rolled-up bill.
"Oh Ms. Madeline, please....I can't accept. You've done enough just by buying dinner tonight!"
"If you call me Ms. Madeline one more time, I'm gonna knock your block off! Listen Tonia, I just told you I'm financially OK to do this kind of thing, and I know for a fact that you are financially OK NOT to! I've been where you are, honey cakes, and I wished that I had a person to look after me like this. Besides...it absolves all of my indecencies in a way. I told you I wanted to be nice for a change. Please, let me do this. Please." Toni stared deep into sincere eyes. Then she flashed that devilish dimple at Madeline and squeezed her hand.
"OK, but only if you call me Toni, and if you promise to me that your intent is not to make me a slave to this 'power' thing going on."
"Promise."

CHAPTER 38

Concerns from another realm

Nearly two weeks had passed since Nilé's encounter with Mr. Stapely, Jordan, and the group. For the most part, she brooded throughout the day. She managed to get some editing done, but lost a contract as a result of not having met a deadline. Her heart felt sick and leathery, as if it were pounding with great difficulty. Her mind on the other hand was light and fragile, fluttering from one thought to another without responsibility. Her ancestors stayed close by but decided to do nothing until she was stronger. They knew she had no idea of Jordan being possessed by the spirit of Thompson. They knew that Thompson was growing stronger with each day he inhabited Jordan's physical body. They were aware that he had absolutely no regard for Jordan whatsoever and would quite possibly use this opportunity to overpower his very soul and remain in him for the duration of Jordan's life. Thompson had fallen from grace ages ago and became mad with the realization of eternal damnation. Knowing that no rules and propriety applied to anything he did, he for centuries found ways to bide his time, selecting innocent souls to consume just to experience the nearest thing to living again. Souls that never had a chance against his cunning and determination were put to death unbeknownst to relatives and loved ones. These were the men who changed at the blink of an eye and were considered to have lost their minds. Families, lovers, and mothers were left crying for years wondering why their man, father, or son had changed, while Thompson ravaged and raped the women that he inherited.

"He nebba' gon' lay a hand on my baby girl. If he so much as tries, I promise I'll break de rule and gwan on in her mysef, an' strangle de man she love!"

"An' zackly' how dat gonna fix things?" asked Henny. Nana didn't answer, just stared as if promising nothingness a fruitless guarantee. After much silence, Batu spoke.

"Everything hang on the rod o' love. We've come up against this pillar of hate time an' time again. Each time we triumphed but seem like we nebba learned a thing. We thought it was our strength and determination that won de battle. God want us to know that it was our love for Him that gave us grace to win. Grace is de one thing dat' Thompson will nebba have de luxury of gittin'. God been fuelin' us wit grace because of our undying love fo' Him. Thompson gots no poison dat God's grace caint extinguish."

"But what about Nilé?"

"Nilé gots ta git de same grace we's gittin! She got ta git strong in her love of de Lawd. Dat's where we kin help. Dat's where we begin." As the great cloud of witnesses grew in strength and resolve, they felt a new and fresh participant eager to do the will of God in the spirit of a child named Monnie.

CHAPTER 39

Chess moves

"Now here's what you have to do to win Mr. Stapely's favor. You have to cater to his every need without being obvious. When he needs a pen, have it ready for him, and make sure it's opulent. I have a drawer full of pens that if totaled could pay three months of your rent! Mr. Stapely needs material assurance. His self-worth is neatly wrapped in fresh currency. Now…he'll ignore you for weeks and at times will try to unnerve you with brash and ignorant opinions that if you let them get to you will do more damage to your spirit than good. So be careful as you approach him. Beguile him with your charm; he's a sucker for a pretty smile, and Lord knows, you've got one of the prettiest! Study him, anticipate his every whim, and in time, my dear, you'll have him telling you secrets!"

"With all due respect, I'm not interested in secrets. I have enough of my own that I'm trying to unload. Since Monnie's death, I resolved to do away with them. Seems they do more harm than good."

"Oh sure, honey, I agree. But the ones you're not s'posed to know of are extremely valuable, leverage wise. Just think of them as a bargaining tool. That's all! You don't have to do a thing with them if you choose. But it's nice to know that one day one secret you know can be used to move a mountain."

"Good morning, Madeline." Mr. Stapely breezed past the two women with an air of self-righteousness, then stopped, and turned quizzically looking at Toni as if she were a new piece of furniture that he hadn't ordered.

"Who's this?"

"Mr. Stapely, this is Tonia Saunders, our new assistant."

"I don't need a new assistant, I have you."

"Of course you do, and that's the way it will stay, but Mr. Stapely, in that you've just about got your finger in every pie that comes out of the IFU oven, in order for me to assist you efficiently, I find that I too need assistance!" Pointing to Toni once again as if she were a chair, he asked, "Is this in the budget?"

"Don't be silly, Mr. Stapely! Now I know for a fact you have to remember the morning I broke down in your office. I darn near soaked your carpet with tears, crying about how I have just too much to do. In fact, it was your suggestion that I hire an assistant, and you assured me that it was in the budget, and that if it wasn't, you'd see to it that money would be freed up somewhere! I don't know how you did it, but as usual, you held to your promise and now I have myself a wonderful assistant…and she really is wonderful, Mr. Stapely." Mr. Stapely inspected Toni with the eyes of his great-grandfathers past. Somehow, she could feel his imagination taking liberty to view and even touch places that she had covered with a bra and sweater. His eyes were not searching for efficiency nor did they care about the budget. His eyes sought solace in the warm spicy brownness of Toni's voluptuous curves. There was a sickening double entendre felt in his response that he was sure that she *was* wonderful that made both Madeline and Toni look down at their feet. Then Toni remembered what her grandma Mumbia once told her, "Be keerful, wit feelins. Dey wild and powerful like de weeds. Don't give um' sanction ta ruin ya garden!" She immediately tightened and looked up into the eyes of Mr. Stapely.

Her soft amber eyes prompted Mr. Stapely to march into his office ordering Toni to earn her keep by bringing him his cup of coffee.

"Don't let that get to you; he's doing that to test your metal! You march right in there and be the professional that I recognized in you the first day we met. And don't let that old dog run over you either! Stand up to him…but professionally, you know." Madeline watched and feared that all of her instructions were too much for Toni to handle. She worried that Mr. Stapely would crush her fragile spirit with his harsh manner. Moments later, Toni found herself alone with Mr. Stapely as he requested she close the door.

"Have a seat, Ms....uh...what was your name?"

"Saunders, Tonia Saunders."

"Yes, Ms. Saunders." Toni sensed a nervousness masked by authority in his tone. Instantly she looked at his hands and they were visibly shaking. The evidence of a schoolboy crush was all too obvious to Toni, and she found strength and power within as he feigned importance. It was her turn now. Though it had been a while, this scenario was familiar and invigorating to Toni. She felt an internal gratefulness to the man for allowing her to feel desirable again and affording her an opportunity to strike back at him for the shame he brought two undeserving women moments ago.

"Are you from nearby?"

"No. I'm from Atlanta, Georgia."

"Atlanta! What would make you want to leave a booming city like that?" Tilting her head slightly as if questioning the sense of the question, she hesitated, crossed her legs, and swung the one on top back and forth just enough to allow her shoe to slip down, exposing a soft creamy two-toned heel that seemed to mimic a bowl of vanilla ice cream covered with warm caramel. She watched him see it, then playfully responded, "This job...Mr. Stapely." Then, feeling like a horrified mouse at the mercy of a cat's instincts, Mr. Stapely desperately searched for an escape from humiliation, recovering in tone and indignation.

"You couldn't find work in Atlanta? Are you running from something, Ms. Saunders?"

Toni appreciated his chutzpa, but she wasn't finished with him yet.

"Perhaps I'm running *to* something."

"Well, uh...I certainly hope you find it. It's not good for an attractive woman as yourself to be searching for something, and can't find it."

"I didn't say I was searching, Mr. Stapely. All I mentioned was my running to something...and I prefaced it with perhaps." At that, she flashed a big smile long enough for Mr. Stapely to fall into her dimples. One half hour later, Madeline looked up from her desk and saw Toni closing Mr. Stapely's door. Madeline's inquisitive look was settled by a wink of Toni's eye that reassured Madeline and made her feel proud.

"I have to run a few errands for Mr. Stapely; I'll need about an hour away from the office. Will that be OK?"
"What's he got you doing so soon?"
"He wants me to drive to some town called Trappe and look at the area. He gave me a map, said I was to pay particular attention to the deterioration of a house a few blocks from an old train station. He wants to know if it is inhabitable, at least as far as my standards are concerned."
"Humph! Why is he sending you? You don't know a thing about this area. Maybe I should go with you." There was a hesitation, then Toni whispered, "Madeline, Mr. Stapely mentioned that you would try to go with me. Then he specified that I should go alone. Something about my being Black and blending in with the town folk would draw less suspicion. I'd really prefer you coming along with me, but I don't want to go against his direct orders, ya know?"

There was a long pause as Madeline studied Toni's eyes and tapped her pen on the desk. Her instincts read beyond the explanation as to why Toni was to go alone, but she couldn't get around them.
"OK, go alone, but call me if anything comes up. When you come back, tell me first of your findings, hear?"
"I hear you." Toni pulled her cell phone from her purse and keyed in Madeline's direct line.
"Be no more than an hour!"
"Yes, ma'am."

The drive to Trappe was direct and took about ten minutes. The town itself was shabby and poor. No sooner than a turn in any direction from the main road would find you driving on yellow dirt through either fields of corn or soybean sprouts. There were signs along the way advertising fresh corn or live rabbits for sale, and a few of the roadside markets were abandoned. All Toni could see were Black folk tilling what looked like property that they owned, as the patches of land were small with handmade fences distinguishing the boundary lines. Women smacked at fresh white sheets and denim overalls as they swayed in the midday sun while the men either chopped wood or yanked vigorously at stubborn mowers that would not start. The house that Toni was looking for was set a bit back from the dirt road. The grass around the fence was high, and weeds had taken over the cornfield across the way. Toni made a mental note of her first impression as she parked the car close to the gate, being careful not to get caught in a nearby ditch. She hesitated before leaving her car, saying a short prayer for protection. As she concluded her prayer, those weird feelings she had about the place were removed, and she walked toward the porch with bright and hopeful eyes. What she took into her soul was that this place at one time was a home filled with love. Although the porch and swings were now dilapidated and starving for paint, the bones of the house maintained its character. Looking around to the back of the house, Toni was surprised to see an SUV parked. As she walked toward the back porch she shouted, "Hello! Anybody home?" Peeping into one of the nearby windows, she was again surprised to see a beautiful fat cat jumping off its ledge. Standing still, she could hear the rumble of what sounded like a motorized chair and then she saw her.

"And who the hell might you be?" asked Angie.

"Uh, my name is Tonia Saunders. I'm looking at houses in this area, and this one looked abandoned so I thought I'd take a closer look…."

"Did you see a 'For Sale' sign anywhere while you were busy poking around?"

"Uh, as a matter of fact, I didn't…"

"Who is it, Angie?"

Nilé appeared at the door, wiping her hands with a towel. In Toni's mind, she looked nothing like her surroundings and wondered why a refined "city-looking" woman would be in a place like this.

"Some squatter that got caught wit' her hands in the cookie jar!"

"I'm sorry, ma'am. My Name is Tonia Saunders, and I was looking at houses in this area…just looking. I wasn't going to occupy this place if that's what your friend here is implying. I just wanted to take a closer look. Even though this is an old house, it looked to me like it was at one time beautiful and full of love….I can't explain it, I just wanted to see it better, that's all." Angie's heart wasn't moved but Nilé's was. She invited her in, offering her a cup of tea. Toni's first impulse was to say no and bolt out of there, but there was something about the warmth of Nilé's voice that urged her to stay.

"I gather that you're not from around these parts, huh? Most of the folks know each other." Toni was measuring her responses, aware of the fact that she was given strict instructions not to divulge any information about IFU.

"Funny, I sort of gathered the same about you. I mean, you don't look like everybody I've seen so far, and…do you know the town folk?"

"Uh…excuse me…just who here is in charge of the interrogations?" Angie quipped. "You here are the trespasser, so I think you should be answering as opposed to asking!"

Nilé wasn't at all pleased with Angie's style but allowed the statement to hang in the air, realizing that her friend had her best interest in mind. They were travel weary after having at the last minute decided to pack up and live on the premises to put a stop to any efforts to secure Nilé's land without her knowing about it. They were looking at hours and hours of cleaning and restoring to do, and right now all they really had on their minds was to scrounge up a meal on a potbellied stove that neither one of them knew how to use. As Nilé bent sideways trying to find a pilot to light one of the burners, Toni slid out of her chair and politely demonstrated the correct way to light the burner. Blowing out the long wooden match, she timidly smiled at Nilé and admitted, "Your friend is right. I'm sorry. I am from out of town and live in the city nearby. I was driving around and saw this house that looked like my grand momma's back in Atlanta, and I guess I felt a flash of homesickness and decided to take a closer look." Nilé was embarrassed to have allowed Angie to be so mean. She put the kettle of water on the burner and admitted that she too wasn't from Trappe, but had once lived here.

"This in fact is my great-grand momma's house. I used to come here when I was a little girl, and now I'm being asked by some university to relinquish the home built by their very own hands so that they can build research facilities." Angie was visibly perturbed. She sensed that Toni was up to something. She also felt that Nilé's naiveté about people in general was at risk of being abused. While Angie watched, Toni and Nilé began to establish what looked like the beginning of a budding relationship, and Angie's head was about to spin. It was time in her mind to take control.
"Look Tonia, I know we got off on a bad note. That having been said, and all the other stuff here today that's been said, I'm a cripple and need my rest. Nilé, by now I'm sure you've gathered, is too sweet to tell you that you have to go because we are both tired, but I'm not! Maybe someday later in the week you could stop by and we can talk some more, but you can already see that this place needs a lot of work and we are two tired sistas! Please…please come back another day, OK?"

Toni took the message with dignity and understanding. She was inwardly delighted to have met a woman so intelligent and in many ways like her. There were so many similarities about their grandmothers, and they laughed and shared the same stories about outhouse experiences and eating raw corn from the cob. She thanked Angie for being so candid and even stated that it was good for Nilé to have a friend like her to keep her on track. Nilé found Toni in many ways charming. Angie on the other hand found her full of the stuff that filled the old outhouses.

CHAPTER 40

Roughing it

"You're late! It's been exactly two and a half hours."
"I'm sorry, Madeline, I found the place right quick but coming back I took a wrong turn and got lost."
"Why didn't you call me?"
Toni had to think quickly. "Pride, I guess."
"Pride? Well pride's gonna dock you a full ninety minutes on your next paycheck! You make good and sure you never allow your pride to get in the way of your job responsibilities—do you understand?" Toni noticed that Madeline enjoyed reprimanding her as her demeaning tone cut into her essence.

"Do you have a report?" A sick feeling of being at a crossroad between honesty and deceit consumed Toni. She wanted to tell Madeline how she met the proprietor and learned that she had no intention of giving up the land without a fight. She wanted to let her know that Nilé had done her homework and researched the area stating that the grounds where her great-grandmother built her home was sited as an historical landmark, and that the townspeople of Trappe mysteriously held that particular place in high regard, urging her to hold on to it no matter what. Maybe it was the way Madeline didn't look at her as she flung her hand out and shifted on one hip. Maybe it was because Toni felt hurt that a mere ninety minutes of lateness could unravel what she had hoped would be a friendship. Maybe it was Madeline's misplaced anger fueled by Mr. Stapely's closed door interview and an assignment given to Toni that should have been given to her. All of these things kept her at the fork in the road. She had been dismissed so many times in her life that it didn't matter that the question was initiating conversation, it was said with an air that assured her that if

Madeline could get this information any other way she would. It was one word, one manner, and one hand on Madeline's hip that made Toni choose her path.

"Well?"

"There's hardly anything to report. The house is run down, and the grounds have overgrown. There's an outhouse by the back, and a God-awful smell coming from the nearby woods. Maybe the townsfolk dump their refuse back there. I for one don't see why Mr. Stapely would even want a place like that."

"It's not for you to see, Tonia."

"I see." The inflection in Toni's response brought Madeline down a peg. She dropped her eyes and began shuffling papers on her desk. "I need you to freshen up and file this paperwork. When that's done, you need to address the projects that I see remaining on your desk. We have deadlines, you know. This is fiscal year closing, and Mr. Stapely is adamant about things being done in a timely fashion."

"Yes, ma'am." Madeline walked away permanently changing the climate of the room to one where first names would not feel warm anymore.

That evening Angie roamed about with Nilé in Nana's old house receiving a history lesson on how Nana was so organized and persnickety about how things should be done. Patwa cautiously inspected crevices covered with cobwebs and on occasion dislodged a pot or shelf, causing a momentary racket that sent him fleeing in the opposite direction. They decided to retire in Eden and Nilé's bedroom, as the feel of Nana's was somewhat eerie.

"I wonder if the sheets we packed will fit this old bed."

"If anything, the bed is smaller, so we can just tuck the excess up under the mattress." They busied themselves dusting furniture and replacing curtains. After a while the room seemed to come to life as the smell of pine cleaner wisped through the air. Once the bed was made, Angie began to adjust her wheelchair to the side of the bed runner.

"Oh, let me help you with that, Ange!"

"Naw…don't help me, I need ta figure out how to do it by myself. Thanks for the offer. You sleepin' with me in this bed?"

"Funny how you just claimed the bed as yours, Miss Thang! Yes, tonight I'm sleeping with you, and I don't care if the lesbian patrol rolls up in here! I need to be next to someone in this house at night. At least for a few days!"

"I know that's right!" Without any further ado, the friends washed up by the old porcelain basin. The water was cold but refreshing, and Nilé was glad that she remembered to bring a bar of scented soap. Nilé made one more trip downstairs to fix a pot of tea and slice off a few pieces of Angie's carrot cake. They chatted until the sounds of their own voices lulled them to sleep. In the morning, Angie was awakened by what sounded like a gang of people outside the window repeating someone's name over and over.

"Nilé, wake up!"

"What's wrong?" Nilé mumbled.

"I need you to go see who's out there!"

"Who's out where, Ange? C'mon give me a few more minutes then I'll check."

"Never mind! You want something done you can't depend on Normals." Grabbing her legs and swinging them over the edge of the bed, Angie purposely made as much noise as she could getting in her chair. By the time she was settled, Nilé was sitting up in the bed on her elbows.

"What are you doing?"

"Apparently what you're too sleepy to do! I wanna know who's out there chanting something about Dog Rights."

"Dog Rights?" Nilé stopped to listen for a moment. Then she broke out in laughter.

"You mean bobwhite?"

"Yeah! Is that who they're calling? Who the hell is Bob White? They think somebody named Bob White lives here?"

"They're birds, Angie! They're called bobwhites because that's what their chirp sounds like! Listen…" Nilé waited a moment and anticipated the next cry. She then imitated the same sound. "Bob…white! Bob…white!" She fell back on the bed cracking up, as Angie tried to disguise her embarrassment by hollering out the window, "Bobwhite, my ass! You better go somewhere with that mess this early in the morning!"

Then looking sheepishly over at Nilé who was in tears, she threw the cloth at her.

"You can go back to sleep."

"I'm up now! I guess I should go get some fresh water for us to wash up in, huh?" Silently both of them thought about how this lifestyle may have been more than they could handle. Nilé was used to hot showers in the mornings and felt bad that the house had no way of accommodating Angie's handicap. She shuffled down the wooden staircase that led to the kitchen. Remembering how to ignite the burners, she then placed a full cast-iron pot on the back burner and set the fire high. Scratching her head, she looked around the kitchen trying to remember where things used to be. To be honest, she didn't recall much about the kitchen, only that it was always hot with Nana in the center navigating her way through pans of green beans to be snapped and pork chops to be seasoned and floured. She called up to Angie to see if she wanted some tea.

"I hate to bring this to your attention, but tea ain't the cure-all for everything! No, I don't want tea, but I do want to pee! Could you bring me some kind of pan or empty mayonnaise jar, so I can relieve myself?"

Moments later Nilé came upstairs with a bucket of hot water, a tall empty drinking glass, and two slices of carrot cake. Tossing the glass toward Angie onto the bed, she stated that that was the best she could do.

"Ange…this may not be a good idea. I mean it's hard on me already…and you…"

"It's gonna take time to adjust! Thas' all! We started this now we gots ta finish it. Hell, Oprah Winfrey and her sidekick what's-her-name did it."

"Gail?"

"Yeah, Gail! And they did it without drawers! I watched it on TV, how they had to live the pioneer life for about a week or so, and the first thing they told them was they couldn't wear no drawers! Now, if them two high ballers can come through, I know we can! Shoot, they used ta sleepin' on two million thread count sheets and havin' their meals brought to them. We can deal wit' dis! Come on, treat it like an adventure!" Their conversation was interrupted by Nilé's cell phone ringing.

"Hello? Toni?... Oh! Yes Toni! How are you? Wow, what time is it? Aren't you up a little early?"

"I know it's early, but I had to call you before I set off to work. Listen, I wasn't completely honest when we met. I work at IFU...as a matter of fact, I'm Mr. Stapely's secretary's assistant." There was a long pause. Then Toni continued.

"I was asked that day to survey the property and bring back what information I could gather. Apparently they wanted me to find out firsthand all that I could about the condition of the house and grounds."

"And exactly what did you tell them?" By this time, Angie figured out that something was wrong and wheeled close to Nilé to listen in.

"I didn't tell them anything...well, nothing that they could sink their teeth into. I didn't tell them that you were staying there, or anything about the history of the place. I just gave them my impression of the physical grounds, that's all."

"Why are you calling to tell me this now?"

Angie blurted "Yeah!"

"Because I feel like something terribly wrong would happen if I didn't. I can't explain it; I just feel it. I don't expect you to trust me at all now, but I had to tell you before I went to work. They're working hard every day...with lawyers and big shots; I mean, they meet and talk for hours about how to get that patch of land. Ms. Nilé, there's something on that land that you must not know about, that's why I thought it best to call. You seem like a nice person; you certainly were nice to me, and you didn't have to be…anyway, I just thought I'd call."

"Thanks for the heads-up, Toni. I really do appreciate it." Toni hung the phone up, feeling unsure but hopeful. A thought of her beloved daughter singing a wistful song she made up for her mother flashed through her mind, coating all the edges of doubt. She grabbed her purse and softly hummed the song as she started out for work.

CHAPTER 41

Choosing sides

The grounds at IFU had become dark and hardened by November's frost. Naked trees lining the walkways served as a warning for muskrats to scamper in desperation through drifts of wet leaves for last-minute meals to stockpile. Madeline grew increasingly threatened as Toni gradually gained Mr. Stapely's trust. Spurred by the motive of simply wanting to do a good job, Toni would provide all he'd request expeditiously without asking questions. She had learned to anticipate his needs even more accurately than Madeline, yet supplied them in a way that had no "you need me" undertones.

One morning when the group was once again gathering to meet about the Trappe territory, Mr. Stapely asked Toni to take the minutes.
"Mr. Stapely! With all due respect, these meetings need to be documented by someone who has a sense of history about the topic at hand! Someone who knows what to edit and what to keep in! Surely you can't expect Ms. Saunders to jump right in and understand all of the intricacies involved in this acquisition!"
"As a matter of fact, I've been keeping her abreast on what's been going on. Besides, I need you to handle more important things such as enrollment, scheduling, and year-end reports. Those things require a sense of history, my dear, and unless you have any other remarks regarding decisions I've made, I believe we're through here." A match set to the driest of kindling couldn't have spread a fire more quickly throughout the room than Madeline's resentment as she glared at the two of them, closing the boardroom door.

"Why are you out here? Hasn't the meeting started?" asked Jordan as he approached Madeline's desk.

"Apparently they don't need me."

"Who's taking minutes?"

"You'll meet her soon enough. Shall I buzz you in?" Jordan was confused and somewhat amused by Madeline's demeanor. He was never crazy about her because she always seemed to be digging for information that had nothing to do with her business. As he entered the room, the group nodded and he found an empty chair at the mahogany table close by the door. One of the trustees was speaking as Jordan looked around, familiarizing himself with members he knew little about. Then he saw her. At first, her head was down and he didn't recognize the heavy frame, but as soon as she looked up, the horror in her eyes triggered flashbacks of an affair gone wrong, and Jordan's head began to spin. Thompson too recognized that she was the force who summoned him, but other than that had little interest in her. He could feel that she once loved Jordan, but neither he nor the man whose body he now occupied had any idea of her daughter who was now working against him on her mother's behalf. Besides, Toni was of little moment, as it was Nilé who Thompson had set his trap for.

"We've made several attempts to acquire the Davis property to no avail. We even increased our offer. Our experts are looking into a background check on Ms. Davis…to see if something in her past could loosen her resolve a bit. That's why we asked you here, Dr. Beslow. It seems delightfully convenient to have become aware of your history with Ms. Davis in Philadelphia, and for that, we thank you. It seems like the gods are with us! We were wondering if you could lend a helping hand, so to speak." Jordan shifted in his chair trying to regain composure. He was nauseated by the idea that they would use him to gain access to Nilé's land and mortified to know that a woman who nearly enslaved him decades ago was sitting at the table taking notes! He felt a raging battle inside, one that fought for dominance in choice, moral choice, and although he knew what he wanted to do and say, he felt as helpless and in pain as a man undergoing surgery whose anesthetization had failed.

"Dr. Beslow?"

"Um...let me understand...you want me to give you information about Ms. Davis? Damaging information?"

"Well, not damaging per se. Perhaps leveraging would be a better word." Toni read Jordan's discomfort and knew that she had to do something to assist her old friend. Dropping her pen, she awkwardly lunged forward to retrieve it, causing the gentleman to the left to spill coffee on his suit and nearby paperwork. Corporate shuffling and overtones of annoyance followed long enough to allow Jordan to clear his mind. He looked over to Toni with an expression of appreciation. She in turn gave him an "It's-the-least-I-could-do" smile. The spilled coffee managed to scald one of the group members badly enough to prompt Mr. Stapely to suggest that the meeting adjourn to a later date. As they left the office, all Madeline could hear was a plethora of "I'm sorry" from Toni, which pleased her indeed. Mr. Stapely blew the door open and barked a command to reschedule. While staring at Toni, he made it quite clear that Madeline was to resume her duty as minutes' keeper. Toni's concern for Madeline's triumph was not what grieved her. Trouble brewed within. A dark immobilizing uneasiness stirred inside, generating a command of responsibility. The uneasiness required her to reach beyond her own fears, as she realized that in a matter of moments she had become the new keeper of secrets.

That night as she laid out her outfit for the morning, she received a phone call from Angie. Angie made no bones about the fact that her call was to warn Toni that if her intent were to sabotage Nilé's efforts to keep her great-grandmother's land, she would suffer a fate worse than death. Toni's soul grew weary as she listened to at least five minutes of not so subtle threats before interrupting.

"Angie, I have nothing against your friend; as a matter of fact, it only took a few minutes to discern that the woman we

are speaking of has a wonderful gift of kindness. She was more than gracious to me, given the circumstances in which we met, and I am forever grateful. I don't know what I have to say to convince you that I am not spying for IFU, though my initial assignment was to do so. I've made a decision based on the woman I met that day....I do have a mind of my own, and it's not governed by my salary or fear of my employer. Truth be told, I just started working for these people recently, and I'm not at all happy about their ethics."
"Oh?"
"Yes. Mr. Stapely, the guy I'm working for, is as trustworthy as a snake. He has no allegiances that are not directly linked to his attaining power and money. The whole university is running off of the same fuel as far as I can see, and that is greed. Why, I was hired less than a month ago, and he replaced me for a secretary that had diligently worked for him for over five years because he was paranoid that she was gathering too much information about this land. I can't make out why he's so paranoid, but the whole thing runs cold in my veins. Let me tell you how, during a meeting, Mr. Stapely asked a man that he had no idea I once loved to coerce Nilé into giving up the land just because he heard him mention that he knew Nilé while he lived in Philadelphia."
"Wait a minute. Run that by me again! What man knew Nilé that you once loved?"
"He's a guy that I knew years ago. I was crazy about him and tried to do everything in my power to get him to love me too, but he was so caught up in his DNA research…"
"Oh hell no! His name wouldn't happen to be Jordan, would it?"
"Jordan! That's right! You know him too?"
"Yeah, I know that Black son-of-a-biscuit-eater! I know he broke Nilé's heart for no earthly reason! I know that if I ever get my hands on him I'ma knock the tar outta him."
"Now hold up, Angie—he isn't at all for the idea; as a matter of fact, he was repulsed by it."
"This is getting really deep!"

"I know, and Nilé has no idea of what's ahead of her. I wanted to warn her, but not knowing all of the particulars, I can't tell her what to do next."

"Well, it's a good thing your boss has you in on the meetings; you can get the info and pass it on to us…that is if you really want to help."

"That would have worked up until today. You see, I deliberately sabotaged the meeting because I didn't want to be a part of it. Now Madeline, his original secretary, is back taking notes."

"Well, you just gotta change that! Figure out a way to get back into the meetings. Look at it as an initiation requirement. Until you let me know that things are the way they should be, I ain't got zip ta say to you. Thas' how I'll know you are really sincere."

Toni stared at the phone that was now simply droning out a dial tone. She wondered what she had done to deserve all of this negativity in her life. As she lay on her pseudo bed of foam rubber and cheap sheets, she prayed to her grandmamma Mumbia to deliver her from her dilemma. Her prayers only lulled her into a restless sleep.

CHAPTER 42

North!

"Let's check out the grounds, Nilé! We've done enough washin' and cleanin'. Let's find out why everybody seems to want this place. Maybe there's oil below. Hell, I might be looking at the twenty-first century Jed Clampett!"

"Angie, don't be crazy. There's no oil. All I know is there was a tunnel at the end of that inner hallway I showed you that led to the woods. My daddy took us there when we were little. He explained that the tunnel hid runaways and that Nana and Pop-Pop dug cavelike dwellings all throughout those woods back there. I went once but it smelled so bad I never went again. Besides, Nana warned us that if she ever caught us messing around in the woods she'd whup us."

"Well...not tryin' ta be disrespectful, she can't whup us now, can she? Besides, don't you want to know what's back there that was so forbidden? Maybe she hid lots o' money or somethin'."

"Nana died a poor woman. Poor in cash but not in spirit. She was never one to hoard material things. Said all that was prized in her lifetime was taken, so wasn't much use in trying to get what people could take. By the time she passed away, she was pretty much senile, but the one thing she'd do was laugh and laugh for hours on end when she'd sing some song called 'Old Mary Don't You Weep.'"

"I know that tune. It's an old Negro Spiritual." At that moment, Angie began to sing the song. When she got to the part that said, "Pharaoh's army got drowned," Nilé hollered, "That's the part! That's the part that would make her laugh and laugh! I wonder why?"

"Well, the answer might be right back there in them woods. Let's go check it out!"

It took some navigating to get Angie's wheelchair down the narrow steps that led to the passageway. Nilé pushed and pulled, oftentimes leaving deep grooves in the claylike walls that closed them in as Angie scooted down behind her on her rump. As they came closer to the bottom level, the horrible odor increased. They lifted their T-shirts and covered their noses and mouths gasping for air and sweating profusely. Finally, when they had reached the bottom, a certain sense of victory was felt as they slumped over each other laughing and panting. The hall that led to the first pod was long, low, and dark. Nilé handed the flashlight to Angie who had crawled back into the chair. Not much was said as they moved along the passageway. A feeling of wonder mixed with nervousness seeped into their spirits. About fifteen minutes had passed when Angie hollered, "Look! A door!" Nilé pushed harder compromising the packed-in earth that seemed to forbid their reaching their destination, then she crawled over Angie to open the door. She remembered that she would have to throw her shoulder into it as Nana did in order for it to open. She silently prayed that it would look the same way as it did in the dream. As soon as the door gave way, Angie scrambled to work the chair through the threshold. Fortunately, it was not hard to do as the rotted wood around the door was pulled away by the force of her motorized chair.

There it was, just as Nilé remembered. It was a room about ten feet in diameter with walls just as high, tall, and smooth. A man-made seat as wide as a cot made of earth rimmed the walls about two feet from the ground. The shelves still held old dusty mason jars halfway filled with dark liquids or what looked like tree bark and leaves exhumed from the woods. Nilé felt proud as she listened to Angie taking it all in. The colors seemed more vibrant, and the coolness of the pod was welcoming. Nilé reached into her jeans pocket recovering a few packs of matches. Angie pulled out a zip-lock bag filled with tea candles. Silently they lit them all, and the room's paintings danced to the tune of the candlelight show.

"Here is where you get your sense of color and design, Nilé! Look at all of these beautiful pictures! There's not a square inch that hasn't been painted!" As they examined the room, they realized that a rug of woven leaves had been painted on the floor, the center of which had been worn out and faded as a result of gathering together in prayer and dancing. One by one, Nilé's ancestors urged the visitors to take in and praise them for their awesome work. And they did, so much so that they found themselves crying and praising God for allowing them to experience a jewel of history that had been hidden in the depths of earth and stone. Every nook and cranny was examined by the new explorers until Angie asked, "How'd they get out?"

"What do you mean?"

"How'd they get out? There has to be an escape hatch or something. You don't do all this diggin' and paintin' and have no way to get away! Where's the door that leads them out of the woods?" Nilé felt defensive toward the implication that her ancestors hadn't designed an escape. She looked around in desperation. Nothing. Then she remembered something her grandmother had whispered in her ear. *"You'll have to go against your name to find your freedom, chile."* As soon as the thought passed through her, Nilé cried out, "NORTH!" The Nile River runs north! I had to come to the south, against my name, to discover that my Nana's secret passages go north! We have to figure out which way is north!" In amazement, they both looked at each other knowing that the message was revealed to both of them. While Angie tried to assess where they were positioned using the logic of the house and the distance they had traveled, she wheeled her chair around and around first pointing to one wall, then another. Nilé stood quietly, searching deep in her soul for the answer. She looked at all of the surrounding pictures. Each one seemed to tell a story of the trials and tribulations that the escapees had suffered. Each one held deep within its design a message of hope. Finally, her eyes rested on a painting of a star. Beneath the star, a blue and white teardrop was painted. Another and then another was painted below. Every drop became more animated in color, as the swirls of paint cracked and splashed against their boundaries, eventually forming what looked like a river, twisting down and around the other images of sorrow and grief. She followed the path of the river until her eyes rested on a dark patch of earth below the man-made bench. What at first looked like another star painted in light brown she later determined was a hand. Dropping to her knees, Nilé crawled under the ridge of earth and placed her hand on the brown image print, then pushed. The earth gave way effortlessly to a dark and tunneled passageway far beyond what her eyes could see. Angie watched as Nilé disappeared into the tunnel.

Almost an hour went by before Angie cried out, "All right, Nilé! It's getting late and these dang candles only got about a minute left to them! We seen enough! At least I have!" Her panic turned to relief when she heard the scuffling of Nilé's body drawing closer to the room.
"Whew! I thought I'd never get back!"
"You ain't the only one! Girl, where the hell did you go?"
"There's loads of 'em, Ange! Loads of passageways that all empty out into another room! None of the rooms are as beautiful as this, but they all have drawings on the walls and a picture of the river! If you follow the river, it always leads to a hand and when you push that hand..." Nilé began to weep uncontrollably.
"And they said that we had no more intelligence than that of farm animals. We moved about their land as mules, suppressing the genius of kings and queens!" She wheeled her chair closer to her lifelong friend. Reaching toward her, she placed her arms around Nilé and hummed a melody that she had never heard before. A song of sorrow and hope. A song beset with moans and tones that made the soul feel better, even though no words were said. A song that was as old as pain and as new as a dream in the heart of an unborn child. She hummed until they both emptied themselves of the heaviness that the day brought them. Then, in silence, they headed home.

CHAPTER 43

Unrequited Love

"Somebody in de back chambers!"

A heavy wet whisper that had never seen the light of day warned Nana and her relatives of an intruder. It was the voice of one of the Stayers. She didn't want to interrupt their celebrating the day's triumph. She too wanted to rejoice but felt the presence of that which did not belong to them close by. They had allowed themselves to remember personal anguishes just enough to move the energy forward to a place where Nilé and Angie could feel it. All of this was extremely difficult, yet their determination made it happen, and the success moved their souls to where they were overcome with praise.

"Somebody dere right now! We must hurry to see who!"

Nana and her group instantly heeded the warning. Through worship, they had fed themselves heartily from the Spirit of God, and it rendered them in tune with each other and the mind of the Creator. Nana led the posse who needed no light to guide them. Whisking through corridors at the speed of light, they'd stop momentarily at a crossroad or door, then decide as a group to move east or west of the main tunnel. As they proceeded, the awareness of an intruder in the back chambers grew stronger until they all knew who was there moments before entering the room. Speaking to each other, they warned that a display of anger would weaken them. Henny moved toward the front of the posse. She knew the mind of the intruder intimately. She also knew that though countless times he tried, he was never able to dominate her spirit. "Let me speak." She whispered with authority. The women lined up behind her knowing this time she was right.

She fluffed her hair, straightened her shoulders to lift her ample cleavage, softly cleared her throat, and slid through the door.

"Hello Thompson!"
"My Love! It's been years."
"What brings you here?"
"I think you already know, darlin'. She's almost as gorgeous as you. Could never find one quite like you…you know how hard I tried."
"She belongs to me, Thompson. She's one of my own." They stared at each other long and hard. Then he spoke.
"You don't want to get in my way. You know what I can do."

"You are absolutely right. I don't. However, I couldn't convince my kinfolk. After all…she belongs to them too." Suddenly the others fell behind Henny making a personal appearance—one by one through the slats of the old door behind her. Thompson took it all in without saying a word. His chest began to heave with passionate anger and excitement as his very essence was driven by an insane belief that there was no woman he couldn't eventually control or oppress if he put his mind to it. One by one, the souls of Black women appeared. One by one, each held on their faces memories of his having personally scarred their lives. Each expression stimulated him. Each penetrating stare aroused him so that his eyes rolled back and he began to caress himself. He hadn't the intelligence to realize the battle would be tremendous. He hadn't the wisdom to understand what was at stake. He was consumed by his own arrogance and perverted desires. He recalled the fragrance of their resistance, their screams, the begging, and they invited and allowed him to delight in the hell that he had created for them. He had no idea nor did he care of the outcome of each of the men he inhabited who eventually had taken and, in many instances, killed his victims. He had no idea that he was standing on the territory designed specifically for his final demise. When all seemed too much for Thompson to endure, he smiled and chuckled, "I'm touched that you've taken the time to prepare a party just for me!" Looking around he cried out, "Why… such painstaking details! I'm overwhelmed! How are you lovelies? I see you're no worse for the wear!" Spreading his arms out, he asked, "Does all of this belong to you?" Each woman controlled her anger and said nothing as they stared at Thompson. Then Henny spoke. "This is the last time I will warn you. Leave Nilé alone. Leave this town, Thompson. Jes' leave."

"Only if you come with me, my dear."

This had been an age-old request that Henny denied time after time. Centuries of cunning followed by emotional and physical destruction of countless women in the name of love was the pattern established by these two who would not yield to each other's influence.

Henny's first encounter with Thompson was in the old country. She was a young girl changing at the speed of puberty with everything on her vibrating with excitement. She had been promised to a young farmer whose parents were of noble standing. She, however, had no interest in him, as her eyes were set for a warrior who wooed her each time he came into her small village. Because she was already promised, she had no recourse but to run away with the warrior who, after he had taken her innocence, left her to fend for herself in the brush. She knew she would not be able to return to the village where she would bring shame to her family, so for three years, she lived close to the roadside, and allowed herself to be taken by passers-by for meager portions of food and shelter. By the time she was sixteen, she was very good at what she did and as self-sufficient as a man, hunting, building, and eventually planting enough roots and beans to sustain herself without the help of any man. Her thirst for sexual pleasure, however, had become quite intense, and she'd find herself setting her most elaborate traps for her most desirable prey, men. They'd stay with her for a while promising her everything in exchange for her love which she gave freely. Yet, in the depths of every man's soul, there is a need to anchor his heart to a foundation of trust. Each time a new man would pass through the area where Henny lived, she would find the twinkle in his eye far more brilliant than the one with whom she was staying. In a matter of weeks, there would be new gifts and promises coming from the thatched roof of a woman who only responded to the intensity of the moment.

One morning while Henny was wading in a nearby river, a new prospect caught her eye. As he neared the riverbank to cool his head, she decided to entice him. Reaching for her jug, she allowed her wrap to fall from her shoulder, exposing a large firm breast that teased the river's surface with a dark and glistening nipple. The farmer watched yet made no attempt to approach her, and Henny's ego was a glutton for punishment, large enough to receive what the normal woman could not bear. Stubbornly, she continued her provocative dance but to no avail, so in total frustration she marched up the bank with jug in hand proceeding toward her hutch rationalizing that the man must have been castrated during battle or born with a feminine eye. That night, as she offered her body to her current lover, she could not take her mind off the man at the riverbank. Closing her eyes, she imagined being beneath his shoulders giving and taking in equal shares all that the night's passion had to offer. That night her confidence had been dismantled. That night she no longer wanted the physical pleasures that strange men could offer. That night the only thing she wanted was what she was not allowed to have, and that need consumed her. That was the night she fell desperately in love with Thompson.

CHAPTER 44

Thanksgiving Day

"Good morning, IFU administrative office! How may I direct your call?" Although each greeting Toni presented in a professional manner, she felt lifeless as she answered the phones. The office was so quiet she could hear her heart beating. The only thing cheerful about the room was her sweet-dimpled Monnie who sat gazing back at her mother on the steel-gray desk. Toni felt even more miserable when she turned on the radio only to hear Christmas songs being played so early in the season. It was a gruesome reminder of how she would inevitably spend her holidays, alone and depressed. As she stood to file a few papers away, the phone rang again. Before she could complete her salutation, she was interrupted.
"Toni?"
"Yes, this is she."

"It's me, Nilé. I hope I didn't catch you at a bad time. I'd have called you at home, but you never gave me that number..."
"No, no...that's OK. There's nobody here today. It's Thanksgiving holiday break, you know. I volunteered to hold down the fort because...well, just because." There was a silence of understanding felt by both. Then Toni broke the awkwardness by giving Nilé her home phone number.

"Listen, I feel really awkward calling you, but I just had to. Angie mentioned that you knew a guy by the name of..."
"Jordan Beslow...yes, I do. Angie must have told you that I dealt with him years ago. It's over now, Nilé, really it is. I don't know why I was so obsessed with him in the first place. His mind was always somewhere else."

"Yeah, I know what you mean. Umm...can we meet someday, I mean just to talk. I feel I need to talk to you, I don't know why. Something strange is happening. I mean, meeting you, IFU wanting my Nana's land, Jordan...don't you feel like there's a connection?"

"Yes I do! In fact, the connection was so strong that it's what compelled me to call you in the first place, but Angie got the message. Nilé, this business about IFU wanting your land goes much deeper than what they want to portray."

"I believe so too. Nevertheless, here's what we will do! Let's you and I go out to dinner one evening, that way we can talk in private..."

"Talk in private about what?" Angie, who was rolling into the living room and overheard the end of Nilé's sentence, interrupted the conversation.

"Um, Ange...I'm on the phone with Toni."

"What can't you say to Toni around me?" Silence again.

"Listen Nilé, if it's all good by you, I can come over there. I don't mind Angie. She's got your best interest at heart." Reluctantly, Nilé responded.

"OK...then...how about Wednesday evening?"

"Wednesday evening? Thas' when I'm gonna be cookin'! Have her come over for Thanksgiving supper! She ain't doin' nothing that day, is she?" Toni's heart leaped with joy. What a wonderful solution to a terrible situation. She could kill two deadly birds with one turkey! That nagging question dangling in the back of her throat about Nilé and Jordan's relationship could be quelled all while she was eating a home-cooked meal.

"Thanksgiving day would be great! What time do you want me there?" Nilé deflected to Angie who had begun orchestrating the entire event right up from under her.

"Come 'round two or three. I know you country mammas like to eat early. And come with an appetite! I'm not cooking for nobody to be prissy around my food."

Thanksgiving morning was particularly cold and dreary. Toni's first thought was to be thankful that she had somewhere to go that day. Around twelve o'clock, Nilé called Toni to ask if she needed a ride. She realized that the busses would take forever, and Trappe was a remote town. Toni agreed, and they set a time and place to meet.

Pulling up along the roadside, Nilé smiled as she watched Toni's round body sprinting toward her car. She was so short that she had to hop up just to get into the SUV. Instantly, her warm giggle and deep dimples evoked a safe feeling within Nilé, as she pulled off, telling her that she conjured up the whole "I'll pick you up" thing just to have a few moments with her alone. The ride back to Nana's took about twenty minutes, and that was plenty of time to reacquaint themselves and ask questions that neither one of them really wanted to reveal around Angie.

Walking into the old house took Toni by surprise. What she saw the first day had totally disappeared. Warm colors, fabrics, and textures now replaced the once mouse-brown decor. A fresh coat of "pastel mango" paint brightened up the living room walls, and wildflowers picked fresh from the woods flirted with nearby lacey curtains. Pictures with oval mahogany frames hung with regality from the walls to reveal a loving family with a history begging for exploration. Laundered doilies were starched, ironed, and positioned back in their original places, and the old rag rug boasted colors not seen in years after having been vacuumed for the very first time ever. Thick and masculine soulful aromas of sage and thyme blended harmoniously with the feminine sexiness of cinnamon and nutmeg, all under the orchestration of Angie's masterful hand. As the two women strolled toward the kitchen, Nilé took her time introducing Toni to members of her family whose portraits hung on the walls. They were a collection of pictures dug out of the family's old cedar attic by Nilé. She had also taken the time to frame some of her drawn portraits, as she explained to Toni that though she did not know the people, she believed in her heart that they existed here.

The dinner table was set. Nothing fancy, but Nilé felt particularly proud to see old chipped cream-colored bowls Nana once served dinner in holding collard greens and candied yams once more. Angie had outdone herself. As she rolled up to the table, she whisked off her flour-dusted apron and wiped her brow.

"Whew! Now this is a time when I'm glad I ain't got no feelin' in my back 'cause I know for sure it would be cryin' out by now!" The ladies laughed, and Toni was the first to comment on the wonderful spread. Each joined hands around the table and took turns giving thanks to their Father in heaven for this occasion. When all had been said, Angie began to sing in a low and sensuous tone "Now Thank We All Our God." It sounded nothing like the worn-out hymn to which Nilé had been accustomed. Angie coaxed each of the woman's spirits to search deep within their souls, as she birthed new life into the lyrics. Montages of past and current memories sped through their minds. Celebrations, heartaches, moments of fear, and occasions when all was well with the world were remembered. They sang all three verses with deliberate adoration to a well-deserving Creator, and when Angie was finished, both Nilé and Toni were soaked in tears.

"Well, what are we looking at each other for? Les' eat!"

The dinner was delicious and conversation was light and easy. Nilé bragged about her friendship with Angie, and they reminisced about the good-ol' days, until Toni was bent over with laughter. Eventually, gravy and cranberry sauce were spilled on a white-linen tablecloth and butter-soaked biscuits turned cold. The old house walls seemed to swell with the pride and happiness of days remembered. All while these things happened, Angie picked at parts of the turkey carcass with her finger while grunting in highly animated tones.

"So now that you know all of my past deep dark secrets, thanks to 'Miss Thang' here, tell us about your growin' up. Was it as crazy as ours?" Angie's segue was casual but deliberate.

"I'm afraid it wasn't nearly as colorful as yours. As a matter of fact, not much color was in it at all, save my grandmother Mumbia."

"Mumbia? Was that a made-up name or her birth-given name?"

"She was given that name at birth. What I know about the name is that it comes from her grandmother who hardly spoke a word. When she was born, she pointed to her and said Mumbia. We later found out that that was my great-great-grandmother's place of birth. I looked it up once and found out that a place called Mombia is located in Zaire, which is located in almost dead-center Africa. How my ancestors got yanked all the way from central Africa remains a mystery to me. Anyways…Mumbia is what she was named, and Mumbia is what she will always be in my heart."

"Sounds like you really loved her."

"More than life itself. At least I thought so until I lost Monnie."

"Who's Monnie? Don't tell me you one of those families whose names all begin with the same letter! I never understood that."

"No, it's just a coincidence. Monnie is a nickname for my daughter Monica." Toni knew she had opened a can of worms and was not sure if she wanted them spilled all over the Thanksgiving table.

"You have a daughter? Why ain't she with you—how old is she?"

"She would be thirteen in December, but she passed away."

"Oh my GOD! I'm sooooo sorry! I wouldn't have pressed if…"

"It's OK. Seems like my whole life now is beset with a bunch of 'I'm sorry's.' Everyone eventually stumbles into the reality of my pain. It's not your fault." Fat and heavy tears rolled down baby-doll cheeks, as Toni tried to regroup. Nilé slid her chair close to Toni's and rubbed her back.

"You know, Thanksgiving is a time when we are called to remember. Even though you have painful memories, it's good to remember her today. It means she's with you right now." Nilé had no idea where that statement came from. She was not one to speak of what she called "spiritual spookiness," yet the words spilled easily from her tongue. Moments led into hours as each of the women took turns remembering loved ones who had passed on. As they spoke of them, they came and sat at the table of Thanksgiving, smiling and grateful to have been invited and remembered.

"Seems like they're all here with us, don't it?" Angie whispered. "Maybe thas' what they wanted...us to come together to remember something. Ya know all of this is happening for a good reason. Maybe we're the ones chosen to discover something."
Folding her napkin in an accordion shape, then unfolding it, Toni responded to the comment. "I believe that there is a connection too." All eyes were on Nilé.

"What?" Never being one to get into conversations of this nature, she backpedaled defensively.
"What! You know what! Look at this! We have no Godly reason to be sitting here in Trappe, Maryland! We should be in Philly, layin' back on a couch watching TV on a wide screen. Why are we here? And, don't get offended, but who the hell is our guest? We don't know her from squat but she knows Jordan! How's that sound? Is this all a coincidence or a crossing of paths orchestrated by God Himself? Don't get all spooky eyed on me, Nilé, you ain't got no reason to get scared talkin' about this. God is all up in this here situation, and I for one ain't one to go looking another way when I feel His tug."

"What's Nilé afraid of? Our bringing up the spirits of our ancestors, or why we're here?"
"BOTH! She can't take talking about what she has no control of, as if Normals got control of anything...."

"Now wait just a minute! SHE happens to be right here listening to you talk about her, and SHE can defend or put herself down better than either of you can!"

"What are you afraid of, Nilé? Are you afraid?"

Nilé searched her heart for an answer. She wanted to say, "Yes! I'm afraid!" over and over again but knew that she'd be besieged with pep talk that would not sink in. Finally, she muttered in frustration, "I don't know what I'm afraid of, I just know I am. Every step leading to this day has been a step taken in fear. This is not me. I don't do things like this. I don't even know why I didn't take the money and sell the land. Look at this place; it is so not worth 1.5 million dollars!" Toni's eyes nearly popped out when she heard the value placed on the property.

"Oh, Miss Nilé, we are here for a reason! The ancestors don't want us to sell this patch of land and they're calling on you to find out why! If you sell, you'll be more sorry about it than if you stand up and fight for it. Trust your gut. Trust the ancestors."

"Trust Jesus!" Angie hollered.

It didn't take more than an hour for Nilé to drop Toni home, then turn around, and pick her up again.

"That girl lives in an apartment with no furniture! She doesn't have a friend in the world, and I can't imagine what loneliness she must be feeling with no family around." When the two decided that she would live with them, Toni found them at her complex honking and shouting up at her window.

"Girl, git' your tail in this car!"

"What are you here for? Did I forget something?"

"Yeah! You forgot how to lean on friends. Pack up an outfit for tomorrow and bring your butt right on back to this car. Hurry up! It's cold!" Toni stuffed her only nightgown and all of her six outfits in a plastic grocery bag and ran down the stairs. They giggled and dreamed all the way home—planning the next step in the journey of their lives, somehow knowing that they would travel together.

CHAPTER 45

Into his own hands

Jordan had already accepted the fact that he was not himself lately. Everything he thought had a negative quality to it. He seemed annoyed with any idea that was not on his agenda, and he had no issue with letting people know if they were not on his page.

The Trappe land acquisition was particularly irritating. He could not see how a handful of financially proficient white men were having such a hard time coaxing a naive Black woman out of her property. He didn't understand why this particular piece of land was so highly revered and, if it could not be acquired, why they didn't move on to purchase land closer to their campus for considerably less. Jordan had exhausted all that the university could offer by way of laboratory equipment. He along with a few engineers had designed a device that needed manufacturing, but the pipeline of bureaucracy held that up too. Everything was being bottlenecked by the acquisition. As he dressed, he mumbled and pointed to nearby furniture with accusing gestures. He spewed highly judgmental assessments and definitive solutions to the matter at hand and scolded the entire group for not allowing him to be an integral part of the acquisition. Each opinion he imagined grew richer with anger. Every dark idea that poured from his mind found its way through uncharted corridors leading to his heart. Acting as a thin layer of disdain, those imaginings quickly hardened and he physically felt his heart beating with great difficulty. Each beat convinced him to see through the eyes of malice. Soon he wanted desperately to destroy the entire lot of the IFU administrative committee along with their self-proclaimed piety to expose the whimpering squabbling group that they really represented. Their ineffectiveness was keeping him from great research. These thoughts consumed him and devoured any concerns that may have tried to grow in his head about Nilé. As far as he was concerned, she too was in the way, and any bad blood created between them could be ironed out later...after she gave up the land...*his* land.

He decided to drive to the town of Trappe to see for himself why it was considered such a find. Toni received his call to cancel a meeting at 9:00 with Mr. Stapely.
"Of course, Dr. Beslow. As a matter of fact, he's right here—would you like to speak with him?" Toni was surprised to hear the hesitation and strained rejection of her offer. Mr. Stapely had arrived early specifically for the meeting and had his hand out to receive the call. It was only when Toni said, "Oh, I see..." and feigned concern for Jordan's health that Mr. Stapely could determine that the call was a cancellation. As she heard the pitiful excuse fabricated word by word, Toni looked over at her picture of Monnie. A sadness developed as she thought that half of her beloved was lying to her at the moment. As she stared at the picture, she developed a sense of urgency to call Nilé almost as if Monnie was trying to tell her to warn Nilé.

"OK Doctor, I sure hope you get the rest you deserve and starve out that cold. You sound terrible!" Hanging up the phone, she felt convicted, realizing that she too was as much a liar as Monica's father. Then she called home.

"What did you forget this time? For not having much, you sure do forget a lot of stuff!"
Angie's playful phone discipline was thwarted by Toni's tone.
"Angie, put Nilé on the phone. Jordan just cancelled his 9:00 meeting with Stapely, and I just feel it in my gut that he's on his way over there."
"Over where? HERE? For what? Oh hell no!" All of the emoting drew Nilé to the room.

"What's going on?"

"Jordan thinks he's gonna bring his tail up here and....here, talk to Toni." Throwing the phone onto the couch, Angie spun away in disgust. Nilé listened as Toni filled her in with the details. It was not until 10:45 that day that Jordan was greeted by the clicking of a shotgun behind him.

"Tresspassin's a dangerous thing 'round these parts." Jordan recognized Angie's voice and began to turn slowly toward her.

"You can stay right where you are, sweetie; you look good from all angles...I ain't gotta see you face-ta-face."

"Angie, what is this all about?"

"Stole the words right out from under me! S'pose you go first."

"I just wanted to see what all of the hoopla was about around this land. I hardly thought it had escalated to this level. What is it about this God-forsaken patch of feces-infested woodlands could you possibly feel remotely compelled to protect and keep?"

"Nice pitch but save it for sympathetic ears. Ain't none of your business why we wanna keep it for real, for real."

"We? You have a vested interest in this land as well?" Angie felt sick for a moment, as she scrambled about emotionally dodging the amused inquisition.

"Yeah we! You got a problem with that?"

"As a matter of fact, no! It makes the challenge all the more interesting. It seems like everyone wants this land for some selfish reason or other. *Your* fighting for it simply builds up the ante. I'm curious...what's in it for you?"

"What on earth is going on, Angie?" Nilé was walking toward the two.

"I'm 'bout to find out if this man's guts are as fine as his sweet candy-coated shell! Thas' all! You ain't gotta worry 'bout none of this. He ain't stayin' here long." Nilé sensed that Jordan was not in the least bit threatened by Angie or her shotgun. He seemed to be entertained by the whole scenario, and both Nilé and Angie soon felt themselves caught up in a sick battle of wits that Thompson had full control of.

"Why don't you put that thing down? You'd have used it by now, and you look like a poster child for some B-rated western...you holding a gun in your paralyzed lap." Angie had become accustomed to his malevolence and spewed back hateful insults, realizing that she had absolutely no power unless Nilé grant it to her. Nilé was completely entangled by the gaze in Thompson's eyes as each soft sentence spoken to her deadened her resistance. Henny watched helplessly as she had promised not to inhabit her grandchild of distant generations. She remembered her vow to let go and let God do His work, yet she knew that Nilé was no match for the wiles of Thompson. Thompson knew he was gaining more and more control. He knew that there was something holding Nilé's ancestors back; otherwise, they would all have seized him. His smile grew wider. His voice became sickening venom that paralyzed Nilé, even though she knew she should not listen to Jordan. It was not until Mumbia, who had responded to Toni's plea for assistance, arrived that the playing field leveled. She stood strong and solid, as her granddaughter approached the three of them standing at the edge of the woods.

"I thought I'd find you here!" Toni's sudden appearance threw Thompson off.
He quickly regained composure and asked, "Working for or against the ladies today?"
Listening to her grandmother whispering, "'Member whut I said about weeds. Dey gots no business in ya garden!"
Toni giggled a little, then quipped, "All you need to know is that I'm working **hard,** Jordan. You know what happens when I work hard." The curiosity on the women's faces ran counterpoint to Thompson's respect and acknowledgement of Mumbia's presence. Thompson was infuriated, remembering how she was the one who initially summoned

him to do *her* bidding. That he faithfully honored her request years ago, only to find her opposing him now, was an unpardonable outrage. As Toni spoke with Jordan, her stock went up as far as Angie was concerned. Her poise and confidence in handling this man seemed unreal, as there was nothing that he could say that would shake her resolve. It was the resolve of two women who loved one child, and that was no match for Thompson. The conversation took long enough to pull Nilé out of her fog. She too began to witness a facet in Toni's personality that ran counter to her seemingly sweet disposition.

Thompson, realizing he was now clearly outnumbered, threw his hands up and nervously laughed, "OK! I give up! Shoot me already! A friendly visit has turned foul, and I am the first to admit having something to do with it. However, ladies, I admitted that right up front. I HAVE SOMETHING TO DO WITH THIS LAND! And now I am learning that EVERYBODY has something to do with this land! Wonder what it is? Wonder what it is, indeed! Well...as much as I hate to be the one to break up this delightful tête-à-tête, I sense that I've worn out my 'unwelcome' as it seems. Good day, ladies! I trust I can gracefully walk away without being shot in the back? Even though the gun isn't loaded!" All of the women looked down at the shotgun and noticed that the bullet chamber was wide open and empty. Both Angie and Nilé were obviously embarrassed, but Toni held her ground, staring through the feigned amusement of Jordan and advising Thompson to back out gracefully. Realizing that she was onto him, he tipped his hat and bellowed a self-fulfilling laugh as he drove away, leaving a cloud of dust and gravel in his wake.

Nilé marveled at the resolve of her new friend. Although she was at least a decade younger, she stood fearless and undaunted by a man who time and time again rendered Nilé helpless with a simple smile. Angie too was impressed, but knew that the timing of Toni's arrival was divine. She was only too pleased to find an ally who could see past the man's exterior into his heart of ice. Still responding to the energy of her ancestors, Toni knew that she had to act quickly, as Jordan would be contacting IFU's administrative council to advise of her link with the Trappe territory.

"I've got to get back to work. They think I went home to pick up the thumb drive that I had borrowed from Madeline. This is going to get messy. They have no idea that I live with you…showing up just may have cost me my job."

"They don't have to know that you live with us. You still have your apartment address. Cut off your landline and tell 'em that lack of finances led you to do it. Any call you receive should be coming to your cell anyway; something you can control a little more."

"OK, that's covered, but what reason do I have for showing up here today?"

"Just get back to work. God will give you a reason." Angie answered.

At that comment, Nilé spun around and hollered to Angie, "Ange! You ought to be ashamed! God is not going to lie for Toni!"

"I never said He would. But I know two things. One, that God made her come here to risk what she didn't even realize was at stake, and two, God is able. So, go on—get your three-foot-tuff-as-nails-dimple-flashin' butt out of here before the hounds come around sniffin'!"

"She's right. I better go. Love you both!"

CHAPTER 46

"Somebody in de back chambers!"

The chambers that the Stayers had spoken of were to Nilé and Angie, for the most part, unnerving. They had happened upon them one day while searching the underground. The chambers were not like the other pods. They had no murals. There was nowhere to sit, and the walls for lack of a better word were breathtaking. Rows of a particular linear pattern repeated, covering every inch, from floor to ceiling. A circle or triangle of sorts interrupted the rows periodically, then the pattern would continue. There was no color, just the black of the earth interrupted by geometric patterns of white lines. Upon close examination, one could see stonelike white lines were carved or wedged into the walls. They were not painted, as would be one's first impression. The exquisite pattern of these stonelike lines, their distance perfectly measured and symmetrically placed in accordance to the next pattern of lines, rivaled any ancient or modern mathematical genius. Not one line was farther away from another, although some were notably smaller in width and depth. The variation of design created a subtle alteration in texture. By this means, the texture shift created an illusion of distance and close proximity almost to the point where one would have to extend the hand to feel where the wall actually was. The temperature within the chambers was at least five to ten degrees lower, as the walls were discernibly cool to the touch. Found in various locations of what now had become an underground network of intersecting pods, all the visual aspects about these rooms were threatening, yet paradoxically, their serenity compelled one to remain within them for healing. A sense of closure could be felt, an infinite accomplishment that answered and then transcended the fear of hopelessness. There was peace in the chambers. Every beat of a heart was finally validated, and each emotion, at long last, felt.

It was decided that the back chambers would be the meeting place for the ancestors from now on. There, Mumbia was introduced, welcomed, and embraced by new friends.

"We appreciate your joining forces with us. Your great-grandchild has told us about your journey to Jordan and his connection to your loved ones." Mumbia replied, "Jordan alone is a weak and confused soul, but I must warn you that he is being inhabited by a very powerful force." There was measured silence. Finally, Nana responded.

"We know of Thompson, Mumbia. You are standing in the graveyard of his conquests, concubines, and conduits!" Mumbia looked around. Suddenly those dry iced white lines revealed certain organic curves that suggested the structure of bones. Skulls and scapulas (now exposing their once ambiguous geometric forms as white spheres and triangles) were strategically interspersed among the rows and rows of tibia, fibula, and even phalanges embedded within the walls. Some of the spirits of the victims stood tall and solemn along with Nana, her ancestors, and the Stayers. There also were bones in the walls not represented. Bodies of men killed during battle and struggle and then, without ceremony, dismembered, bleached, and implanted by the Stayers into the dust from which they had been formed. Each room of the chambers represented a memorial of colorless pattern. A visual memory of lives intermingled and now indistinguishable placed side by side, white bones against the black earth remaining eternally equal.

"How many of deese 'im responsible for?"

"All in this room, Mumbia. All." A shudder ran through Mumbia as she looked around assessing the gravity of Thompson's evil.

"What him plan ta do wit' 'cha kinfolk now?"

Nana spoke, "He's helping Jordan and white men in the nearby university where your granddaughter works. The school wants to buy this land...our land. They say it's for research. They's right 'bout dat! De head 'ministrator, Mr. Stapely, is kin ta James T. Brokes, one o' da highest members of Pharaoh's Army. Dat man, one day jes' up and disappeared an' none of de family could git ta de bottom of dat!" Nana chuckled and looked around the room. "Stapely got reason ta think his great gran-pappy disappeared on my land. He 'bout as right as de love o' God! Now he want ta uproot everything in this town ta find out if his hunch be true. In doin' so he be uprootin' the good wit' the evil, an' my soul remember too much uh went into dis heah land. Ain't no white man gonna take it from my kin. 'Sides...Stapely want Jordan to trace DNA for proof! Lawd can only tell whut would happen to de town ifn' they find out who kin ta who killed Pharaoh's Army. Deese chirren had nuff' sorrows. Dey don't need ta suffer at de han' of a Black man bein' used by a white man."

"Seem like de nex' move ain't ours ta take. Yo' granddaughter say no, right? Now alls we kin' do is watch."

"Watch an' pray."

Meanwhile at the office, Madeline was busy completing a report that was due for a 3:00 meeting that day. She hardly noticed that Toni was gone until one of the board members requested paperwork from another project. The request aggravated Madeline who never liked to be taken off her track, so in response she buzzed Toni to collect the information. As Toni's intercom buzzed, she could hear it from the hall. Instead of going to her desk, she casually slipped her jacket off and stuffed it into her purse as she walked into the lobby.

"Heard you buzzin'...what's up?"

"Toni, Mr. Gustov needs the first-quarter report for the Tasker Project. Would you grab that from the stacks down the hall? I'm over my head with last-minute details for the three o'clock."

"Sure! Do you want me to take them to him?"

"No...I think he said he'd pick them up after the meeting. I just need you to pull them."

Just then, Jordan sauntered into the lobby. Surprised to see Toni there, he deliberately scratched his head and feigned bewilderment.

"Didn't I just see you moments ago?"

"Wouldn't you know if you did?" was the response from a woman annoyed by the efforts Jordan was making to blow her cover.

"That's just my point. Unless you have a twin, you'd almost have to be at two places at the same time! How's that possible?"

"If you saw me at both places, how's that possible...unless you have a twin too?"

"Look! I don't have time to listen to two grown people not having a clue! Obviously neither of you know where you are now—which is in my way! Toni, I thought I asked you to get a report. Dr. Beslow, with all due respect, what can I do for you quickly?"

"I'm looking for Stapely."

"He won't be back until 3:00 this afternoon. Is there a message I can give him?"

Jordan paused and looked at Toni. The stare was long and hard. Toni looked back without flinching. She had the prayers of thousands behind her and she stood strong.

"No. What I have to tell him can wait. Good day, ladies." Both women not looking at Jordan mumbled back with detached repose, "Good day." By the time Jordan was in his car he had decided to drop the whole "tattletale" move and get on with his life. After all, what did Toni's presence at Nilé's home have to do with the big picture?

CHAPTER 47

The 3 o'clock meeting

"Gentlemen, the day we've been waiting for is finally here. All of the numbers have been crunched, and all but one of the contacts has been made. Both the state and county have considered and approved our petition to acquire Trappe as a suitable town for the University to utilize for research purposes. We all agree that it is a positive move toward redevelopment of an otherwise unproductive wasteland. The townspeople were advised of the acquisition. Most refuse to move, however, despite the reasonable offers given them, but that is of little moment."
"Has Ms. Davis been told?"

"No…not yet. I wanted to know if there would be someone willing to break the delicate news to her. She seems like a nice enough woman, but she offered no room for negotiation. Her unwillingness to listen to reason was a bit unnerving. Anyway, I will do it, but I truly am in no position to console her, as she sees me as her complete and total nemesis."

"I'll break the delicate news to her!"
"Dr. Beslow! We were almost unanimously hoping that you would step up to the challenge. It seems most appropriate. After all, this facility is for *your* research and, well, your having known Ms. Davis previously helps all the more, I'm sure…"
"Not to mention our mutual Blackness!" A deafening silence struck the room. No one would have ever expected Jordan to step out of character, not even himself, but the obvious setup was nauseating, and Jordan had to voice his disapproval some way or another. Besides, Jordan's current "dual" thinking compelled him to make bolder moves, as Thompson was aware of the ulterior motives of each man present, and

even though he did not reveal their agenda to Jordan, Jordan felt the unsavory and clandestine racial heaviness that drove the gathering. It felt too much like he should not have been there. Watching eyes that seemed accustomed to peering through hooded sheets, he witnessed their spirits twitch slightly with discomfort at his statement. Then he watched as one by one the rage grew and engulfed the room. How dare the man whose descendents once plowed their fields speak to them in this manner, particularly when it was for his research that they beseech his assistance?

"I demand you take that back!" shouted Mr. Stapely. "It was rude and uncalled for!" The eyes of all in the room supported Stapely with moblike hysteria imploding within each member. Although both Jordan and Thompson enjoyed the emotional raucous they had initiated, it was Thompson who kept the event from turning into a disaster.

"Gentlemen. At ease! This is the new millennium! I was under the impression that enough generations had passed by so that a Black man could actually crack a racial joke below the Mason-Dixon Line without feeling as if he had to leave town. Was I wrong? My goodness! After all, she and I are obviously Black; we do have that in common. That fact in and of itself would ease the tension that I know is inevitable in this situation. Right? Exactly what was uncalled for in my statement? If anyone should take offense, it should be me, as I was only stating the obvious. Is it not obvious that I am indeed Black?"

"That's not the point, and you know it!"

"The point is you need someone to broach Ms. Davis with this God-awful news, and I'm your boy...ah, um man. Right?" He flashed his charming smile and dug into his trousers for his cell phone. Moments later, all had witnessed his arrangement to meet Nilé the following morning for breakfast at the Trappe Station Diner.

Nilé had expected the phone call. This time she was not alarmed nor emotionally moved by the Thompson/Jordan butter-cream voice spilling from the receiver into her ear. She remained disenchanted as she felt him smiling when he confirmed the time that they meet.

"Ten o'clock is fine, Jordan. I'll see you there."

Looking out the window toward the woods, Nilé shrugged her shoulders attempting an apology to her Nana. She knew what news Jordan was bringing. Gossip had made its way to her too. Her eyes began to fill with tears as she walked slowly in the direction of all that she had discovered. Hers and God knows how many other family histories would be dug up and destroyed within the months to come. She felt totally responsible and frightfully helpless. She should have rallied the townsfolk up and petitioned the local and state officials just as her enemies had. She did not fight enough. She never fights for anything. She's too afraid. Standing in front of the wooded area, Nilé burst into tears.

"Oh Nana, what have I done? You brought me here to fight for this land, I know it, and I just let it go. I just let it go. I am so sorry." All she could hear was a faint melody sung by her Nana strolling through the corridors of her mind.

CHAPTER 48

Groundbreaking news

The day of the groundbreaking was overcast and rainy. A flash-flood warning issued throughout the county triggered a call from the administrative board to Mr. Stapely to reschedule, but he overruled the suggestion. He argued that the University had waited long enough for this event, and besides, a little rain would be an asset to the construction workers because it would soften the terrain.

Jordan dressed slowly that morning. He examined his emotions, questioning why he was not jubilant about the day's event. He wondered if it was because he still felt something for Nilé. No matter how hard he tried, he could not come to terms with having been used as a pawn by the University. Besides, his research and theory were unraveling more and more each day, though he did not have the guts to admit it. Stapely depended on him to reach a scientific conclusion that would prove that the Caucasian race's dispassionate resolve to gain power by any means was genetic. It would be Jordan's discovery of what one race lacked…pituitary melanin (be it a result of mutation or adaptation) that in fact led Caucasians to become an oppressive people stopping at nothing to prevail in power. He realized how so many would be hurt, uprooted, unemployed, and devastated for the cause of a theory that had become by now irrelevant to Jordan's very being. Most of all he cringed with disdain at the thought of Nilé's inheritance being lost because of his theory.

Nilé's friends from the town of Trappe had gathered in her house. As the rain began to fall, all who could not fit into the first floor of the home huddled on the porch. They brought fresh breads and rolls, thermoses of coffee, and warm smiles.

There was a sadness that each man and woman felt, but no one spoke of it. All they talked about was their recollection of Annie and Pop-Pop Davis. Most didn't know them personally, but had heard stories of how these two had done so much for the townsfolk of color. Nobody ever came out and said that Nana and Pop-Pop had literally built an underground railroad; they just spoke of how many wrongs were righted by the hands of Nilé's great-grandparents. They all vowed that the memories would not die. They all promised that their children and grandchildren would be brought to the site, not to marvel at a research facility, but to hear the stories of how, before the University took hold, there once stood an old wooden house with a basement that led to a tunneled trail...and that trail was the backwoods to freedom.

Local news reporters set up platforms close to the actual groundbreaking location. Mr. Stapely insisted that he push the first shovel into the ground at the very entrance of the wooded area. He had even leaked that the evacuation might possibly turn into an excavation of sorts if his intuition served him correctly. He wanted all of the stations to cover the event, and his mysterious leak had everyone's curiosity piqued. City officials buzzed about shaking hands with University bureaucrats, as Mr. Stapely tried to suppress an all but giddy feeling inside. As the crowd grew, station crewmembers began silently queuing reporters to begin their narratives.

Nilé took in a deep breath. "This is it!" she said to all who gathered on her Nana's porch. "I suppose we should go to witness this groundbreaking. Listen...I'm very sorry about the outcome..." A deep and wise voice from the crowd spoke.

"Shhhh...now don't you start up wit' no apologies, Miss Nilé. We knowd whut you wuz up against from de start. We is here to support 'cha. 'Sides...too much done gone on in dis land fo' us ta think it's over. Now we done what we could do. Our fight is through, but de Lawd ain't even broke a sweat yet! We heah ta watch and pray fo' justice!"

Nilé smiled at the crowd through her tears. Angie broke the silence by shouting, "Well, let's git this show on the road! We need a song! Anybody got a song in their heart they would like to share?" The same voice that had rebuked Nilé began to hum a tune that was vaguely familiar to Nilé. Angie instantly caught on and joined in. One by one as they walked toward the woods, they sang with heads held high. Reporters and city officials became irritated by the sound and tried speaking over the song that grew louder and louder as they neared the woods:

> *"Ah don't feel noways tired*
> *Come too far from where I started from*
> *Nobody told me the road would be easy..."*

As they reached the next line, the women and the men separated their voices into a call and response pattern. The sound began as a whisper, each note multiplying in harmony as the women singing repeated the words. The voices of the men bellowed in baritones that repeated what the women were chanting in harmony:

> ***"I don't believe He brought me this far****...I don't believe*
> ***I don't believe He brought me this far****... I don't believe*
> ***I don't believe He brought me this far****... I don't believe"*

As they reached the edge of Nilé's property, known as the woods, their voices resounded personifying the solidarity of a people who had done their best, and all they had left was to stand.

> ***"I don't believe He brought me this far****...ta leave me!"*

As cameras were swung toward the small group of singing townsfolk, Mr. Stapely hurried the speaker, and stepped down off the platform. Together they held a shovel with a large red bow attached to the handle. Placing their feet on the edge, they on cue pushed down into what appeared to be softened earth. To their surprise, the ground did not move. They moved their shovel a few inches backward. Nothing. After several attempts, they decided to use the bulldozer to dig the first hole. A stringy unshaven hardhat-clad man in the booth inside the cab chuckled as he happily shifted his toothpick to the other side of his mouth. With a sense of pride and power, he changed gears, then pushed and pulled levers. The crowd watched as his intricate moves choreographed a "bulldozer dance" of sorts, causing his vehicle to look like a clumsy ballerina with pointed leg and pointed toe lifting into the air. Another pull of a lever would force the huge leg to plunge its metallic toe toward the earth. The final shift sent the shaft of the dozer plummeting toward the spot that separated Nana's land from her woods and then.... SNAP! All present that day witnessed what looked like a crayon's attempt to penetrate a diamond. The shaft of the dozer completely broke off, and one of the cables flew through the window of the cab and smashed into the chest of the driver sending him hurling twenty feet into the woods to his death. The tractor itself had lifted about twenty feet into the air upon impact, and when it slammed back down, the cab separated from the body and bounced a few times. One of the other construction workers jumped out of his rig and ran to assist. All of the nuts and bolts in every one of the rigs scheduled to dig into the woods that day began to rotate to the left until each and every jointed component of all the tractors at the site buckled and collapsed as a result of their lack of reinforcement. Both spectators and workers ran frantically for cover. Mr. Stapely tried to regain control of the event, but spectators had already reached the panic level, hurling umbrellas and shouting at a feverous pitch. News reporters excitedly captured details of a groundbreaking gone wrong, documenting to the world on video how the all-but-celebratory occasion for the administrators of IFU had been mysteriously thwarted, as construction workers simultaneously backed out what remaining equipment they had and headed for the highway. Mr. Stapely was filmed screaming at the top of his lungs, "I'm warning you—this is a breach of contract! You will be held accountable for this! Come back here!" All while the poor and soaking citizens of Trappe, Maryland, again continued to sing:

> "*I don't believe He brought me this far to leave me!*"

In the midst of the craziness, Nilé felt a surge of courage race though her veins as she began to mumble inaudibly yet repeatedly with the voice of her great-grandmother, "Git! Git out an' git offa my land!" With fists clenched and raised high, she shouted until her voice cracked, "Git offa my land! Git offa my land!"

Angie in awe of her friend's newfound courage began to laugh and to hold her fist high, screaming, "Git offa' her land!" One by one the town's people picked up the chant as reporters swung their cameras onto a rain-drenched Nilé standing in the midst of her grandmother's property claiming and taking back all that was stolen from her personal life and that which would never be taken again. With each horrible memory of how she lost battles through fear, she cried out, "Git off!" Each wasted year, each heartbreak, every injustice, all unwarranted guilty feelings she, through her lips and tongue, renounced and removed from the corridors of her very being every time she spoke "Git off!" In addition, Nana was there coaching her, rejoicing with the other ancestors. They all were soaked with the downpour of Life's living waters drenching their once-unfulfilled dreams with the celebration and reality of an unexplainable now.

Mr. Stapely stormed over to Nilé. His eyes blazed in fury and his smile was unnerving as he spewed, in guttural tones, promises of unfathomable misfortune to be issued to Nilé by him personally. Knowing that the battle won had nothing to do with her strengths and abilities, Nilé stared right back, unshaken, and whispered, "Bring whatever you think you have, Mr. Stapely. Bring it."

CHAPTER 49

The last Stayer

It was three years to the date of the Trappe groundbreaking that Mr. Stapely died. Each year prior to his death, his antics ranging from civil suits filed against Nilé to favors cashed in on politicians who issued summons after summons to appear in court for various frivolities was used to strengthen Nilé's resolve in keeping her great-grandmother's land. Each year she discovered more about the pods underground. The townsfolk slowly revealed information held in secret for decades. During afternoon or Sunday teas, they would gather around her living room and reveal whom they were personally a kin to in Nana's list of runaways and Stayers. They spoke of potions that could heal diseases that the "Guvment still lookin' ta fin' cures fo'." In addition, they recalled a language still spoken fluently by the children of the Stayers. Their stories told of several attempts to destroy the old house, several fires, and finally of the recent fabricated bomb that blew up and gutted Nilé's SUV. Each story reminisced how, like her ancestors before her, Nilé was not frightened enough to move.

It was not long before "Nilé folklore" had been developed and spun all over the county. She and Angie would laugh when they heard children weaving tales far more elaborate than the ones of that infamous day.

Her finances were bled dry, and she had to give up her place in Philadelphia. Owning a home was not all it was cracked up to be. She was used to calling maintenance when something went wrong, now she had to shell out cash to replace hot water heaters and frozen pipes. Her freelance job as a copywriter kept the month-to-month bills at bay, but the court cases and attorney fees ate her alive as Mr. Stapely had intended. Angie had gone back home to keep up her business, but came down frequently for support. She always seemed to know instinctively when Nilé needed encouragement. Frequent visits to the county library kept Nilé's sanity intact as she researched all she could about the town and its inhabitants. Nilé also set aside precious time to "renovate" the pods she discovered. During those three years, she found that the network extended almost to the edge of Delaware, where the tunnel's end lay at the mouth of the one hundred second pod.

The oldest survivor of the Stayers was a woman by the name of Janie Kepshanks. She was as she said "too old an' stubborn ta die!" and the townsfolk believed that she was at least one decade beyond her one hundredth year of living on earth. Janie Kepshanks remembered Nana and Pop-Pop well. In fact, it was Janie and her sons who helped "break down" the remains of old man Brokes. One day Nilé visited Ms. Kepshanks upon invitation. Her granddaughter was caring for her and knew of all the stories around Nana's house and the pod stations. Because Old Ms. Janie was weak, her great-great-granddaughter Shelly urged Nilé to visit and hear of the stories while Janie was still alive to vouch for them as true.
"Shelly, I can't thank you enough for having me over."
"The pleasure is all mines. Gram is in the back room sunnin'. Wanna go see her?"
"Oh yes, please." They walked silently through a narrow hallway leading to a large room on the left filled with sunlight. Two enormous cats were sitting in the windowsill, and one smaller cat curled up in Gram Janie's lap.
"Wuz wonderin' when you'd finally sho' up. Took ya long 'nuff!"
"Gram, Ms. Nilé wanna know 'bout alls dat went on when you wuz a youngin' at the Davis home. Kin I begin ta tell her?" Gram Janie peered out the window and nodded. Then she spoke, "You kin tell her but tell her right. Dis be history

and no tales ta be tolt. Tell her good. Tell her right. She deserve ta know de facks!"

"Yes Gram." Looking over to Nilé and sheepishly smiling she sighed.

"Where do I begin?" Gram snapped, "At de beginnin'!" Nilé thought she would ease the tension by asking the first question.

"Did my Nana ever explain why she created the pods?" Before Shelly could begin, Janie spoke softly.

"Funny how sityashens kin move a soul. Yo' granpappy lubbed de groun' yo' granmammy walked on. Said she tole him one night dat he wuz ta count de welts on her back. Count em' all she said. When he done finished countin' she tolt him that number dey counted gotta be reckoned with in her lifetime. Turned out fo' every welt she bore on her back, she built a pod-o-freedom. Said her back look like a map, and felt like it been dug up like de sod she had ta dig over an' over. She figgered it wuz God's way o' tellin' her whut she had ta do on earth. Pop-Pop said each night she'd ask him to look it over an' tell her where the next pod was to be dug. Pop-Pop would see crosses where the scarring was thick and tell Nana that he knew where to dig. Said God Almighty tol' him just where to dig. When dey'd get to a place where the earth was softer, he knew to open up the tunnel and make a pod. One hun-ned two stripes she bore. Mo' den three times mo' den our Lord an' Savior. An I'zes libbin' witness dat dey's one hun-ned two pods is in dat dere ground. Said she wouldn't die till de las one wuz built! Can't tell ya how many done traveled through ta freedom." Then she chuckled. "Even de ones who died is still free!"

Nilé spoke softly, "I understand...in death they gained their freedom."

"Naw! Eben befo' dat! Jes' believin' they would some day be free, no one standin' over their backs ready ta whup 'em made the weakest ones dig. Lawd know I seen em' cough up blood an' mix it inta de earth for mortar. Dey blood, dey vomit, everything dey had, dey gave to de pods. Dey faith free'd dem long befo' dey saw de light of day."

Nilé thought long and hard before she asked the next question. She had the utmost respect for Ms. Janie and didn't want to offend her, but the question sitting at the back of her throat continued its annoying routine of erupting to the brink of choking her until she had to speak.

"Ms. Janie…. I never understood how people claim to be free in the midst of obvious oppression. I mean…you said yourself that you witnessed dear friends of yours mixing their blood with the soil in the hope that their effort would someday bring them freedom…"
"YOU said dat!" Janie quipped. "I nebba said nothin' 'bout 'in da hope'—whut I said wuz dey faith free'd dem long befo' dey saw de light of day!"

"But Ms. Janie…so many of them died in the process. There was no literal light of day for them!" Ms. Janie looked long and hard at Nilé. She was studying to see if Nilé was mocking her.
When she determined that Nilé was clearly confused, she spoke slowly and deliberately, "Das where you wrong, baby chile! Dey was free da moment dey decided to become free. Da moment dey said to demself 'No more!' dey was free. Sho'…dey bodies was runnin' from a massa but dey minds was free. C'ain't nothin' hold back yo' freedom once yo' fear is gone.

"Humph! De 'mancipation proclamation didn't do nothin'! Massas far an' wide just got meaner, an' mo' determined ta hold on ta us. So whut somebody says we free? We didn' feel it. Naw…it was only when freedom turnt meaner den slabe'ry dat most of us 'cided ta do somthin' 'bout it! There come a point in a mind when freedom become mo' den a word swimmin' 'round in yo' head. It become a notion that kin break somthin' as powerful as fear! Das' what it's all about! Ya either side up wit' fear or side up wit' freedom. C'aint do both! Shoot! Da first step you take on the day you says youse runnin' send a surge o' freedom thru' yo' body so strong....humph! Fear take a look at dat kind of fix on a mind an' cain't do nothin' but git out de way!"

Nilé thought about the times her mother forbade her to go to certain parties when she was a teen. Then she remembered how she and her girlfriends would plot and plan a way to get her out. Fear would warn her, but her desire to be at the party was far greater than the consequences. She realized that she indeed was free the moment she decided to go. She saw herself dancing with FM; she felt her body undulating to the rhythm of each record. She would not take no for an answer, even if it was final, and although that was all she could use to relate the feeling, somehow she now understood.

"Y'see, chile, dis body I'm in done felt pain so much it don't hardly hurt no more. An' had pain dat nebba touched my skin dat hurt much worser! You watch a woman take a fryin' pan to de head o' yo' chile, you feel pain beyon' yo' chile's. Dat busted head you know in time will heal up, but what kin ya do fo' a busted soul?"

Nilé then thought about Nana. How many times had God allowed her soul to be busted before she could stare back at fear and make it move out of the way? Nana through Janie urged and enlightened her granddaughter, and while Janie was tired, she was obedient.

"Dis' ol' body caint fo' de life of it figger out why it's still here! All it wanna do is lie down 'neath some shady tree an' reacquaint isself wit the clay from wenst it come! I don't wanna feel de rain no more, I wanna drink it in."
"Maybe it's de po'shuns, gramma, keepin' you alive?"
"Whut, da' livin' po'shuns? Shoot, I done stopped takin' de po'shuns long time ago! Tol' Jesus He didn't hafta keep me libe' no mo. But my soul keep cryin' out...Gotta stay libe for

one mo' day!...an' I don't know why. So every monin' I wakes up to fine myself still feelin' de rain an' not drinkin' it." Then Janie did something that she seldom did with people outside of kinship. She urged Nilé to come close to her. Close enough so that she could smell her skin. Out of respect for the old woman, Nilé moved near her, uneasy but curious. Janie in silence smelled Nilé's hand, then arm. Turning her hand over, she moved the very center of Nilé's palm toward her nose. Nilé's stomach became queasy as the old woman closed her eyes and inhaled with what seemed to be pure delight the essence discovered within her palm.

Moments later, she opened eyes filled with tears. She looked up and spoke into the very spirit of Nilé saying, "I feel lak I done what I wuz kept 'live ta do. I c'aint do this no more. You brought her to me, now aks de Sabeyor ta let me in." Nilé in panic began to withdraw her hand, but found that old Ms. Janie had a grip that would not let her go. Pleadingly she begged Ms. Janie who continued to look past her frightened eyes. Finally, as if a cool breeze from inside every corridor of Nilé's being had opened, a force of breath came from her, blowing into the face of Ms. Janie. Then in silence, she witnessed the old woman look around the room for the last time, close her eyes, then whisper, "Amen." Days later she and Ms. Janie's family stood at the threshold of the wooded area just beyond Nana's yard where they sang spirituals remembered by the oldest of the Kepshanks clan, the last of the Stayers. When the singing and praying had ended, upon Nilé's permission, they took old Ms. Janie's body and walked it deep into the underground of the woods to the pod known as "The Chambers." There, Ms. Janie's granddaughter, Shelly Kepshanks, and two other young women began the age-old tradition of breaking down her body and bleaching her bones, taught by Ms. Janie herself. Only Shelly knew the arrangement of every bone in that pod. Only Shelly knew where to place Ms. Janie. As the night grew old, Shelly's young cousins came out of the woods, leaving Shelly alone with her beloved great-great-grandmother. Amidst the comforting wholeness of ancestral narration, love filled that chamber in epic proportions as Nana and the others welcomed Ms. Janie home.

That evening Angie sat in the small but cozy living room sharing a cup of tea with Nilé. "You've grown so much in the past few years I hardly know you!"
"Yeah? In what way, Ange?"
"Well, first of all, you're hardly afraid of anything anymore. You seem to look for reasons to fight! Don't get me wrong now, I like the new Nilé, seems like you've come to realize that, like your name, your spirit flows in the opposite direction of what life wanted to carve out for it. Just look at you! You're writing up proposals for the development of a public school in Nana's name—for God's sake! You're researching financial investments, learning about stocks, good golly, Ms. Nilé! You ain't actin' like a Normal!"
Nilé looked away to somewhere far beyond the perimeter of her parlor.

"I can't believe it's not that hard."
"What did you say?"
"I can't believe it's not that hard. It's like I'm hydroplaning on God's energy. Every time I want to do something that used to paralyze me with fear…now that fear is gone….I just can't believe it's not that hard. I realize that evil is not wise, Ange. There is no wisdom in evil. Yet I was afraid of it. I mean, how stupid could I be? I went through life, quoting scripture verses so that they could soothe me, instead of owning them, wearing them, moving through them. Why did I fear fear? I mean, for God's sake, there it stands in front of all of us, big hairy and ugly. But if you get a chance to look closely, you see that it only has the ability to be itself. Afraid! Afraid that you might discover what it really is—which is nothing to be afraid of! From the beginning of time, Ange, evil has been disconnected from wisdom. It tries to replace wisdom with power but…it can't. It just can't. There

is no power in anything attained without wisdom, and evil is afraid that we will come to realize that someday."

"OK babe…you're getting too deep for even me! I'ma go to bed now, and try to thaw out that brain-freeze of a statement you just laid on me. Nighty night!" Nilé continued in her line of thinking, rocking her chair and agreeing with thoughts that she knew were not her own. They were new, fresh, original, and smarter than she was, yet they belonged to her. As her mind spiraled off into universal concepts, a loud thumping on the door interrupted her. Peering through a small window, she recognized the moonlight tracings of Jordan's profile. Opening the door, he felt her spirit that was much larger than the room she occupied, and his heart recoiled for a moment.

"I will not stay; I know I am not welcome. I need to see the pods. I just need to see them." Nilé studied his eyes, which were darting back and forth as if something or someone was chasing him.

"Even if I took you now, you'd not be able to see anything. It's too dark. Even in the daytime the pods are dark, Jordan."
"Don't you have a flashlight? This is the twenty-first century for cryin' out loud!"
"Yes, I do, but in deference to the ones who built the pods, I will not light them up at night."

"Stapely said you were full of voodoo! He said you had some sort of magical gridlock on these grounds. Everybody's afraid of this place! Well, guess what, Nilé? I'm not! I'm not afraid of it or of you. Remember, I knew you before you became a legend! There is something about those woods that I have to see. Something you are deliberately keeping from me! You jeopardized my research for that patch of stench that sits on your .property. The only two women I gave into will not forfeit my entire life's dream."
"Two women?"

"Yeah, two women, and you know it! One I know had me spellbound, and now you're trying this surreal out of this world 'can't touch that' bullsh…"

"Who is that, Nilé?" Nilé backed up for Angie to see Jordan. "Just who I thought it was an' I got somethin' for ya this time!" At that moment, she hurled a hatchet toward Jordan's head, and it missed him by inches and imbedded itself into the snow-white woodwork around the door. Neither Jordan nor Angie flinched, but stared into each other's eyes with the intent to back down the other, through venomous stares of rage.

Nana and the ancestors appeared with concern. As they neared, Nilé for the first time acknowledged their presence but assured them that she did not need their assistance. Then, she spoke. "You want to see the pods? You may see the pods. But like I said, not before sunrise!" Then, opening the door (no wider than Angie's mouth), she motioned for him to come in.
"I have a room in the back if you want to stay the night." Jordan too was nonplussed, but following his instinct, he walked in, pulled the hatchet out of the door, and handed it to Angie, as he found the room down the hallway.

CHAPTER 50

Revelations: The Final Chapter

Dawn tiptoed in, timid and sweet. A soft veil of clouds covered distant hills as thin as an angel's petticoat. The local "Bob Whites" were announcing his name throughout the fields, and this morning, instead of tea, Nilé brewed coffee nice and strong to serve as an aromatic alarm clock. Angie was the first to appear in the kitchen.

"G'mornin'! What's with the coffee?"
"Would you rather have tea?"
"Naw, I just felt like being difficult. We got something to go with this?"
"Nope! I was waiting for you, my dear!"

Angie began scrambling around the bottom cupboards, where they had rearranged the baking goods for her easy access, grabbing flour and all the basics to whip up a coffee cake. Hearing sounds from the room down the hall, they looked at each other.
"I almost killed a man yesterday."
"I know."
"But in defense of me, something's wrong with that man, Nilé!"
"Something's been wrong with mankind, ever since the fall, but we honor a God of second chances."
"Oh if I knew I'd be havin' breakfast with the pastor, I'd a rolled up in here wit' my Sunday hat!" Nilé realized Angie was upset about the judgment, as the room grew loud with silence.
"Ange…Jordan is not the same man that I met and grew to know in Philadelphia. You're right, something is wrong…with him…but I'm not afraid of that." She threw her hands up in the air in exasperation. "There I go with the

fearless talk again, but Angie, I really am not afraid! And because of it, I see more clearly and I'm less distracted by 'what ifs.' I feel I can address Jordan's needs without jeopardizing my own."

"Since when did his needs need to be addressed by you?"
"Since I found him on my doorstep, stating specifically that he needed to see the pods. My great-grandmother's pods!"
"It's your home, it's your life, I'm just a guest, Nilé...do what you gotta do. I just hope...yeah, I'm gonna say it...I just hope that this fearless encounter affords you the opportunity to see things more clearly as it relates to the two of you 'cause in matters of the heart, you is still actin' like a Normal!"
"If we could rewind the tape a few years back, I can recall when you were pushing me toward the man!" Just then Jordan entered the room.

"Good morning, ladies. I...uh...want to first apologize for doing whatever I did to warrant an axe being hurled toward my head. I am truly sorry for having stirred up that kind of emotion." Angie felt the stillness of the room urging her to speak.
"No. I need to apologize. You didn't say anything to me, and for that reason alone, I shouldn't have tried to kill you. I couldn't even plead self-defense in a court of law. ...But, in defense of myself, Jordan, something's wrong with you!" Nilé looked at her lifelong friend as if she was crazy.
"You're right, Angie. I feel like I'm losing my mind. No, I know I have my mind, but it seems I don't do what MY mind wants to do. The only thing I know is that who I really am inside needs to see those pods, Nilé. I don't even care about the research. Well, yes I do, but not as much. I need to know...something, I don't know...."
"We'll eat something first before we go. You cannot walk through those grounds without having something in your stomach. You need strength emotionally and physically the first time you encounter the pods."

The sun had regained the morning's confidence as it playfully tapped the shoulders of those who walked toward the woods. The spring grounds were dewy yet firm, hardly yielding to the feet and set of wheels on it. Yes, for some strange reason, Angie came along. The pod hallways, adjusted after months and months of teasing enough earth away to accommodate the width of a wheelchair, waited in silence for the arrival of three. Jordan gasped and grabbed his jacket covering his nose and mouth the moment he entered the first pod. Nilé lit a match even though he was holding a flashlight. She ceremoniously walked to the age-old tin plates nestled snugly within grooves dug out in the walls. There, she pulled tea candles from her jacket and placed them on the tins. All stood still until every candle was lit.

The room shimmered and waved as if trying to balance itself on stilts. Nilé and Angie watched as Jordan's eyes became accustomed to the magical whimsy of colors more brilliant than life itself dancing around his senses, numbing the pungent odors to a tolerable level. His eyes were like that of a child, and seemed to be communicating with something intangible. The sisters witnessed him timidly touching the walls, following lines and memories that he swore he recalled but could not rationalize as events that happened in his lifetime. In silence, they watched until he reached the first portal. Jordan turned around and pleadingly requested, "More."

Room by room he was transformed by what he witnessed. Crying, he nodded his head in agreement to walls that spoke only to him. Angie and Nilé understood because they too had been changed in the same way. A few hours passed by before they could engage in conversation, and even then, it was labored and fragmented.
"Those jars?"
"Potions created by the Stayers."

"Stayers?"

"Runaways who chose not to go north, living and dying within the pods, helping others."

"Did anyone survive?"

"We don't know."

"This is not all?"

"No."

As they left one of the pods, his spirit was quieted, desensitized by an hour's worth of experiencing an elaborate highway structure that turned into a pod every eighth of a mile from its predecessor. The enormity of the endeavor no longer overwhelmed him. Instead, it instilled a newfound pride for a people, his people, who portrayed on the walls with black skins seasoned with indigo blues and pomegranate reds, telling story after story of how they got to where they were. He could no longer find validity in his project. Morning years wasted he questioned why his reality never lined up with truth. He was a scientist for God's sake! Why didn't he research the history of his people before drawing a conclusion about them? What made him regard them with such disdain and why? Why…despite all of the evidence staring him in the face, could he still not love Blacks? Still, even now? Was what he felt inside keeping him from loving Nilé? Did he run from Toni because she knew all along of his self-hatred? Why was hate the bottom line driving force in all of his accomplishments and failures?

Then, Nilé advised Jordan of one pod that he was yet to see that was not like the others. Turning left, a direction not typical to the usual, they walked in silence toward the pod known as the Chambers. As they neared it, there was a heaviness that grew within them. Each step was labored, as they searched inwardly to draw strength to move forward. As they reached the portal, they saw Shelly, awakened by their footsteps.

Nilé asked, "Everything OK, Shelly?"

"Everything OK, Ms. Nilé. Everything be OK. Why you here this early, Ms. Nilé?"

"I want to show a friend the Chambers."

There was a long pause as the two looked deeply into each other's eyes. Shelly's gaze of surprise was depositing her fear into Nilé that the resting place of Ms. Janie's bones was still fresh, and the darker softer earth might be revealed if they were to see it now. Nilé answered her concern with a look that quelled her concern. Somehow, Nilé knew that all would be fine. Trusting in the power in Nilé's eyes, she turned toward the door of the Chambers and opened it slowly. Unbeknownst to everyone else, Shelly immediately recognized that the earth that she had disturbed had somehow disguised itself as hard, old, and showing no signs of ever having been touched. Nilé was aware of the ancestors' presence, while Jordan, experiencing abysmal sorrow, fell to his knees and wept uncontrollably. It was there where Thompson removed himself from Jordan's body and stood among the ancestors while Shelly in obedience closed the Chambers' door.

Every single soul represented by bones embedded within the Chambers was present in the room. Nilé for the first time saw her male as well as female ancestors, with Pop-Pop Davis in the foreground, smiling.

"It's taken too long fo' dis' time ta come." Nana whispered.

"Dis' been my dream since I saw what happened seem like a million years ago. I c'ain't say I knew all de part of it, but I knew ta follow de Lawd fearlessly 'til some sense be made of da mess and heartache had done been made ta dis' family line since the day we came ova'."

An account was given by a self-proclaimed griot in Nilé's family line. He recalled how as Nilé's family was pried from their ancestral ground of Africa to America, Henny and Thompson continued their love-hate relationship that sailed across a dismal ocean almost as unforgiving as their affair.

How, when alive, Thompson knew at the shore of that riverbank in Africa where he stopped to refresh his head that Henny (sending overt and embarrassing sexual overtures his way) was the voluptuous woman he was once promised to wed. How his anger grew larger than the stories returned to his village about a beautiful woman who ran away in rebellion lived on the outskirts of the village, and gave herself to any man who pleased her. He vowed that she would never own the love he once held inside his heart for her. The love she forbade him from the start. He promised to punish her for what she had done. It was not until they crossed the waters and countless maidens of her lineage were ravaged and killed by white masters and maverick male slaves who embodied the soul of Thompson that Henny realized who he was.

One day, to be sure, Henny slipped into the spirit of a twelve-year-old girl only to experience the lustful eyes of Thompson staring at her. During a most horrific moment for that girl, Henny rendered the child unconscious and allowed Thompson to do his bidding, as she feigned resistance, loving in all actuality every moment of it. This was the man who had rejected her. This was the man she finally had! Thompson, realizing who it was beneath him, lost himself for one moment and like a child beseeched Henny to agree to love him and him alone forever. Henny, seizing the moment, wrenched the flash of weakness from his heart and crashed it to the floor. As he spiraled downward through the tunnel of rejection, she reminded him of the total humiliation she felt by his rejection at the riverbank. With insurmountable rage, Thompson killed the limp and fragile body of an innocent child, and the two continued the battle generation after generation until they reached the life of a woman named Annie Davis. It was something about Nana's spirit that persuaded Henny to stand her ground, forcing Thompson to realize that she would always be one step ahead of his cunning, and as a result, Thompson, unable to get to Nana, saw to it that she was whipped unmercifully time and time again with the lash of his frustration.

Neither Thompson nor Henny had any idea that Nana's pain and suffering were used to strengthen her resolve to free hundreds upon hundreds of slaves. The tales brought on by the diaspora would prove time and again of the vilest methods of cruelty being used by God as a pawn to eventual triumph of a people. Generations of unrequited love had woven an incredibly delicate web of painful deception, and the very tool used to free enslaved Negroes was now being used to complete the journey that Nilé needed to take for her own freedom. Nana had completed her part of the task. Nilé had helped, yet there was something more that needed to be done…something that only a beautiful chocolate-brown little girl with long fat braids framing her face like giant parentheses could supply. Monica stepped forward and handed a lock of Jordan's hair to her mother, Toni. It was the very lock used to conjure Jordan into her bed. Toni held it in her hands for a moment, and then turned to Nilé.

"This is what's kept you two from ever coming together. Take it. Maybe by you having it, it will bring to you the same joy I had as a result of my union with Jordan." As Nilé looked down at the thick soft cord of tangled hair, she remembered how it used to fall into her bosom while they made love, and she longed for those days. But today, all eyes were on her as if an entire universe was hanging in the balance waiting for her response. She turned to Nana to ask what to do, but somehow knew that the decision to be made would be wholly hers. It was at that moment when she began to understand the reasoning behind her maddening journey. For her ancestors, the journey had finally ended, but for Nilé, it had just begun, and as desperately as she wanted both love and freedom, she saw firsthand what happens to it when perverted.

Her first lesson toward freedom was to learn what love wasn't. It wasn't contrived, nor could it be coerced, nor could it ever be promised or compromised. For that type of love flew in the face of freedom. She could see how yearning and desire sought after love, yet their eyes peered through nearsighted lenses. She knew that Jordan was not hers to love. When she allowed the hair to slip through her fingers, it was as if a magician released a flock of doves into the air simply by waving his hand. That's when love was released. That's when it flew.

Love first flew into Jordan's emptiness who saw Toni the way she always wanted him to see her, with loving eyes and an incredible sense of remorse, realizing that the deep-dimpled chocolate-brown child was theirs. Love then rose like a phoenix out of the ashes, in the hearts of those witnessing. Everyone there understood love's own resolve to remain bound, until truth allowed it to be free, delivering a lifelong friendship its payment in full, while Angie cried and cried, trying not to believe that she could feel a tingling in her legs. And finally, love came down to kiss the brow of a woman who was named to reflect the paradox of her life—a woman ever running in the wrong direction, yet being the very source of freedom for her family. And, because love was faithful, she knew she too was free.